Instagram: @danielcharle

To my editor and friend, Mia Walton @my.book.memories. I am extremely appreciative of you and your hard work on making this book the best that it could be.

To my cover artist and friend, Lydia Jones @lyds_makes_things. Thank you for yet another tremendous cover. I am very lucky to have you on my team and I look forward to the future for more projects.

A special thanks to my arc team who made the novel what it is today.

Courtney Sharpe @thesharpereader

Kristy Bugg @readingyouastray

Heather Warner @shutup_heather

Madison Lai bookish_book.lover

Mia Walton @my.book.memories

Nicola Emma @booksinthebath

Nina Nin @ninnanin87

Kirsten Aucoin @aucoinkirsten

Casey Skeen @caseys_reads

Maureen Carney @bookwormdownunder

Amanda Calhoun @calhoun.crew

Taylor @readwithme_xo

Tiffany Case @tifflovesthrillers

Hayley Bjon @thatbookishvixen

A MANOR OF MURDER

A man who'd gone missing in the storm was the first indication of what was in store for the stranded. Two dead bodies would soon follow. The first had been found in the kitchen, stabbed in the back with an antique blade and blood pooled under the body.

The next had been found in the main study, the man's body draped over the desk. A wireless telegraphy machine idled in front of the body. The blank pieces of paper before it had been smeared with blood before a distress call could be made. A third body, unaccounted for, had not yet been found.

The urgent message of panic hadn't been sent.

The last victim, a man desperate to give an account of his findings before dawn's break, had come so close. The dead man had valuable information and the killer stopped him. Destroying any evidence, the killer struck the man before a message to his office could be sent. The victim was killed before he could so much as scream.

The lifeless body remained much like the first until the stranded found it.

What had once seemed to be a beautiful place to spend time with old friends and family, had now turned into a night of terror which the Smallhorn manor would not forget.

Chapter 1

Emma Squier hadn't visited the Smallhorn manor before. It was something long overdue, as her best friend regularly reminded her. When she finally arrived, it was even more stunning than what her friend described.

In the eve of January 1927 winter had come strong and a great storm had been building for many weeks.

A dark shadow brought over from the forestry land eclipsed the neighbouring woods of the manor. It ushered an ominous touch. Emma gazed at the clouds.

She looked over the roof of her taxi to the far distance and the rolling hills covered in pine trees. She inhaled deeply, smelling the piney air which drifted from them.

Emma had never seen as much of the countryside as she would've liked. Born in London, she barely left the city. She always thought that the city was all she ever needed for the rest of her life. It was a safe and comfortable place. It had been her home for all her life. As a young woman who'd recently found herself, coming out to the country left her feeling a little out of her depth.

She looked around the manor. She'd never seen such fresh grass before. It was still as ripe as any blade in the royal parks in London, even under the stormy clouds. It was almost primal being so far away from home. From what she knew, the next residents lived over a mile away and the main village of Sherrington was even further.

She hadn't the faintest clue if her friends' family had any electricity out this far. The old manor didn't look like it did from the outside, leading her to picture only old-time candlelight and lanterns.

'The Smallhorn Manor, miss.' The driver said, leaning over his shoulder to get a look at Emma through the window.

She ducked back down and peered into the vehicle to meet his gaze.

'You'll be alright, yeah?' The driver asked.

Emma could barely see his eyes under the flat cap he wore. He squinted and his mouth clenched. 'You know there's a storm coming?' The older gentlemen warned. He held his cap down with his hand as a whiplash of wind busted through the open window.

'I'll be with my friends tonight. I'm in safe hands.' Emma nodded with a smile which was good enough for the driver to peel away and leave her. He didn't take long to get out. He wanted to beat the storm and get home safe to his own family.

As the vehicle tore down the dirt road, it eventually faded from view, allowing Emma to get a full sight of the woods around her.

Trapped in by them, the manor nestled in the centre of the invading trees. It was a secluded residence, hidden from the public eye.

She turned on her heel, gripping the leathery strap of her duffle bag which held all she had for the night. Looking up at the manor, she noted how it rested silently, perched upon a hill of freshly trimmed grass. She smiled at its magnificence, the trails of her taxi rumbling away in the distance.

This is it. I'm here now. The taxi is gone and there is no turning back.

There had been a reason why Emma had postponed her best friend's endless invitations to visit the manor. It was something that Emma dreaded thinking about as a child and even as an adult, the fear remained.

As she pumped her legs up the hill towards the manor, the feeling of fear growled louder in her mind as the manor loomed up before her. She couldn't help but think about all the horrible, scary stories her best friend told her about the manor. Though it was beautiful and the kind of place where a medieval princess would live, Madeline would always tell her about the manors dark past.

Many ghosts were said to haunt the manors rooms and halls. They were everything from past owners to servants and even knights. Madeline, Emma's best friend, claimed to have seen and heard them many times as a child. Almost all the time, she would speak about footsteps in her parent's bedroom. She would hear muffled noises in the kitchen where servants and cooks would colonise and the trailing sound of cries and wails which came from the downstairs compartment where a dungeon was later built.

Such stories had remained with Emma for all this time. Unto this day, she still heard them inside her head, dreading the day when Madeline would ask her over to experience them herself. Now an adult, she had to come with a grown-up appearance about her. She couldn't be scared anymore. It would be childish of her, she thought.

As she took a moment to look up at the manor, she described all the details and the sheer size of the historical home, she couldn't help but feel the terror of what she was told within. It looked beautiful from the outside. Even with the grey, overcast skies, the dark of a storm brewing still could not outwit the manor's tremendousness.

The grass was watery-green and flowers blossomed around it. The manor was a beautiful stone with gargoyles mounted upon the roof, strong and bold enough to withstand hundreds of years of history and weather.

Without wasting another moment, Emma chucked herself forwards. She stepped off the rough gravel of the driveway, swapping it for a mixture of sharp stones and smooth pebbles which made up the entranceway towards the manor.

As she cautiously walked up the steep-ish climb, a speck of stone made itself a nuisance, finding it's way into the side of her shoe. She felt the stubborn lump in the side of her foot, dropping her bag with a exasperated groan. She kneeled to dislodge it.

Just as she did, another vehicle came bounding up the driveway from the main road she'd come from. The cherry red motor car braked hard, swerving onto the drive in a hurry.

The engine revved hard as the driver picked up speed for the climb. It raced past Emma, leaving her with a cloud of dust and dirt. The driver seemed to notice her and miraculously, barely missed her.

She felt the metal of the motor cars' side scrape her hip and with this, her heavy coat frolicked in the air.

Before she could stand back up, shoe in hand to shout at the arrogant driver, she noticed just how rich and expensive the vehicle was. A triumphant sports vehicle, rare and something she had never seen in London in fact. She wondered just what kind of person was driving. *A lord or someone part of the Smallhorn family perhaps? Someone rich enough to drive an expensive sports motor car out in the dusty country.*

Emma was furious. The motor car and the driver's ignorance had nearly wiped her clean off the road. Emma counted her lucky stars. She dusted herself off from the dirt on the road which swooped upon her clothing. Emma wasn't the kind of person that you would want on your bad side. Not with what she was progressing to be. Emma Squier had just finished studying law. She had now been made a qualified detective. She wasn't *exactly* a detective yet, but she was going to be. She had just finished university and her internship had only just expired before she got the call from Madeline to come down for the weekend.

Emma had spent so many years at university. She had worked hard and forfeited many pleasures to get where she was today. she'd rather enjoy a short getaway.

She was a hard-worker and someone who'd taken after her father. He'd spent forty years as a detective himself and Emma wanted to follow in his footsteps.

After many years of studying and finally having completed her course, an invitation from Madeline for a weekend break out in the country was exactly what she needed.

Emma watched the vehicle climb up the last of the steep walk. It circled around the centre of the manor's water fountain. The vehicle idled for a moment as Emma gathered her things after placing her shoe back on her bare foot. But before she could fully stand back up, the driver appeared. She could make out the figure of a man and watched as he shut the car door behind him with a loud thud. Before Emma could get a real good look at him, he'd climbed the steps of the manor with his back turned to her.

Emma could see from the clothing he wore and the way his hair remained neat in the wind that he was a man that took pride in his appearance. He adjusted his suit and combed his hair with his fingers before he approached the double-door entrance.

The man never looked back. It was as if he'd never seen Emma down the bottom of the slope – the person he'd almost killed. It suddenly hit that for at least the night, the man who had almost killed her with his car could be staying with her. Emma gritted her teeth. *'Christ,'* she said in a tiny, wavering voice.

With the heat of anger boiling in her blood, she picked up the pace and struggled up the path. She readied herself to confront the man who wandered in.

Once Emma reached the summit of the path she stood there awhile longer. She waited to see which way the clouds were moving beyond the manor. And although the clouds were swirling like black ravens signalling disaster, she rather enjoyed the notion of a storm in a place like this. They seemed to be coming over from the East. Soon they would smother the nearby forest lands. Disaster was coming. *Old, cold London* was ditched for *Old, cold North,* Emma had joked.

Out in the country, it was rich with nature and serenity. She could truly feel the pulse of a long, medieval history. She imagined brave knights throughout all history who'd come from afar, traversing the tumbles of the hillside, flocking through the woods to eventually come to the long-standing manor to rest. She liked that perhaps she was following in their footsteps. Now she had been a weary traveller, hoping to seek shelter in a grand, long-standing manor.

Emma remembered reading Robin Hood. Those stories had her thinking that the lands of England were even more classic and beautiful then how the old stories told them. It was quite becoming.

Emma spun her body around, half-sinking into the stones below. At the far-end of the manor there was a barn shed. The big doors had been left open as if someone was working, walking in and out to deliver and stack burlap bags of seeds and chaff inside. The strong scent of the burlap had helped prove Emma correct as it merged with the piney drift coming from the woods.

She turned to the double doors of the manor. In the side of her vision, the gleam of the cherry red sports car couldn't help but stay with her. It stayed like a bane to her existence, the colour matching her contained anger.

Before long, a disrupting sound distracted her. It had come from behind the door.

The thud frightened her. It did make her jump out of her skin, but she contained her fear before someone could see her. She allowed the fizz in her body to slowly die down, straightening herself up and smiling as the doors opened. Emma was glad to see Madeline in the doorway. A smile as big as hers appeared upon Madeline's.

'Emma, you made it.' She exclaimed.

'After how many years, I finally get to visit.' Emma responded as she awkwardly swallowed the fact that it had been her fault. She pushed the invitations back.

As Madeline came down from the concrete steps, Emma noticed the sparkling high heels her friend wore. Matching them was a velvet dress, coloured with a dashing midnight blue. Strapped around her neck was a crystal-clear necklace, something that her parents could afford her to wear. She looked nice, but nothing of the sort that Emma had remembered. Afraid, Emma wasn't sure what she had stepped into, now seeing Madeline dressed fit for the King's arrival. She greeted her with proper formality which lived up to the Smallhorn name.

Emma hadn't dressed half as fancy as her friend. All she wore was a loose, white shirt with a brown coat and a high crown baker boy hat.

She felt a little underdressed for whatever occasion she had come to, but it hadn't fazed Madeline one bit how her friend dressed. All that mattered was that she'd arrived.

She hugged Emma tightly as if she was there to catch her from falling.

'All this time I thought you were scared of coming. Especially with all those spooky stories I used to tell you.' Madeline teased. She did have a way about her. Somehow, unbeknown to Emma, Madeline could always read her mind. It was as if her feelings were tattooed on her face for

Madeline to read. Emma didn't know how she did it, only assuming it was something she picked up after having known each other for so long.

This time, she could see Emma's hesitance to step inside. She knew what she'd been thinking.

'No, no.' Emma awkwardly stumbled. 'It's just so far away from the city. Coming all the way out here, even the taxi driver had trouble finding the place.'

Madeline nodded. Even people who lived in the nearest town of Sherrington had trouble finding the place. The Smallhorn manor certainly held its own when it came to being exclusive and hard to stumble upon.

It took almost an hour for Emma to get to the manor from the train station. The driver had his map, but the Smallhorn manor was something less discovered. From the way the tall trees of the woods cloaked the manor it was as if nature were trying to reclaim it.. It was a place where enemies from long ago couldn't find. Friends of the family name and folk of the territory had always done their best to keep it from becoming overrun or taken over. It had been a manor owned by the Smallhorn's for the best part of four hundred years.

Madeline was quick to defend the privacy of the manor. She liked the serenity herself. It was polar opposite to life in London, much to what she'd experienced with Emma.

'That's the best part about it.' Madeline concluded. She had always been that way.

When Madeline was younger, she used to speak tremendously about the manor. Emma had just enough of her ear left after Madeline would chew it off all the time.

It wasn't just spooky, ghostly things that Emma remembered hearing. Half of the time it was about all the things she found in the manor. There were antique weapons, knights' armour, old books and scrolls and many precious treasures and heirlooms left from generations past. Better yet, Madeline always spoke highly of wandering the woods with her father, going on walks with her parents and taking a picnic basket to the river on long, summer evenings. It was a way of getting away from the city every once and a while. Madeline would come to live in London with her grandparents most of the time for school, but during the holidays she was almost always back at her parent's manor.

Madeline looked at her home. For four years, she hadn't been back to London, taking refuge with her parents and enjoying the serenity for awhile.

Once released from the hug Emma had peeked behind Madeline, her eyes finding the luxurious motor car parked beside her once more.

'Who owns that motor car?' Emma pouted. 'The damn fool almost ran me over. I shall have a word with him.' Emma said crossly. She peeked behind Madeline's shoulder into the open doorway as if she was trying to see him down the entrance way.

Madeline threw a sharp glance at Emma. *Don't worry,* it said.

'Well, I want to know. I certainly mind being around a man who almost killed me.'

'Oh, he is just in a hurry to get home to see my parents. It is my cousin and my parents very much adore him.' Madeline rolled her eyes. Her parents couldn't talk enough about her cousin's, but mostly the motor car owner, Fillius. Emma could see that she was tired of it already, but there was still a due sense of love for her cousin also.

To break the awkwardness, Madeline's family could be heard from inside. They heard a scuffle of laughter. Voices then followed. They were unrecognisable to Emma and she didn't know what they were saying.

'That is probably him now, talking with my parents.' Madeline pointed out, throwing a smile back towards Emma with her rosy-red lips.

Emma had picked up her bag, feeling a redness swell in her palm from the rubbing of picking it up and putting it back down again. for a moment, she had swore it had started to bleed and drip, but it was only from her sweat.

'Come on, why don't you come inside so I can give you the tour.' Madeline invited her in. She walked up the steps, entering the manor to lead Emma inside.

All at once, Emma felt the throbbing history to which she walked through. There was a certain smell… an old smell, one where the air from the fifteenth century had never left. The scent merged with the concrete walls and the relics left behind, greeting visitors in the entrance hall. It was dark inside. the walls were cloaked with paintings and sets of armour. Emma glared down, almost nudging a twenty-pounder mortar with her knee.

'Father says it's called a *"Bombard"* but I've always known it to be a mortar.' Madeline announced, noticing Emma almost knock into it, like it was a common occurrence to all guests who entered through the front door.

'Fifteenth century that is.' Madeline proceeded with the tour, adding odd little facts and titbits of knowledge along the way.

'My older brother, who hasn't visited in ten years by the way, broke one of these pots. My parents looked at him like he broke the ten commandments.' Madeline joked as she passed the glass shelf, chuckling as she turned out of the hall.

Emma had her eyes fixated upon the pots. They were all Egyptian – something obscure from the rest of the manor. Each pot was painted with different stories upon them, the one with a man raising a spear to a crowd of people, *presumably the enemy* was quite interesting.

Emma lagged behind. She'd soon found herself alone in the hall, stuck in the dark with nothing but the light of Madeline's voice around the wall. She gathered the pace to catch up to Madeline before she lost her.

'So, you finished university? That's good.' Madeline said. She dipped into the next room where she'd taken a seat upon a forest green sofa. Emma stopped at the door, staring inside at what looked to be a sitting room. Covering one half of the four walls in the room were bookshelves full of leather-bound prints, each book thicker than any Emma had ever seen – the library at her university didn't even have books that thick.

Surrounding the bookshelf and lining the walls were paintings of poets and lords. 'They haven't moved in centuries,' Madeline muttered. She hadn't a clue who they were – like most of the paintings in the manor. 'We think they are likely centuries old, but father was never sure.'

Emma watched as Madeline reached over towards the centre table. She fiddled with a porcelain cup. She positioned it on a saucer and poured herself some hot tea.

'How is detective life treating you?' Madeline asked. Madeline wriggled back into the comfort of her sofa with her tea between her fingers. She lifted one leg over the other and sipped at her tea.

'Well, it's not *"going"*, as per say.' Emma replied once she took her seat next to Madeline.

Madeline took a huge gulp of her tea. She almost spat it out at the concern in Emma's voice. Her brows furrowed as she set her tea back down on its coaster.

'How do you mean?' She asked in a worried tone.

'Well, I've only just graduated.' Emma sighed. 'I've been looking for a job in the city but nothing has come up yet.' Madeline picked her tea back up, sipping it again. She was concerned about her friend, but it was only a fraction of the worry Emma felt. She knew it sometimes took a while for things to come through but a few months seemed quite the dilemma. She knew she had to be patient and maybe a weekend with her best friend would keep her mind from going astray.

'Well don't you worry, *darl'*. Something will come up. Probably when you least expect it.' Emma was assured by Madeline's smile. She had a way to interlink her eyebrows with it too, the two made it seem that her words spoke the truth and Emma had always been comforted by her way.

Silence stirred between the two. Emma watched as Madeline took her cup off the saucer. The clink of the fancy, primrose-patterned cup clicked in her mind. As she sipped, Emma could hear the breathing of the manor, the creaks and groans of the foundations below her and down the hall. Suddenly the thought of ghosts had come back to her. She thought she was hearing them, but the building was old. It was bound to make noises.

Madeline watched as Emma's eyes searched the walls and ceiling. She couldn't help but crack a small smile from behind her teacup. Madeline was used to it. She'd heard and seen many things in the manor growing up.

Just as Emma busied herself by looking around the room and up the ceiling, someone hit the door. She whirled her body around while Madeline continued calmly sipping her tea.

An older gentlemen had come in. Emma turned to him. He pressed his splayed hands against the door and knocked lightly. With his entrance, the groans and creaks of the home had gotten louder. Yet with his footsteps across the floorboards, it was enough to drown it out.

'Madeline, you have family at the door.' The man spoke in an impeccable accent, something very much the same to how Madeline sounded, Emma noticed.

'Yes father.'

Emma deduced that the polished man was her father. She had never met Madeline's family before. Not even when she lived in London for all her schooling years.

In an instant, Madeline got up from the comfort of the couch, shoving a forced smile down at Emma.

'Will you excuse me?' Madeline asked quickly as she left the room to greet the latest arrivals. Madeline's father remained at the door. After he politely guided her with his hand around her back, he turned back on his heel. He stuffed a wide smile towards Emma.

'And you must be Miss Squier?'

'Yes. Yes, I am.' Emma raised from her seat, giving a half curtsy to the man. The older gentlemen was dressed marvellously. He wore a grey suit with a brown, buttoned shirt behind it but it was a lazy, about the house kind of suit.

'Are you Mr Smallhorn? Madeline's father?' Emma asked to make sure.

The man bowed his head, his slightly dark hair falling to his brow, letting the badger-like white strip of hair come to view.

'Indeed I am. You must be Madeline's best friend, Emma? She has told us all about you.'

Mr Smallhorn cradled a glass in his hand and held it to his stomach. Emma could just about smell the gin inside with the hint of something peach flavoured, ice tea perhaps.

'Indeed I am. I hope that it won't be much trouble. Seems like this is a family event.' Emma said with a nervous chuckle, to her admission letting the laughter out a little clumsily.

'Nonsense. A friend of the family virtually is family.' The assurance left Emma feeling a little better. Now that she felt welcomed by more than just Madeline, she took her seat back and waited for Madeline to return.

Mr Smallhorn was a very nice man. Emma saw many similarities between him and Madeline, such as the same cosy smile and welcoming demeanour. Emma got the impression the man was proud of his family and every once in a while liked to show off his family manor to guests.

'Just sit tight for a moment whilst I welcome the next guests.' Emma nodded. Right before Mr Smallhorn had departed the room to greet his new arrivals, he said one last thing to Emma.

'I could give you the tour if you like. A lot of history in this place.' Mr Smallhorn grinned as he retreated back from the doorframe. Emma was delighted. She said that she looked forward to it and with that, Mr Smallhorn slowly escaped to return to the front door.

Emma was cautious. The manor, the age, the stories were spooky. Her senses told her that something wasn't right. Now that she was in, there was no turning back.

Chapter 2

'1498 this manor was built. It was originally crafted by Sir Douglas Smallhorn. He was the great, great grandchild of one of King Edwards most admired knights in the hundred years' war.' Mr Smallhorn boasted.

He stood proudly and held his head back with a kingly posture. He kept his hands behind his back and kicked his legs out forwards in a type of slow sway. He'd led Emma all throughout the manor when his duties of welcoming his guests were over. Henry Smallhorn had always been proud to show off his manor. It wasn't just the antiques nor the grandness of it, but it had mostly been the history behind it. He was fortunate enough to be able to spread the facts of his family's inheritance. He was quite proud to be a Smallhorn.

'Ok, father. I don't think Emma wants to hear all about the manor.' Madeline lingered behind. This must've been the thousandth tour she'd had to suffer through . 'You have overloaded her poor head with hundreds of facts already.' Madeline scoffed, finding that the long tour of every room in the old manor had tired her.

Emma shook her head. She playfully smacked Madeline's arm with the side of her hand.

'Nonsense. History is most important and the history of this manor deserves to be told.'

Mr Smallhorn was delighted to hear such a thing. A smile ripened and his cheeks glowed. He kept his hands tucked behind his back as he walked up the few steps leading down a flat carpeted hall where an aisle of bedrooms were situated.

Emma soon realised that the tour was at an end. It was the last corridor of the top floor in the three-story manor. She had seen anything and everything, from the dungeon to the kitchen and all the left behind artefacts, most of them from the early fifteen hundreds. many were of knight and royal origin.

Emma had studied the many weapons hung up on the wall, the most prized of which kept in glass cabinets. She had seen the dresses worn by princesses and the armour of knights on full display. She'd seen all the pottery and tableware which Madeline's father had sworn up and down that *Queen Elizabeth I* had used during her one time stay.

Emma was impressed.

'Everything is all so very impressive, Mr Smallhorn.' Emma said, having never seen let alone been in a building of such old history before. She hadn't even visited the Tower of London before, but she'd heard about the armoury in the White tower. Perhaps the Smallhorn manor could give it a run for its money.

'How did you acquire the manor, if you don't mind me asking?'

Henry chuckled between his clasped lips.

'It hadn't been a case of "acquiring" per say, but more of an inheritance.'

'Well, the Smallhorn family can directly trace our lineage to Sir Douglas. He built the manor, as I mentioned before.' Emma nodded as she turned to a case of antique rifles which had casually been displayed in a glass case by an empty room.

'It is something of a family home, handed down from generation to generation since its foundation. The Smallhorns are cousins to the Douglas family and my family name has owned the manor since the mid-seventeenth hundred's.' Henry's words seemed to fumble for a moment. He thought about what he'd said and realised it was a question to which he hadn't solved himself.

'I don't know exactly how the transaction transpired. I believe the Douglas family died, perhaps in a feud with a knight or royal type. Whatever happened, the Smallhorns legally inherited the manor and have obtained ownership for some time.' Mr Smallhorn declared when he came to a stop at the first room down the hall.

Emma peered down to the red carpet. She gazed at the crown crest patterning along the edges of it. What was once fluffy and springing with tuffs, now the carpet had become flat with use and age. It felt a little crusty under Emma's shoe. She could even hear the thread's crack as she walked forward.

'Everything found in these walls has been kept over the years. Everything should be in a museum, quite frankly.' Mr Smallhorn admitted with a cocked grin. The very words left a bitter taste in his mouth as he didn't quite like the idea of all his family heirlooms in some museum. Emma rather got the sense that he believed everything should be kept in the family. And she was right. Henry Smallhorn went on.

'This is my family and my heritage. Everything here shouldn't and won't change. I will keep this manor as traditional as possible, like nothing has ever changed.'

Madeline chimed in, taking her hand and wrapping it around her father's arm.

'Father is very protective of his family treasures. I wasn't allowed to play with any of them.' Madeline went on.

'And you still are not.' Mr Smallhorn playfully added, but the slight grumble in his voice told Emma that he was still as serious as he was when he told Madeline that as a child. Emma took it as a warning for herself, like it was Mr Smallhorns own indirect way of warning her too. Meanwhile, Emma remembered that Madeline told her how angry her parents were that her older brother had broken that ancient pot in the entrance hall all those years ago. She swore that she could see the trauma on Mr Smallhorn's face as he seemed to recount that day during the conversation. His face blushed with red and his cheeks went all steamy. She could see the dread simmering in his eyes again. He seemed a little obsessed. It had only been a piece of pottery, but he treated his family heirlooms like his own children.

Quite frankly, Emma wondered why he had fixated upon one thing. The rest of the manor was overstuffed, but perhaps he struck fear into his children not to break anything further.

'Alas... My daughter is right,' Mr Smallhorn admitted. 'Please. I feel ever so guilty for keeping you this long. I certainly have talked your ears off.' Mr Smallhorn realised what Emma was only too polite to ever admit it.

Mr Smallhorn stepped down the hall a little. He came to a stop and extended his hand to show Emma the way.

'This is your room for the night,' he gestured.

Mr Smallhorn opened the first door down the hall. It was a vacant room and a room that looked as if it had been untouched for a number of years. There were too many rooms for all of them to be used, but Mrs Smallhorn still routinely washed the sheets and rearranged the room from time to time to make it cosy, paying the maid of the manor well to clean it and the rest of them up over the years.

Emma could smell the dust and the fabric of the clean sheets and the woven curtains. A room that'd been contained for a kept prepared for a number of years, at last being put to use. Emma thought that it was beautiful. A little lonely, rather like herself, but beautiful on the inside.

'Please, have a look.' Mr Smallhorn said. He stepped aside with his hand and kept the door open for Emma to drift in.

And so she did. At first she only sensed its beauty, but now she could see and experience it in full. The Smallhorn's room was now Emma's for the night. It was different from her apartment in London, the difference very profound. Although the manor itself was full of gloom and the grey skies full of a storm, the room seemed brighter and more airy than all the other rooms she had seen. The freshly washed sheets breathed a nice aged aroma into the air.

It was surrounded by old history, yet somehow it felt new.

In the centre of the room, a large quilt covered a queen-sized bed. The velvet red of the quilt matched both the carpet and the curtains and upon it, the family crest was woven into it with golden wool. It was a wonderful quilt and created a cosy room.

Emma stepped inside the doorframe, imaging the age of the room and just how much of it had changed from the beginning. She rather hoped that it hadn't changed from the time it was built until now. Fit for a princess or a weary traveller of some realm. It could've been someone famous and important who over the years had stayed in the very room that she was to stay in tonight.

She imagined a gorgeous princess in an exquisite dress writing at the table before bed. She could only dream to think of those who'd spent many of nights in her room.

'This has always been my favourite room.' Madeline said. She smiled over Emma's shoulder and peeped inside.

'You tried so hard to switch your bedrooms. But this one deserved to be preserved for our guests. Besides, your bedroom is much bigger.' Mr Smallhorn argued quietly, trying to let Emma enjoy the moment.

Three paintings faced the end of the bed. Old and probably worth a few *bob*, Emma thought she recognised the paintings, but Henry couldn't help himself from spilling more facts.

'That there is Geoffrey Chauncer. The one in the middle is William Shakespeare and the one on the end is Elizabeth. *Good old Queen Bess.* She is my favourite royal of all time, in fact,' Henry Smallhorn stated.

'I know, I recognise them. You know, I did study English history for a semester at university,' Emma said.

'I am impressed,' Mr Smallhorn clapped, making Emma think that no one who ever stayed could guess who the three paintings were.

'I found them in one of the spare rooms filled with all sorts of clutter. I pulled them out and my wife decided it was best to have them in this room.' Mr Smallhorn said, at which point he heard Mrs Smallhorn calling from downstairs. The three heard her voice echoing up the stairs and down the hall. She seemed as though she had been calling for some time as her voice had grown louder and louder at each call.

'Please excuse me.' Mr Smallhorn announced, leaving both Madeline and Emma to fend for themselves.

Emma looked at the paintings once more as she stepped further towards them. A beautiful breakfront rested below them, stacked with thick, leather bound books which looked more natural than ornaments in Emma's view.

She hadn't quite gotten over her room yet. This room combined with the rest of the manor… it left her feeling delirious. She started to think what a shame it had been that she hadn't taken Madeline up on her invitation much earlier.

'Henry… Henry, dear.' The calls from Mrs Smallhorn continued in the background. He had not yet reached her. Emma set her bag down on the bed, her eyes continuously darting around the room.

Madeline showed Emma the bathroom. It had been redone with white tiling depicting roses crawling up the walls. The bathroom was just about the only part of the manor which was new, and yet as she approached it she noticed she found it still somewhat old.

'It was renovated about thirty years ago. It almost killed my father to do so, but it needed it' Madeline said. She pointed out the slim white sink and the chips at the piping beneath. 'It may be the youngest thing in this building which isn't alive', Madeline joked.

Just as the two exited the bathroom a man stepped out of one of the bedrooms. He startled the pair.

At first Emma thought that the stories about ghosts had been true after all, that Madeline hadn't made them up after all these years. Emma gasped, her hand flying to her mouth.

The man stepped back a little – he seemed more frightened of Emma and Madeline's reaction than the pair themselves. The man wore black clothing, his hair was just as dark. He stumbled and hastily smiled at the two girls, his wrinkles cutting deep into his forehead.

'I am sorry. Did I frighten you?' He asked with a calm tone.

'Uncle Robin!' Madeline announced cheerfully, throwing her arms out to hug the man.

'This is my uncle, my father's brother.' Madeline introduced her uncle to Emma. She wanted to shake his hands but noticed they were occupied with two poles, used for fly fishing. The twine was held together by two sticks, looking handmade instead of bought. Like his brother, Robin seemed to like things the old-fashioned way. Emma gazed at the clothing he wore. His army green overalls were made of worn leather, hidden behind his banker's suit where a quiet grey tie blended behind it.

Emma looked up from his clothes to witness the grunting smile of the small, balding man. It was a forced smile, the kind to let her know that he didn't have the time to stand around and chat.

'I'm sorry, love.' He said, turning to Madeline. 'I'm in a bit of a rush.' He said, apologetically holding up his fishing poles.

'I have to head down to the river before this storm gets any worse.' He turned to Emma and bowed his body toward her. 'It is nice to meet you,' Robin said, never even asking Emma's name. He quickly excused himself, stating that he would be late to beat the storm before going to the woodland river for some fly fishing. Robin was an older gentleman. He had been invited to the family reunion that was tonight, he stumbled down the hall, carrying his things awkwardly. Robin Smallhorn was ten years older than his brother Henry. His bones did ache and his knees were sore, but he wouldn't miss a moment of fishing.

'He very much likes to keep a hold of the old things. He found those rods in the manor a few years back.' Madeline said, remembering the many times she'd joined Robin at the river when he would often come over.

'He lives on the other end of England. Cornwall actually. He is a little further away and we don't get to see him so much.'

'Is that right?' Emma replied, wondering why he had moved so far. Sensing it, Madeline caught on Emma's inquisition.

'My father and uncle need a few miles between them. They get on well most of the time, but they do fight quite a bit. It is probably because my father was left the manor by their grandparents. I don't know why it went to him, my father being the younger sibling, but I've always imagined that's where their problems stemmed.' Madeline always suspected that it was the case. 'If it wasn't for fishing being a buffer for their spats and quarrels, they would likely never see each other as much as they do.'

'That sounds awful.' Emma said. She straightened up a little straighter once Madeline mentioned that the manor would be uncle Robin's if something were to happen to her parents. The detective side of her couldn't help but hang onto that little fact.

'You really think he has such a thing is on his mind… Do you think your uncle would want the manor so badly?' Emma asked, thinking that she was overstepping a personal boundary as soon as her words left her mouth.

Madeline was only too happy to entertain the notion, like it was the only time she could confide with someone about the idea.

'It could very well be. He does love this manor, though it would likely take him away from his practice.' Madeline revised, adding that uncle Robin was a doctor back in Cornwall. He had an office and a wealthy home. His children have grown up and are now spread all over the country, but he had everything including his wife and two dogs at home to keep him content.

It would seem that Robin had lived a happy life outside the claim of his family's inheritance. He had moved to Cornwall to build his own life, yet he still loved his family and cherished the home in which he grew up in.

Helping her unpack, Madeline mentioned that just about everybody had arrived. Dinner, as far as she could tell, would be served in a few hours or so. It wasn't dark yet but in little over an hour it would be. It was just enough time for uncle Robin and the other family members who were to meet him at the river to catch some fish.

Robin Smallhorn walked the half mile or so through the woods, following a gravelled path to reach the river. The dark, stormy skies above made the late afternoon look night already. The woods were hard to see through. A thick smog of darkness drifted through them, making it impossible to see through the slits between the trees.

His sore joints and the ache presiding under the soles of his flat feet were all worth it once he had reached the edge of the river. He joined his cousin, Frank Lightfoot and Frank's son, Alfred Lightfoot.

'Hold strong. Keep that line strengthened. Plant your feet in the ground.' Frank commanded, noticing his son's struggle in the river. A strong breeze came down the opening of the river, coming like whiplash from the storm which was increasingly picking up.

Alfred listened to his father. He dug his feet into the rocks in the bed of the water, holding his body firm against the force of weather. He mimicked his father who stood five yards next to him and Robin who was a little further down the river, taking a fiercer hit closer to the storm.

The water rushed through, coursing towards them and disturbing the fish they had hoped to add to their baskets. Alfred's hook bobbed against the ripples, and fought against the might of the water. Even with the water crashing past his knees he stayed steady and strong, anticipating the bite of cod coming down with the direction of the water.

The young Alfred tried his best. It wasn't the first time he had been fishing at the Smallhorn manor. He knew how to handle himself and he'd learned just how rough the river could be.

In his young age, he'd visited at least a dozen times before. He knew the river. He knew it well enough to battle it.

There was a certain way to stand in the water that Alfred's father, Frank had taught him.

"You just stick your feet under a couple rocks on the riverbed and put force behind your back". That was how he learned.

Rain sprayed hard and had not stopped for an hour now. With no sign of slackening, it tapped the water, sounding to the three fisherman's ears like rain plummeting on iron ply... at times it'd be considered a relaxing and cosy sound. But with the storm coming, it was a sign to hurry up with their catches and get inside.

'You've got it, Alfred You've got this.' Frank shouted, stirring his son on to land a fish that had taken a bite.

Alfred felt the pull at the end of his line, but the fish had not yet fallen to his hook. waited for a moment. He waited for the fish to tangle its mouth around the barb before he knew it was his. When he felt the line weaken, he knew it was time to bring it in.

In an instant, Alfred lifted the rod high over his head, yanking the last fish of the day from the water. Frank waddled towards it, carrying a large net to catch it. He pushed his way through the heavy river with all his might, walking rather awkwardly as if he were tearing through quicksand.

At long last, Frank banked it. Finally, Alfred was allowed to be released of his pressure.

'Good work, son.' Frank complimented him. Robin had left his place and had begun trudging up alongside the river, water dripping from his soaked clothing.

At which point, Robin passed Reginald Jackson, who everyone called Reggie. He was perched upon a rock, his bare feet dangled below, he stubbing his heels with every light-hearted kick.

Reggie was a young, sweet lad. He wore his straw hat – the one he usually took outside. On his rock, he began to act like *Jim* out of *Huckleberry Finn.* It was the way he felt so free out in the woods with nothing but a rock for a seat and a charming story to pass his time. Reggie was a young lad of colour, and as much as the world did, the Smallhorns never discriminated against him. In fact, they took him in with open arms and a well paid job.

He'd found work in the paper when the Smallhorn's queried for a stable hand. He Reggie would spend his day's working on the barn and looking after the animals the Smallhorn's kept. In his spare time, he liked to read and he often found himself joining those who went fishing when they'd visit the manor.

After a long day of working in the stables, stacking hay, cleaning the pens and feeding the horses, he drifted down from the barn often and ventured to the river. He would bring along his favourite book, ironically reading *Huckleberry Finn,* and sat upon the same rock by the river.

He must've read it a hundred times over. He enjoyed the serenity of reading by the cool lapses of the river, hearing the splash and sway of the water hit the rocks before him, but he also liked to come down when the Smallhorns came to fish.

Reggie stuck by the family, having finished his work and enjoyed the fresh air. He wore a droopy straw hat which protected most of his body from the harsh summers under the sun, and the unrelenting rain during the winters. 'Caught anything, Mr Smallhorn?' Reggie asked, simultaneously peering down into the bucket which Robin carried. It was full with four fish, a couple of trout and a singular cod.

He gazed at their red bellies with the black dots which speckled their flair.

'Once you commit yourself to a course of action, anything is possible.' Robin said as he showed Reggie the bucket more clearly.

Four was enough for him. He never caught anything more and was lucky to catch two on most visits.

'Even in conditions like this.' Robin added.

The worst day of fishing still beat any day of work, which was one of Robin's favourite mottos. He lifted his eyes to the clouds rolling in and at the same time, like it were magic, the thunder grumbled in agreement with his words.

'You sure are lucky, Mr Smallhorn. You think we have enough?' Reggie asked. He lifted his hand upon the top of his hat to keep it down as a topple of wind cascaded from the far end of the river.

'There will be fish aplenty,' Robin chuckled. He patted Reggie on the back and the two shared a smile.

'We should get back. That storm is coming in something fierce.' Robin said, knowing full well that the fish he and his brother introduced to the private river for them to catch had to be limited, and at the same time the weather would reel them back inside.

Reggie jumped off his rock, his feet landing inches from the shards of cracked, smaller rocks below.

'Where are your shoes, dear boy?' Robin asked, taking care to notice that Reggie almost cut his feet.

'I left them in the barn, sir. I like to keep them off by the river.' Reggie had his reason to which nobody else could quite understand but him. He liked the way the wind barrelled through his toes and the spray of the water kept them cool. Now he could see it. Now that Robin pointed it out for the first time, he really did understand why everybody thought he was trying to be like Jim.

'Come on, we best get inside. The weather is coming over fast.' Robin and Reggie made their way towards the Lightfoot's who had enough of the day already. The others weren't so crazy about staying out too much longer. They did their best to supply the main course for tonight's dinner, but Reggie would've liked to stay out a little longer. He didn't care about it getting too late or the weather coming in. The storm would've been a striking moment for Reggie. He wanted to mark the event in his memory, staying out to feel the utter arsenal of something so strong that it had been feared for weeks. People all over Northern England had been preparing for it for some time, expecting power outages and having to fend for themselves for at least the weekend.

Reggie slipped the book into his back pocket, feeling the roughness of his old, torn pants against the back of his hand. Parallel to the river stream, birds flocked from the trees, joined by bats. They had been tricked by the clouds, thinking it was already dark. The birds scurried away from the storm, sensing the might of it, but the bats stayed strong, simply moving because dozens of birds did.

Reggie took the lead up the path. He hummed quietly to himself, clutching onto a gnarled tree which leaned crookedly over the bank, almost completely felled to the rivers edge. By the amount of times Reggie had hooked onto it, just a few more times and it would surely break.

The four worked their way up the path. They passed fallen logs and hanging trees. It was much darker now and Reggie didn't notice a leaning branch which poked him in the cheek like an arrogant finger. He lifted his body and swatted it away to break the un-sturdy thing, making sure that no one else would face its trouble.

The wind was unbearable now. Even with the cover of the woods and the trees to break it, the foursome struggled. With heavy buckets full with fish and long nets and rods tucked in the pits of their arms, it was always harder coming back than it was going out.

Reggie made it out of the woods first. He gazed up at the manor that was a hundred or so feet away now. The wind hit his back as he turned away from it, facing the main barn in the distance. The wind seemed to hold him back, pressing roughly up against the front of his body. With its frosty touch, his spine tingled with a drop of ice-cold fear. He became both frightened and worried at what he remembered when he saw the barn in the distance, realising he had to get to the barn before the weather got any worse.

'What is it, dear boy?' Frank Lightfoot asked, noticing Reggies' troubles.

Reggie stammered and choked, hoping that his ill service would not come to bite him once he was to tell Mr Lightfoot of what he had done.

Henry Smallhorn had reprimanded him many times. He didn't like it when Reggie left the barn doors open as he often believed that his prized horses would escape, or a hunger-stricken fox would sly its way in.

'I forgot to close the stable doors.' Afraid, Reggie was just about to leap forward and race away towards them but Mr Lightfoot stopped him in his tracks.

'In this terrible wind, especially with more to come, those doors will be off their hinges.' Mr Lightfoot predicted. Frank sighed. He knew that Reggie couldn't close the barn doors all by himself. They looked like they'd need a team to get them battened down, each door as big as a castle's drawbridge.

Frank scrunched up his mouth with a frown and looked to Reggie, knowing full well that he could never close the huge, double barn doors on his own. *He would have trouble with them in still air with those twig-arms anyway.*

'Come on. I'll help you out. Seems like a two-man job.' Frank Lightfoot said, urging forwards to reach the barns as soon as possible. He dropped his net and bucket, leaving it to his young son to carry as well as his things.

Alfred Lightfoot and Robin Smallhorn walked the rest of the way up to the manor. Each struggled to carry their piled-on things and the wind took them, swaying the buckets full of fish that they could almost slip out and escape.

As the two reached the side entrance to the manor where the door opened to a laundry for them to place their muddy shoes, the two watched the last of the struggles of Reggie and Frank Lightfoot. They were yelling and holding the doors down like they were trying to wrangle up a couple of wild horses. Frank was a little stronger, able to force his feet into the ground and gain an inch or two every five seconds, but Reggie – as he feared - had trouble. His scrawny, twig-like arms couldn't hold it, leaving the two men questioning if they should set aside their things and race back down to help.

'Forget it, Alfie.' Mr Smallhorn said. He jerked, turning from the steps leading inside. He read Alfred's stares. The young man wanted to leap from his place, like a border collie bound for rustling up the sheep. Daylight was almost gone, and night had come through. Alfred grew worried.

'They are grown men. Your father was in the war, wasn't he?' Robin Smallhorn proceeded to say. And with it, he crawled out of the darkened, evening weather and into the shade of the laundry. Left in solitary, the safety of the manor looked insurmountably safer than bounding off down to the barns to stay out a little longer. Alfred almost kicked himself. He grunted as he hobbled in after Mr Smallhorn. When he did enter, he accepted Robin's advice and assurance that his father didn't need help.

Chapter 3

Emma looked grimly out the window, knowing that the weather was only going to get worse. But she didn't care. She was safe inside for the weekend.

The manor sure did look like it could hold off anything. The walls were a titan of steel that had withstand a tonne of bombardment over the centuries. A little storm didn't faze her.

She spent the day meeting Madeline's family. Madeline had carted Emma around by the scruff of her shoulder, parading her from one person to the next, forgetting each name as it was told to her..

The Smallhorn's were certainly quite a large and rich family, Emma figured out. Everyone looked nice enough at first glance, but Emma still never met who had almost run her clean over. She remembered the back of his head, the slicked back, oiled, black hair and the slight curls which tucked under his ear. She burned with anger at his carefree attitude, that he hadn't come to see if she was ok then nor now. She wondered where he'd got to.

Emma was told to head up stairs to her room and prepare for dinner. She wore a dress which Madeline kindly lent her. It was a sort of faded pink which she quite liked. Over her shoulders she wore a knitted fleece to keep her warm. It was exceptionally cold inside the manor, and outside it was much worse. The poor, little flame on the table beside her couldn't keep up. It bobbed and flickered off its wick, changing and fluttering to the sounds creaking up the walls and down the corridor – much to what Emma was used to hearing by now, but nonetheless still spooky.

Emma peered out the window. She watched the grey clouds sweep over the green fields leading up to the woods. The fog glided over the ground, searching for unwary ankles to curl around. The rain squeezed from the clouds above, soaking the scenery and weakening the sturdy trees. Emma watched the rain spit and drip down the glass of her window. She studied the droplets race each other as they streamed down the window. As she did, she brushed her hair. She tugged at it, pulling off strands of weakened hair that had been collected by her brush. It was then that her eyes were drawn to something.

'KEEP GOING!' A man shouted from outside. The wind tore the words up the hill and to Emma's window. When she heard the shouting, she looked down towards the barn in the distance. She moved forward to get a better view and witnessed two men whom she hadn't met. It was Reggie and Frank Lightfoot. After a long struggle, the two had closed the barn doors with a single, last grunt.

The older gentlemen dropped his weight to his knees. He was out of breath and thankful that the job was complete. He stood back up and put his arm around Reggie, congratulating him.

Being a detective, Emma had the sense to turn away from her staring and leave them to be. Her curiosity got the better of her and she decided to stay for a little while longer as the young lad – who she could only presume to be somewhat of a farmhand - had walked away from the older gentlemen. Reggie walked up the slope and back towards the manor before disappearing out of sight, leaving Frank Lightfoot alone.

Seperated, Mr Lightfoot stumbled across the grass, walking diagonally away from the barn, leaping over the small rocks and pebbles which separated the path from the grass. He headed closely towards the woods, his hands busy rummaging through his coat. He pulled out a pipe, wielding it around like a blade. He began to fill it, his searching eyes taking on a guilty look. This made Emma feel like he wasn't supposed to be smoking. He didn't want anybody to see him, just in case they would tell his wife, Emma supposed.

The smoky trail curled up from Mr Lightfoot's pipe, joining with the rolling fog. She watched him stare out into the woods for a little while longer, his fist balled up against his hip to relax.

So, she sat there, watching and knowing she had to go back downstairs for dinner soon. But Emma had been intrigued. She had by no means explored the entirety of the manor nor met everyone yet, but she felt as though she could remember the names and faces of those she took the time to stare at. The man outside looked oddly enough like Madelines' father, maybe a cousin or something, Emma thought.

'What are you doing?' Emma spun around out of her chair. She gasped, thinking that indeed a ghost had come crawling from all the groans and creaks behind her, but it was Madeline.

Her words came out a little deeper than her normal speaking voice – it was an inquisitive voice, almost the kind that caught her up to no good.

Emma's hand remained clamped to the armrest. Her eyes bulged as she still tried to register that it was Madeline.

Just before she could ask how long she had been standing there, watching her stare, Madeline walked forwards. Her high heels clicked against the floorboards as she walked in, softening when she reached the carpet.

'It's nothing. Just looking at the weather.' Emma persisted. Her heart throbbed and her eyes never died down from their fright. She looked like she'd been up to something. She didn't want to admit that she'd been spying on Madeline's family.

Madeline had made her way to the window. She kneeled over, searching beyond the rain-filled glass to find nothing but the darkness of the woods and the grey clouds swarming the lonely land.

'Oh, it does look quite nasty out there. It has really picked up, hasn't it?' Madeline said. She never mentioned that Frank Lightfoot had been standing outside.

Emma's brows narrowed. She couldn't believe that she hadn't pointed him out.

Emma joined her at the window. To her surprise the man who was once there no longer was.

Emma stumbled. The man would've had to move as quick as the lightning in order to have disappeared so quick.

Just as Emma thought about the lightning, a new bolt brightened the sky. Thunder grumbled a second after, fizzing the blood in her body once more.

'I didn't scare you, did I?' Madeline asked. She cocked her face to one side and scrunched her eyes in a playful manner. Emma didn't know what it was, but her best friend found it hilarious to scare her at times. Like always, Emma had played it coolly, never giving Madeline the prize of spooking her.

'No. Of course not.'

But Madeline knew. It was made clear by the obvious gulp which Emma wished she could bring it back up like it never happened.

'You ever get weather like this?' Emma asked. Her tone was changed, almost awed. London sure did get its grey skies and rain every there and again, but nothing compared to what had come thus far.

'Every winter brings a storm quite like this. But this one is meant to be the worst in years, so the papers say.' Madeline replied, as the two listened to the window shake.

Emma kept camouflaged to the mystery which shook in her head. She carried on with polite conversation, all the meanwhile wondering where the man outside had gone. He seemed to disappear as quick as the flash of lightening.

Madeline looked at Emma, puzzled. 'Is something wrong?' she asked, as she stepped away from the window.

Emma shook her head. A smile fell from her lips and her expression had glazed over.

Madeline never believed a word of it. She looked over Emma's shoulder, back out into the window for some time. She thought that whatever it was which distressed her, it was coming from outside. But Emma had gotten up from her chair, blocking the rest of the window to stand before her. She showed her the dress, diverting the conversation in an obvious way which left her to gawk and reminded her of the reasoning as to why she came up to Emma's room. Madeline clapped her hands over her mouth.

'The dress suits you perfectly.' She gasped.

Emma twirled a little, she picked the tails of her dress up and lifted them a little to puff it up.

'I just came down to let you know that dinner will be served shortly. You can come down whenever you like.'

She told her that she would be down immediately, right after she had put on a special perfume she'd brought down from London.

Madeline closed the door behind her, leaving Emma alone. As soon as she did, she leaped back to the window, crunching her knees into the chair. Erratically, she searched the green hills and the outskirts of the woods but there was nothing. She approached the window closer, getting a look at the barn in the corner of the glass once more, but there was no one there either. It was strange. The man must've come back in, Emma supposed, though she hadn't seen him. It did cause her some alarm - it was unwise to stay outside in such weather for too long. He must've snuck back to the manor when she wasn't looking.

She tried to convince herself with some sound reasoning, though the detective side of her kept bringing her thoughts to the front of her mind.

Shaking the mystery out of her head, promising to revisit it later, she clambered out of her room and headed for the dining room.

Emma walked the halls of the manor all by herself. She couldn't help but think that something had gone wrong. It didn't seem right. No one could move that quick. She was the only one to see him. She held this valuable piece of information, just hoping that nothing had gone wrong.

All the time Emma had been guided by the clink of cutlery and the raucous chime of voices with the occasional boom of laughter which came from downstairs. Her gentle study of the manor halls had come to an end and the encroaching voices had turned her away.

The voices led her out of the maze of the manor, safely bringing her down the entrance stairs where she was led into the sitting room where Madeline had brought her before.

Nestled against the open-door frame, Emma peered inside to see the dining room at the other end of the manor. Bodies of people floated by, momentarily blocking the candlelit room, carrying plates of food and fancy bottles of wine.

The jumbled conversation of a dozen voices and the sudden shock of laughter grew louder as Emma came closer. It was funny; the more people she'd believed were coming for the dinner and the more voices she heard, the more she felt alone. The only person she truly knew was Madeline, but even still it had been a couple of years since she had seen her.

It had all seemed a tad strange as to why Madeline had invited her. The *"family dinner"* had sounded like something of a personal matter and the foreboding storm did bring about a bad omen.

She moved with caution, blending in with the darkness of the hall, keeping close to the walls. An unfamiliar smell drifted from the dining room as dinner was served. The aroma that was generated by the ovens washed across her face and with it, a dry unpleasant smell. It was then that from the laundry room closed behind her and she smelled the fishy scent of the overalls.

Emma hoped that it wasn't fish for dinner and that there was something else. She never did like fish.

'Have you got the vegetables, love?' A calm voice said from the kitchen, bringing Emma's hope to life. She'd be happy with steamed vegetables.

As Emma found her way close to the doorframe, she peered into the dining room. Most seats were filled with family and friends of the Smallhorns. People were smoking, filling the room with a cloud of what looked like remnants of a fire.

Emma moved to her left, finding an empty seat that looked destined to be hers. She took her seat and was unrecognised by anyone, including Madeline's mother. Mrs Smallhorn had been occupied, toing and froing from the kitchen. She carried huge stacks of plates to set upon the table.

Emma got comfortable. She tucked her dress over her seat and bunched in closer to the table, dragging her seat forwards. She took a moment to look at the food and wine upon the table, trying to decide what she'd go for first. Amongst the clouds and trails of smoke, Emma caught the glare of a man before her that she didn't recognise.

Richard Gottfried was his name, as Emma found out. He was the local doctor and close friend of the Smallhorns. He owned a small practice in Sherrington and recalled many calls to the Smallhorn manor throughout the years. Madeline could remember him being there to check her temperature and prescribe her the best medicine when she lay sick in her bed. The doctor and his wife had indeed grown attached to the Smallhorn family.

Dr. Gottfried was a man of African descent. He mentioned that his father was born in Nigeria and his mother in London. The two were prominent and well-respected doctors also.

Richard Gottfried looked at Emma. 'I don't recall seeing you, dear.'

He spoke with a calm, ashy and grandfatherly tone. His teeth shined from behind his smile, making Emma believe that everything he'd say would be authentic.

'My name is Emma Squier, sir.' Emma whispered.

Dr. Gottfried nodded and noticed the dress that Emma was wearing. He recognised it as being something that Madeline had worn for her eighteenth birthday, just a few years ago. The doctor had an exceptional memory and his presence at the manor was more than necessary for a doctor, but as a friend, he was quite frequent.

'I have never heard of an *Emma Squier* before.' He furrowed his brow. The wrinkles upon his large forehead creased to his inquisitive nature.

'I'm a friend of the family. My best friend is Madeline. She invited me tonight.' Emma bunched up a little closer. As she finished, the housemaid wandered in from the kitchen. She converged upon Emma, noticing that her wine glass was empty. It was promptly filled and as she left back to the kitchen, Dr. Gottfried opened the conversation back up.

'Couldn't be much of a friend.' The doctor chuckled. Emma watched as his belly up over the tabletop as he bellowed with a deep laughter.

'To invite a friend on this terrible night – the night of the *great storm*. Doesn't say much about the rest of us and the family coming out, huh?'

Emma forced a smile. She turned to her wine and lifted the glass up to her lips to disguise the fact that it wasn't so amusing.

'Sorry if he offends your tender ears. He can get a little silly.' The woman next to him chimed in.

'That's quite alright. I suppose it isn't the best of nights to come out.' Emma giggled.

'My name is Millicent Gottfried.' Mrs Gottfried frolicked her gloved hand over her chest. She bowed her head to introduce herself and Emma couldn't help but mimic.

'I am Richard's wife.'

'Twenty-eight years strong next week,' Dr. Gottfried added as he hooked his arm around his wife.

'It's certainly blowing a gale out there now, isn't it?' Mrs Gottfried said as the wind hit the wall behind her, hard enough to spook her. She spoke as posh as posh could be. The clothes she wore and the neat-stacked wig she placed on had told Emma everything she could possibly want to know about her.

Her husband could afford her lavishness. Emma bet that she would live in the manor, if only she could. 'We have known Madeline ever since she was a child. Her mother and I are exceptional friends, you know.' Millicent sipped at her wine. Emma noticed that her lips were tucked against the glass. She was almost sucking the edge of it as if to dilute it.

'And what do you do, miss?' Mrs Gottfried asked. But Emma's attention was elsewhere. She faced the end of the dining room, looking outside the window, past the thin mesh of the curtains. Outside she could see a glow of orange, coming from a lit match.

Someone was smoking outside on the side porch, seemingly not afraid of the weather which whipped against the manor walls, carrying twigs and leaves from the woods with it.

'Miss?' Mrs Gottfried said a little louder. She wrangled Emma back into the conversation. Emma quickly steadied her gaze back to her after she realised she'd trailed off.

'Oh. Well, I studied law in London. And now I am a detective.'

'A detective?' Mrs Gottfried's voice pricked up a tone. She sounded like an impressed aunt who was ready to go back home and show her off to the rest of the family.

'You hear that, love?' Mrs Gottfried said, tapping her husband's shoulder.

'Yes, I heard.' Dr. Gottfried said, as he sipped at his wine.

Emma felt as if she could lie a little. She wasn't really a detective… Not yet at least. But with no one else around who knew, she could juice herself up a little.

'Yes. I have come across some work recently. It is out in London. They have me mostly solving cold cases for now.' Emma didn't care that she lied – though it wasn't of a 'detective-to-be' nature.

'It just warms my heart to see young people delve into such an exciting career. Things had certainly changed since I was as young as you are,' Mrs Gottfried said and just before Emma could be asked just what kind of cold cases she was given to solve, Mrs Smallhorn swooped from her end of the table to join the conversation.

As Prudence Smallhorn leaned over the table, Emma felt her heated breath around the collar of her knitted fleece. She was a little uncomfortable, but she sensed a motherly feeling from her already. She made her feel right at home.

'Eat whenever you like dear. Please don't wait around for the others to join us.' Mrs Smallhorn instructed. She wrapped her hand around her neck, rubbing the sparkling, diamond necklace with a rose-red ruby which dangled in the centre and matched her dress. Emma couldn't help but look at it. The rose-red ruby enticed her – *something that I could never afford.* Emma thought now that the shine had become trapped in her eye.

Mrs Smallhorn liked to show it off. She wore it like a tattered boa. Such a beautiful gem to match a beautiful lady, that's why Mr Smallhorn bought it for her many years ago. She cherished it and every once and a while, Emma did notice her fiddling with it between her fingers across the table before she came over.

Emma never knew that diamonds could possibly be overlooked by anything else, but that ruby was stunning. Now that she'd seen it up close, she wondered just how much the Smallhorn name was worth.

Emma cleared her throat. Her eyes trailed from the precious gem the best they could and she gained the courage to ask her question.

'Who is out on the porch. Do they want to come in?' Emma asked. She pointed to the window where the flame burned brightly, looking rather like an oil lamp brightening behind the window.

'Oh him. That is my brother Billy.' Mrs Smallhorn answered. Emma sensed that there was a little hesitation in her voice.

Emma hadn't known who it was. The man outside had been a virtual recluse for many years since his life was rocked.

Billy Javers was the craven man's name. He was the man who stood out on the porch, welcoming the wind and heavy rain. He watched the night sky and the lightning when it ripped behind the clouds. He liked it when the light showed for a second, where the woods would come to life under the weather's glow. He didn't care for the danger of thestorm. He liked being a witness of it, feeling the spray hit his face as if he were on a cruise ship. But Billy wasn't *normal*.

'My brother, Billy… he is not a well man.' He stood outside a while longer, waiting for his pipe to extinguish. He liked the cold brush upon his skin and how it wandered under his coat. It felt like a touch… a touch so cold and un-human that he'd clung onto.

He felt alive in it.

Emma didn't want to pry – and nor did Mrs Smallhorn want to give the dark history of her brother to an up-and-coming detective, but she thought she ought to tell her. There was no telling what Billy could do. Emma needed to know what he was capable of to be sharing a home with him for the night.

Billy Javers sure did sound like a monster set loose that the family loved too much to ever let go of.

'Where do I begin?' Prudence stammered. She cleared her throat and took up the vacant seat next to Emma. 'My brother was released from prison about six months ago. He went away for many years on the suspicion of murdering a young couple in London. No one knows if he truly did it or not, but *little Billy* is still my brother. My parents were torn, but I stuck true to his innocence. We all love him, but prison changed him. He cannot help but wonder all the time if we think he did it or not, and it drives him crazy.' As Mrs Smallhorn spoke, Emma's eyes never left the window. Her eyes soared through the peep of the curtains and the glass. She stared at the flame and rolls of smoke which came out of it, having in fact never seen his face.

It was as if she'd been staring at a monster – a monster who's details she could temporarily see whenever he blew into his pipe and the sparks burned to reveal the side of his face.

Emma gulped. The young detective that she was was taught never to fear anybody in the name of law and order. But Billy was someone that she became immediately on edge about.

She hadn't remembered hearing of a *Billy Javers* nor his crime in London. She thought she may have glanced over a news article of a piece in her study about the crime, but she couldn't recall his name ever coming up.

The utter mystery of his figure kept the fear living for as long as he didn't ever show himself in full.

'But what is he doing out in the storm?' Emma asked.

'He has become utterly desensitised to things like rain, or thunder,' Prudence answered.

'But won't he get cold out there, or hungry at least?' Emma pried some more.

'He won't come in for dinner just yet. He enjoys his serenity.' Mrs Smallhorn whispered, hoping she wouldn't speak too loud in case he heard them.

'There is a case for you to solve.' Dr. Gottfried boasted, simultaneously stabbing his butter knife into the fish on his plate.

Mrs Gottfried instantly jabbed him with her fleshy, bony finger and stared daggers at him.

'Richard!' She hissed. But Emma and Mrs Smallhorn never minded.

The Doctor knew of Billy's history. He even volunteered to help and examine him for his trauma, but Billy wouldn't budge. Billy barely spoke or desired to be with anyone nowadays.

'It's best that you don't say anything to him if you come across him. If he finds out what you are, it may trigger something.' Mrs Smallhorn casted her warning. Her brother did not take kindly to lawmen or detectives.

Emma stared at him in his duffle coat once more. Now his body was there in the window, but his back was turned.

'Yes, Mrs Smallhorn.' Emma obliged and just as she tore away from the table, Madeline entered. She sat next to Emma, coming into something that she hadn't known, yet she sensed what they were talking about.

'Poor, old uncle Billy.' Mrs Smallhorn hissed at her to be silent, being so close to the wall where Billy was.

'Oh he won't be able to hear anything with that storm going on. Besides, all I'm saying is poor uncle Billy.' Madeline re-iterated.

As a kid, *"Uncle Billy"* and his problems were just about all she heard growing up. She remembered her mother telling her over and over again about the trial. Madeline hadn't been born then, but her mother did tell her what she'd experienced. Madeline had known him to be a reformed man, but the tapestry of prison had not changed him. In a way, Billy had still been imprisoned by his torment. He had become a man who had grown in prison for a few years to become monster-like in the view of people beyond the Smallhorn family.

Though he pleaded his innocence more times than what he could count, as he sat in jail, he slowly grew to realise that the truth could be different. After a while, he did in fact believe that he was guilty. Prison warped his mind. Confronted with guilty men and a home that locked him in with conviction made him believe it. It was a terrible thing.

'Till this very day, I still don't know if Billy did it.' Now tones of grim horror settled into Mrs Smallhorns voice. 'He kept alive. He hadn't gone to the extreme of ending his life by the riddles of torment which cursed him.'

Prudence looked out to him. He really did seem like a monster now. He wasn't Billy anymore, but it was never his doing. 'Perhaps it would be best if he stayed in prison, the way it changed him,' she said. It hurt just to admit it, but she thought it right.

She looked on at Billy, thinking that the monster which had him overrun was still out there. That was the reason why he stayed alone. That was the reason why he liked the darkness and the horrible lashes of the weather.

It was the worst thing that Mrs Smallhorn could think of. Her brother was unwell and from time to time, she thought the worst. She did often believe that he was a guilty man, being allowed to walk a little earlier than what he should have. But on this night, it was a happy occasion, to have friends and family over on a night such as this one.

Emma whirled around and looked down the end of the table. There was that man… The man who almost ran her over. Noticing his look and the way he groped the back of his head to pull his hair down, Emma knew it was him. Dressed in a different suit, but it was him. Crème white it was, almost the same complexion as his skin. He sat next to his brother, Alfred. Both brothers were absent from their father. They hadn't seen him since it was still light out. Next to them, that empty seat remained vacant. Neither of them said a word nor looked away from their glasses. It was as if they too didn't feel like they belonged without their father's influence in the family,

'What is that man's name?' Emma whispered to Madeline. Madeline paused at her food. She looked to Emma's plate before answering her. It was lightly filled with the things around the fish from Mr Smallhorn only lightly picked at.

'You mean the man next to Alfred?' Madeline pointed with her butter knife, chomping down on a lumpy bit of fish.

'That is my other cousin, Alfred's brother. His name is Fillius.'

Emma now had her man. A name to the craven figure whose face she would never forget. With a grunt and her leering stare, she swore to have a word with him when she got the chance. Thinking that her stare would stand out like a lighthouse, he never looked. He was so concentrated on his glass of wine and the fish upon his plate which his brother more than likely caught.

Just when Emma was about to peel away and give in, she held her stare for a little longer, leaving just the right amount of time for Fillius Lightfoot to look up at her.

The two were caught in a lock. Silently, he fluttered his eyes at her, the candle flames upon the table helped to glow them, and they excited the cobalt blue in his eye. Although she disliked the man, she couldn't doubt that he was handsome.

He gazed at her and a faint flush of red tinged her cheeks.

'Oh, my goodness. That may be the best thing ever.' Madeline squealed, tugging at Emma's arms as she realised what had happened.

As soon as she spoke, she snapped Emma out of her trance.

'Don't be silly.' Emma winced. She realised what had happened. Now that she looked into his eyes, she'd almost forgotten about the troubles beforehand. Now Madeline would never let it down.

Thankfully – for Emma's sake, looking down the end of the table, Madeline made the discovery that no one else noticed.

The attention was diverted as Madeline noticed the empty place by the Lightfoot brothers.

'Where is uncle Frank?' She shouted and disrupted the sectioned chatters around the table. Everyone went silent and looked to the Lightfoot siblings. Madeline had indeed been right. Their father's absence never bothered them, they'd only believed he'd taken his time in his room to get ready after fishing. Of course, there was the other thing… They usually knew what he was up to – even though he never suspected they knew. They always knew that he went out for a smoke, hiding away and ditching everyone to get five minutes to himself. Frank wasn't supposed to smoke anymore. He was meant to give it up months ago, but he still snuck one in from time to time. The brothers never brought it up of course, but now that everyone was aware, Fillius spoke up.

'He has just gone out for a smoke before dinner. He's made a habit of it.' Fillius shrunk back into his seat. He wiped his awkward smile away with his napkin and returned to his meal.

'Now that you mention it, I haven't seen uncle Frank since the early hours of this evening.' Madeline's father announced. 'He did return from the river, didn't he?' Henry asked.

Emma barrelled her vision down towards the end of the table, reading the concern upon Mr Smallhorns face. They were equally concerned.

'I haven't seen him since he went fishing. Have you, dear?' Mr Smallhorn asked as he turned to his wife.

'My brother could be up to no good anywhere. It is likely that he is still out there fishing.' She boasted in laughter, keeping her glass waved high by her shoulder. Clumsily, a little wine dribbled out from the corner of her mouth, Emma noticed.

'Well… that is odd. Frank out, in this weather?' Henry Smallhorn was puzzled. The dining room went silent at which moment a monstrous roll of thunder burst. It sounded as though it ruptured just above the roof and it was lucky that the power hadn't gone out.

Emma listened to the shaking of the chandelier above. The crystals rattled like a farm barn shackle at which point she remembered what she had seen.

'I saw Frank outside just before dinner. It would have been an hour ago at least. Emma announced.

'You saw my father?' Fillius answered, breaking the unmatched tension between the two.

'By the barnyard', Emma said.

'That's right. He went and helped your young stable hand', Robin Smallhorn chimed in, remembering the stable door incident before coming in.

As everyone chatted amongst themselves about Frank's disappearance, it gave Emma the chance to return to the window where Billy was outside. He was still there, smoking away at his pipe, unfazed by the stormy weather swarming the manor.

Emma turned to Madeline, whispering in her ear to keep her words from being overheard.

'You ought to tell me more about uncle Billy. Maybe I can help him.' Emma expressed. She couldn't help but feel fascinated by the man. In fact, the whole Smallhorn and Lightfoot family were a little odd to her. In one night she had learned the many secrets of Madeline's family and it was something to which she was not expecting.

'You think you can?' Madeline asked. She moved her hands across the tablecloth, linking her fingers together to find out more about what Emma was trying to say.

'He is a little difficult to talk to, you know. Affected, but clever. He is also a very ordered person. You know, the type who would alphabetically place his books on a shelf and would collapse if one hadn't been right. A man who would make sure all the creases are out of his bedsheet in the morning. Prison taught him to be like that. You know... over the top about things.'

There was a moment of silence and then Emma said, 'All right, Madeline. Just give me five minutes to talk to him. Nobody else has to be around. Maybe I can truly find out what had happened that night. I can help him, if you allow me to try.'

Madeline sighed. Nobody ever could before. He never spoke. He never saw anyone and most of all he despised anyone in the law department. He barely let Dr. Gottfried near him as he saw him as one of the prison doctors in the infirmary instead of a friendly doctor trying to help.

'Ok. I will try and – ' before Madeline could finish what she had to say, she noticed her family jump out of their seats. The groans of the floorboards as chair legs scraped across them sounded at once. Emma whipped her head around, turning to see the Lightfoot brothers as they rose, dumping their napkins over their plates.

The two had missed what was said and didn't know what was going on.

'What is going on, father?' Madeline called out over the table.

'It's fine, dear. The boys and I are just going out to have a search around for uncle Frank.'

Henry followed the Lightfoot's steps. He got up and dumped his napkin over his plate. He wasn't happy that his dinner was to be left cold, but he – more than anyone - wanted his brother-in-law found.

'I want to go out with you. Let's go Emma, it'll be fun.' Madeline said in a childish way. Her very words brought Emma back to the very day when she and her were eight years old and Madeline tempted her into stealing a candy bar from right under the shop owner's eyes. *Poor old Mr Twiggs.* Emma always felt bad for it. Perhaps it was just another motive to make herself someone of the law.

Old man Twiggs never saw them coming, not with his half-blind eyes. On that day, Emma never expected Madeline to act out in such a way. That's what made it that much more dangerous. If she wanted one she could have paid for one a hundred times over. Falling for her gullible tone the same way as she did back then, Emma leaped from her seat, prepared to lend any assistance she could.

'You girls stay right here. I don't want you heading out into a night like this. It's bad enough we are.' Mr Smallhorn said. He reached for his coat and strapped it around his waist.

Everyone listened to the storm hit the manor walls from the inside. They could only imagine how bad it was out in the stir of it. No one wanted to go, but the fear that Frank was in trouble had been the manor's main concern.

'Are you coming, Robin?' Henry asked, interrupting his brother's enjoyment of his drink. Robin coughed it up and spat a little of his wine back into the glass. It wasn't his intention to go out into the storm and he'd much rather finish his warm meal, but he would join his brother.

'Yes, old boy. Just finishing up on the wine. You need a good drink to be man enough to go out in that weather.' Robin said. Like a medieval king, he stabbed the glass back down on the table with a fierce statement.

'I'd go with you. But it's my damn legs you see.' Dr. Gottfried said with a mischievous smile. He held his right knee, his hand passing his gut as he truly felt that he was a little overweight to go running out in a storm like so. The Doctor was an older gentleman. He feared he couldn't hold himself upright against the lash of the storm. He was of decent health but could no longer physically do what he used to be able to.

Excused, the Gottfried's stayed behind to finish their dinner. Next to them, tucked in the shade at the very end of the table were Madeline's grandparents. They were her mother's parents and seemed to visit the manor quite frequently.

Madeline's grandfather wriggled in his seat. He had been eager to get up and join them. He buttoned up his coat and even pulled down his flat cap tight on his head. He was ready to enter the storm for another mission, but his wife held him down.

'Want me to blast a couple of shells in the air to wake him out of the dark?' George Lightfoot asked. He waved his cane up in the air, showing that he still had it in him.

Emma couldn't help but giggle a little, thankfully to no one's attention. The old man could scarcely hold himself up in a light breeze by the look of it.

His wife – Madeline's grandmother - poked him with her bony fingers.

'Haven't you had enough already?' She asked as she turned to his half-empty glass of wine.

'Father, please stay here with the girls. And make sure Billy doesn't go walkabouts.' Mrs Smallhorn pleaded.

'Have a look around the home, dear. We will look outside for a while. Wherever he is, we will find him.' On that note, Mr Smallhorn left the room, accompanied by his brother, Robin Smallhorn, and Frank's sons, Alfred and Fillius.

Emma listened to the hurrying footsteps scurrying down the hall. The sound disappeared as they reached the front door, the heavy pounding of the rain becoming all that could be heard.

'I'm going to search the house. Mary, can you help me?' Mrs Smallhorn called out, at which point the maid burst from the kitchen, spoon in hand and unaware of what was happening.

The two split off – Mrs Gottfried finally having the courage to summon herself to the search party and join Mrs Smallhorn and Mary.

Now everybody was looking for Frank Lightfoot.

Chapter 4

'Some doctor. You'd have to have your wits about you, really.' Madeline whispered. Dr Gottfried had let them get away. He had fallen asleep in his own chair and he snored loudly like a roaring lion. The two were bursting with laughter, as they made it to the front door.

Emma wanted to enter the storm. She wanted to look for Frank too, outside of the rest of the manor's recommendations to head out. Emma had the zeal for truth.

The two turned back down the hall to check if Doctor Gottfried was still asleep in his chair. They could see him from down the hall, still snoring in the dining room.

The poor, old man had fallen asleep in his seat, talking about the old spitfire's he'd seen at the aerial bases of the war. He was a medic before purchasing his practice in Sherrington. Madeline had heard his stories before. But as he got older, he never seemed to remember which ones he had told last.

Emma was beyond keen to go out on the look with Mr Smallhorn and the others. Her inquisitive nature and her sense to investigate was embedded in her DNA.

Emma looked out the window beside the front door. She looked up and down at the path leading out down the green hills and then her eyes fixed on the torchlights scattered around them.

'Everyone is spread out looking for him,' Emma said to Madeline whose hand had tightly squeezed the doorknob.

'Here. Take this.' Madeline ordered as she handed Emma an old, dented torch. Emma handled the cold metal. Her finger looped around the greening brass. She turned it on and pressed the torchlight to her coat so as not to reveal herself. Madeline slipped one out of the shelf herself, banging the side of it with her hand. Before Emma could wonder for too long why the Smallhorn's kept so many torches by the door, Madeline opened the door.

Emma rubbed her hand harshly across her lips and followed Madeline out of the door and into the night. It was raining, and not the gentle kind of rain that someone could put up with while on a walk down the street. Even with an umbrella, it was unbearable.

The rain beat down like pellets of ice. It was hard and feisty, enough for Emma to want to crouch and place her free hand over her head to stop the rain from hitting her head.

Emma was left a little bewildered. Out in the darkness, there was no light beyond the grounds of the driveway. Although the oil lamps hung on the porch beside the double doors did their best to keep alight, it was pitch black.

'Down there,' Madeline announced. She pointed her torch light down to the woods after she searched for a while.

The yard between the manor and the outskirts of the wood seemed a long mile apart. Emma turned to face the many torchlights below, seeing no bodies behind them, just the light. Now she could see them. Over the mound of the drive, she peered below to see the torchlight down the slopes. Pocketed, they searched the outskirts of the woods. The flashlights were almost hypnotic to her, like staring out into the night sky, a blanket of darkness pocketed with twinkly stars.

The storm chucked the two about. Emma rooted her shoes to the pebbles of the drive, but it wasn't enough to hold her down. She looked at Madeline. She weakened and went up to the car parked out front to steady her ground.

It howled and whacked her about. She shouted and held her hand over her hood to keep it down.

Emma thrust herself forwards. She joined her friend, splatting her hands flat upon the rounds of the tyre guard of Fillius Lightfoot's motor car. Once a menace, now her saviour. She didn't have the time to dismantle the irony, instead she focused upon a strange smell which overtook the woodland scent and needled strongly in her nostrils. Whatever the new scent was, it must have been close and strong to come through the storm. It wasn't a pleasant one like the breeze through the trees, but a horrible, stinging one.

'Do you smell that?' Emma drove her voice into the hurl of the storm. Madeline caught it, just barely. She turned to Emma, squinting her eyes and gritting her teeth to yell back.

'Yes. What is that?'

The assaulting smell was rusty and oily. Once Emma could point it out, she leered down to the back tyres of the car and looked to the exhaust. She suspected that there was a leakage but she couldn't see a spill. The pebbles were cleaned and washed with rain. There was no way of telling.

There was no way that the two could make it down the valley and into the outskirts. Emma hadn't the faintest idea how the Lightfoot's and the Smallhorn's had done it. To make matters worse, Madeline's father had spotted the two perched behind the vehicle. He called from where he stood at the beginning of the path leading into the woods and towards the river. He waved his torch in the air, calling Madeline's name.

Miraculously, Emma could hear it. It funnelled with the wind and caught the breeze to make it up the drive to reach them. She tapped Madeline's shoulder to let her know, but she already knew. She poked her head up, spearing down the slopes. She picked his voice out of the wind as it came up from the valley and back to the manor.

'Father?' She whispered with a smile. She peaked up from the hood of the vehicle, showing her face. He saw the torch in both their hands, alerting him that they had defied his orders.

'Get inside. It isn't' – He yelled, but the wind slapped the rest of his voice away, taking it to a different direction so she couldn't hear it.

Madeline's head was thudding hysterically. The beating rain and the sudden lightning strikes were getting to her. Madeline tried to steal her nerves as all she wanted was her father to come back to safety. It was too dangerous out here and she feared the wind would take him. The woods were a dangerous place at night and she knew it. She remembered a time when she wandered out one night, having left her favourite teddy outside by the barns when she was just eight. There was dry thunder that night and when the light of the lightning cracked over the clouds, she remembered seeing a fox coming her way. She had never screamed so much in her life. She was never more scared than she was back then, but now it was all coming back.

She could feel the dry rasp of her breath in her throat as she tried to scream out to him. To Emma's ears, it was more like a whining sound which she couldn't break out of. The wind gusted, making a hungry, rumbling sound to separate it and all the nice sounds of the woods, but it was even heavier by the close-matted branches of the woods beside Mr Smallhorn and his brother.

At the moment of the standoff, Robin looked on. He clapped his hands over his eyes, wiping them clean of the rain and wind. He fixated upon his hair. He dragged the weakening threads over his balding patch, disguising it better so no one would see it.

He stood still like that for a long time until he realised that both Emma and Madeline had snuck outside. He could see the dread building in his brother as he tried to call out to them to go back inside, but the look of disinterest on Robin's face was apparent in the background of his brother's shoulder. He was on a mission to find Frank Lightfoot. The recklessness of Madeline and Emma was only delaying the search.

'It's no use talking to them from here. Go up there and shove them back in.' Robin yelled simultaneously as he was whacked in the cheek by an errant twig taken by the wind.

Angered, Mr Smallhorn began to trudge back up to the manor. Part of his mind fretted with fury at his daughter for putting herself and her friend in danger, but he just wanted them to be safely inside.

Once he'd completed the climb and made it to the pebbled drive of the manor, he paused for a second to smell the oily scent. It hit from out of nowhere and then he noticed the car. He didn't have much time to think about it before Madeline rushed towards him. He embraced her hug as she used the opportunity to try to pull him inside and out of the storm.

'I have to look for Uncle Frank,' He yelled, refusing to let Madeline guide him inside. She must've thought he had turnips growing out his ears to be able to think that she could overpower him. He wanted nothing more but to get his daughter and her friend back inside.

Emma watched from the vehicle as the two argued back and forth. She couldn't hear what they were saying, but she could see the anger and frustration in both of their faces as they each took turns debating.

Suddenly, a bolt of lightning smacked the roof of the manor. The surge came down with fury, paralysing the building immediately. Emma fell back against the vehicle in shock. She had never seen lightning so close and with so much ferocity at the same time. Sparks came from the roof and with it, a sizable chip was carved into the gargoyle above.

As Madeline and her father remained crouched together, holding each other to keep safe, Emma directed her torch to the gargoyle leering down. She saw the damage that had been done to it – she was surprised that it was still mounted and that it hadn't fallen and smashed onto the roof of Fillius's vehicle by now.

As she looked, she saw that a little piece did in fact tumble down. It chipped from the gargoyles arm and plummeted down the side of the manor, hitting the pebbles hard. The crash had sounded as loud as the lightning. She and the others had been too attached to the crumbling fall of the gargoyle. They had each been thankful that it landed away from them.

She was dimly aware of the complete darkness inside the manor now. The muffled voices of those still inside were panicky. The power had been lost – as everyone thought it would be at some point. But at this time, it seemed even more inconvenient.

'Is everyone ok?' Mr Smallhorn scrambled, reaching for his daughter to make sure she was ok. He turned to Emma, wide eyed and frightened. 'Emma?' He asked. She nodded; her mouth wide open to what had happened. The only light was the occasional lightning in the distance and the faded torchlight in each of their hands.

Emma came closer, leaving the safety of the vehicle. She shouted inches away from Mr Smallhorns ear. She asked if there was any sign of Frank. He made a small, caged sound. He had grown a little weary. There was a strain in his heart and the power of the storm had seemed to aggravate it. He breathed in heavily, chucking clouds of breath back into the cold, dark night. His lungs became unable to cope with the cold. As he breathed in the heavy, cold air, it started to change him. He coughed. It was raw in his throat, and he felt as if he were coughing from the pit of his chest.

'Please just get back inside you two. Madeline. Go see if your mother is alright. She will probably have a bird knowing you are out here.' Realising her father's distress in his weak posture and tired tone, Madeline knew that taking his orders would be much better for his struggling health than not. Reluctantly, but assuredly, she got up and readied herself to go back inside. Mr Smallhorn straightened himself and dusted the dirt from his knees. His coat was sopping wet, but he had a tougher time seeing that Madeline's dress was ruined.

He figured that he couldn't make it back down to the woods again to continue the search. Not in his turn of conditions. He wanted to scope around the manor, hoping that he would run into Frank around the back, knowing the risk of running into uncle Billy. But before he could turn on his heels and begin and before Madeline could regroup with Emma to go back inside, a caterwauling call came from beyond.

It was from somewhere unknown, seeming like a dream or an allusion that someone had been calling from afar.

'Help me. Someone please.' The unknown voice screamed continuously. Carried by the lashing wind, it was difficult to know where it was coming from and just who it was. Emma flung the light of her torch down the slopes, the beam glazing over the pebbles until it revealed a body.
Hesitantly, the three treaded forwards, each hearing the continuous screams come closer and closer. Emma crept closer towards the edge of the drive. She passed the vehicle and she let her torchlight glow. The muffled voice she heard was pinpointed. She began to feel as if she was a lifeguard looking for a drowning swimmer at night, a task that seemed almost impossible over the raging weather.

She was halfway down the slope when she almost fell over at what she saw. From her right, that shrill sound came again, much like the whirling winds.

'What is it? Do you see anything?' Mr Smallhorn called.

Emma didn't answer. She didn't need to.

Out from the darkness came a man. Emma watched as he struggled up the remainder of the slope. He threw his hands out, slapping them against the pebbles in a feeble attempt to catch a grip on the slippery slope. He looked as if he'd just struggled to the water's edge from a riptide. His face was bloodied, his hair bashfully swept over his eyes. As he struggled trying to get his body over, Emma's heart was hammering like crazy.

Her feet locked to the ground. Her body was stunned, frozen by the chill of the storm whacking her back as a constant reminder. The strange man locked eyes with Emma's for a minute longer until his entire body crawled out of the darkness. His feet, however, were left to dangle in the grass behind him.

The man fell flat, exhausted by the effort. His body was lifeless and as soon as he stopped moving, Emma was freed from her invisible bonds. She raced over without a moment's waste. She tilted her head forward, piercing through the wind which tried its best to keep her away. She crouched down, patting her hand on the man's shoulder. Now she could hear him breathing, heavy breathing craving rest and respite.

'Oh, my goodness.' Mr Smallhorn and Madeline came over, at which point the man started shouting erratically.

'Somebody, please help me. Please. Get me out of here!'

Mr Smallhorn took over, gently forcing Emma aside. He helped the man up on his knees and got a good look at him. The man looked up at him. His eyes were tiny and red with panic. Just as the rest of the searchers came to help, Mrs Smallhorn and the rest of the house came out of the darkness. They all converged on the man, circling around the situation.

'Mr Bank's?' Mr Smallhorn stammered, now recognising the man.

Mr Banks was sopping wet. His clothes were heavy in water, but it hadn't been the rain – they were too wet for rain. It looked as if he'd fallen into the river. His skin was cold to the touch and he was uncontrollably shivering. The thought crossed Emma's mind that the winter storm was going to give him hypothermia.

Emma waited. She seemed to be the only person now who didn't know who he was.

'You're right. It is Mr Banks,' Dr. Gottfried concurred as he scratched his scuffled, grey, short-buzzed hair.

'What are you doing out here? Why are you covered in blood?' Mr Smallhorn said, peering down at his hand with his torch to see now that he too was smeared with it. He pulled a face – a face of disgust as to where his hands had been.

'Covered in blood?' Mrs Smallhorn said from the steps. She trickled down from them, stepping closer yet still far away not to enter the brunt of the storm.

Mr Smallhorn was right. The rain did its best to wash it away off his raincoat, but Emma could see it now too. It was smeared over his face, pooling in the creases of the wrinkles on his forehead. It was all over his hands and all over his raincoat and pants.

Emma inspected his body with wide eyes, keeping him restrained under the torchlight. She couldn't see any source of the blood, but his arms were cut and his left cheek was also slit.

'What happened, Mr Banks?' Emma asked. She narrowed her eyes, looking down at the man who didn't know her, but saying his name made him think she did.

He was breathing heavily. He looked at her, drumming up the courage to speak. Choking on his hurried breath, he finally did.

'There is a *mad man* out there. He, he… He tried to kill me.'

Emma's eyes widened. She didn't look at Madeline, but she sensed that Madeline had turned to her. Madeline had felt a sudden urgency to look to a person of the law. The outrageous statement made her seek her friend… *The detective.*

'Someone attacked you?' Mr Smallhorn asked, rather wishing that the man had kept his voice at a whisper so as not to scare the others.

'That's right. I was out in the woods just now and someone came at me with a knife. They got me a few times, but I ran away.' Mr Banks closed his eyes. Emma noticed that his complexion was as pale as a fish's underbelly. 'He has lost a lot of blood.' Emma proceeded to say. She felt his wrist. It was very cold. Mr Banks was drifting in and out of consciousness. It could have been the adrenaline of darting away from someone trying to kill him, or he could've been injured enough by the cuts and lost a lot of blood. Emma wasn't sure. All she knew was that she had to take control of the situation.

'Dr. Gottfried.' Emma called past the heavy wind,, waving the doctor over. He refused to come closer than he already was. 'Please take care of Mr Banks.' Emma requested, to which the Lightfoot brothers helped the unconscious Mr Banks up. They carried him into the manor, placing him upon a fainting couch in the sitting room.

Emma straightened herself up. She looked down and noticed the watery blood which now stained the pebbles at her feet. She walked with her finger scratching her chin to which point Madeline sidled up next to her.

'What do we do, Emma? The man says he's been attacked,' Madeline said with fear in her voice. She hunched her shoulders over, slipping the hood of her coat up over her head to keep out of the rain and so her words were unheard by her parents.

'I don't know. I would have to ask Mr Banks when his mind becomes a little clearer. We can begin to sort out what happened when we get him inside and warm him up a little.' Emma turned with her arms crossed. She prepared to follow the Lightfoot's back inside the manor to wait, but Madeline stopped her.

'You don't think it was Uncle Frank, do you?' Madeline asked, fearing even speaking the possibility out loud. 'That is what they are all thinking. I know it. Did you see my parent's faces when Mr Banks said that he'd been attacked? By a madman, mind you?' Madeline persisted. She didn't want to believe it – not even the possibility of it, but everybody was thinking it. Frank Lightfoot was missing and now an injured man appears from the woods.

Emma didn't know. Emma couldn't know. She needed more information to know.

'As I said, let me speak to Mr Banks first.' Emma looked up to the manor, seeing the rest of the family slowly pile inside.

'Come on, Madeline,' Mr Smallhorn shouted from the open doorway.

Emma turned to Madeline one last time to speak in private. She feared what she was about to say. It made it all too very real and dangerous to admit it out loud.

'With the power out and all contact cut for at least tonight, we may be on our own to get through whatever is happening.'

Chapter 5

Howard Banks awoke with a muffled gasp. He thought he had a horrible dream, not realising it was actually a memory of what he had been through.

He went to bed cold but awoke hot and sweaty. It wasn't the river water under his back as he thought, instead sweat. Mr Banks was burning up. He felt the warmth of the candle lights surrounding him throughout his slumber.

He recalled his dream – or what he thought was a dream. In the dream and before his attack, he'd seen a figure behind the trees. Whoever it was just stood there, hiding… *watching him.* He replayed the following scenes in his head, reliving it all over again. He even felt the swipe of the blade against his arm, but in his vision the dig of the blade felt even worse against all odds. The attacker had come out from their hiding place, faceless to Howard. The attacker had chased him across the river. He was soaking wet and with the beat of the rain and the terrible storm, leaving him disorientated.

He splashed through the water, grabbing chunks of it, trying to pull at something to drag himself forward. But it was no use. Each handful dribbled through his fingers, leaving him powerless. He couldn't get out of the stream and the attacker had caught up to him.

A slash to his back. A laceration to each arm and one which went right across his face.

As the water sprayed and crashed around them, the waves created gave him the momentum needed to escape the riverbed. Like a seal escaping the crash and stir of a great white shark, he was given his chance to flee.

Howard chucked himself onto the river bank. His hands were sliced by the jarring shards of rocks but he didn't care, not one bit. He had made a break for it, dashing through the trees and stumbling his way up the hill for safety. His dream had taken him up to the drive of the Smallhorn manor, quite like he had in real life. He hadn't known if anyone was home, nor if they would help him. But the Smallhorns' took him in. They didn't like him so much, he knew that. They had their problems, some hashed out and some left on the backburner. *Thank God I am saved, h*e said to himself, hearing it as if he had said it out loud. Howard's vision cleared as the memories of his dream faded away.

He didn't know where he was. All he remembered was seeing the unrecognisable face that was Emma's. That was the last thing he saw. She had been the one to rescue him from his struggle and save him.

Howard shivered with cold breaths. He gazed up, wide-eyed, to see the face of Dr. Gottfried.

'Ah, Mr Banks. You have found the time to join us once again. My name is Dr Gottfried,' the man said with a chuckle. His gut gyrated as he laughed at his little joke, but Mr Banks wasn't amused. It was quite strange for him to awaken to a smile and a cracking joke. It only made him feel that much more out of place.

Mr Banks rolled over and groaned. He only wanted to know where he was.

He had awoken in a strange room with a strange man leering over him, his throat tight with fear and he only wanted to know where he was. He found little comfort in Dr Gottfried's soothing voice.

Dr Gottfried leaned back from his hover over the fainting couch. He began to prance back and forth to the table. His hands were kept behind his back, his thumbs twiddling as if they were in a wrestle with one another.

'Dr Gottfried?' Howard croaked. 'Where am I… how did I get here?' Ambushed with questions, Dr Gottfried tried to put him to peace as he told him to relax.

His hand spread upon Howard's forehead.

'You had some trouble. Someone out there was after you, or so you say. Do you remember what happened?' Dr.

Gottfried immediately sent Howard back into a panic, but a more contained one. He didn't scream nor retract, but his squeamish expression said it all. *It wasn't just a violent dream after all. It really did happen.*

'You are lucky. Though we are somewhat trapped for the night. There is a detective in the house and we will soon have everything sorted,' Dr. Gottfried announced, sending Howard his assurance. 'You have some nasty bruising and some deep cuts which I have seen and are mending, quite well might I add considering my practice is miles away. Rest now for the time being.' Dr. Gottfried advised, rubbing Howard's head as if he were a young boy.

Howard Banks nodded. He let his head rest back into the comfort of his pillow. He looked up to the abnormally high ceiling and the walls surrounding him.

Howard wasn't a young man, nor an old one. He was somewhere in between. *"In his late thirties, I believe."* Mr Smallhorn guessed when Emma asked. Howard was stressed. From the doctor, there were many questions he had to ask, but the doctor thought it best to leave him be.

'Wait, Doc!' Howard urged for his attention. He reached his arm out to stop him, but it instantly dropped. It was limp and numb beyond anything he had ever felt before. He reached for the doctor's attention, but it was too late. The doctor departed and it was just him and the candlelight.

In the opposite end of the manor, down the hall and in the dining room, Emma sat with the Smallhorn family. In front of her she set her notebook, readied with a pencil to write whatever she could find out.

'Who exactly is Mr Banks?' Emma asked.

'Howard Banks is his name. He is a farmer. He owns the land next to ours, in fact.' Mr Smallhorn replied. There was a bit of a bad taste in his mouth which Emma sensed. She got the feeling that there was a little dispute between the land, where the fences bordered and who got what perhaps. As it turned out, Emma was right.

'My husband and Mr Banks differ in opinions as to what is what and whose is whose. He says he has an extra hundred yards on our end, we say otherwise.' Mrs Smallhorn said, confirming Emma's suspicions.

Emma felt that the way the Smallhorns talked to her had begun to change. They were no longer treating her as a guest, but instead like someone else… *a detective*. Now she was the one people answered to. She was the one asking the questions. She was the one who gave permission to the rest of the manor. The Smallhorns had also sensed the shift of who was in control. It didn't feel right, but Emma knew she had jurisdiction and it was the best course forward.

She was still only new to the field and never had she taken on a case before. She got the sense that some of the others knew this and that they didn't feel the need to answer to her.

Mrs Smallhorn smiled in a cocky way, bringing to light what Emma had been thinking about herself. 'You feel as if you can do this all by yourself. What if there really is a killer out there? What if Frank Lightfoot had tried to kill Mr Banks?' Mrs Smallhorn's smile quickly faded. Her eyes welled with tears and a frown formed in the corners of her lips.

She was afraid.

With the power loss and the sudden appearance of an injured man who'd crawled all the way from the river, this night had come something they all had least expected. The emotions became high and Mrs Smallhorn was feeling the brunt of it.

Emma reached her hand out. In a soothing voice, she calmed Mrs Smallhorn.

'Mrs Smallhorn, I will try my best. If there truly is a killer out there, I have a duty to find them. The only evidence we have is a man who has been attacked. We don't know by *who* or by *what* - but I will find out,' Emma reassured, standing strong.

The injured Howard Banks was an invaluable part of this puzzle. Emma hung on the theory that Frank had hatched a plan to attack him. Out he had gone with the manor full of people and everyone distracted. Not one person would think of Frank as being malicious. Not a single inkling that Frank could have a murderous intent. But Emma wasn't sure.

There was something about the whole theory which made it seem that it was *too* easy to solve. Perhaps Frank was still missing and had played no part in Howard's attack at all.

Emma thought about it but only for a second longer.

'Yeah, and what if you can't? What if we all wind up dead before dawn - what then?' Robin Smallhorn questioned, standing at the end of the dining room just outside the long batwing doors which lead onto the side porch. Robin smoked from a pipe which turned his deep voice husky, making it hard to understand.

Emma turned to face him. She took in a deep breath, making a promise to herself and everyone in the room

'Well then, I must solve this crime tonight.'

She would have one night in the manor, full of people she'd hardly met. Her time had come but in the worst, most admirable way.

Emma turned to her notebook. In bold writing, she made the dispute of land ownership between Mr Banks and the Smallhorns very clear. She wanted every detail recorded and at her disposal when the time came that it was needed.

Fillius and Alfred Lightfoot both looked out of breath as they raced into the room after having been down to the cellar in hopes of fixing the electricity.

'The power is dead. There isn't much of a chance we will see anything until the storm blows over, I'm afraid.' Alfred said, looking at the full table with a worrisome look.

His hands were dirty and his clothes dripping wet. There had been a slight leak in the cellar as the rain had gotten in.

'With every light out in the house, we'll use up every candle before dawn. The landline is dead also, meaning we cannot call anyone for help,' Fillius said after finishing his inspection.

'The phones are dead. The electricity is also out. What are we to do? They say the storm could stay for the entire weekend.' Madeline's grandfather grumbled.

With the power out and no way of contacting anyone from the outside, Emma realised that it was entirely up to her. She gazed at the table and the people huddled around it, falling deep into thoughts as to what she must do.

'We searched for our father along the way. Neither we nor the maid could find him. Uncle Billy is also missing,' Alfred said, making the link that Billy's disappearance may have something to do with his fathers disappearance.

Madeline planted her hands on her hips. She turned to her friend for guidance.

'Where do we begin?' Madeline asked in a flabbergasted voice. Emma got the sense that she was overwhelmed but still wanted to be helpful to Emma. Emma knew it wasn't right - Madeline was just a civilian in the eyes of the law. However, having someone who knew the family and could aid her with any personal knowledge could help her in the end. Emma closed her book, the glow in her eyes lit by the solitary candle at the centre of the table.

The doctor came in from the sitting room, rubbing his hands with a cloth. He wiped the smears of blood from his fingers, having soothed Mr Bank's bleeding head and gashes upon his arms.

'Young, Mr Banks is awake' he informed Emma.

Emma got up from her chair as soon as she heard She needed to speak to him with the memories still fresh in his mind.

'He is still a little wobbly here and there, do be kind with the questions.' Dr Gottfried advised.

Robin overheard the conversation. He didn't like the doctor's advice so much. He was a very opinionated man and also wanted to be in control of the situation.

He lay back in his chair, gazing up at the ceiling and listening to the bashful wind hitting the roof and walls. But now, everything has gone too far.

'Damn it, man. Bombard him with as many questions as you can. He said he was attacked, didn't he? Strike while the iron is hot, I'd say.' Robin Smallhorn demanded. The boastful man was just a tad bit obnoxious. Emma had seen since he'd met her in the hall upon arrival. He had been in a rush to get to the river, and was very pushy and forceful. However, Emma agreed with him this time. Answers were needed.

Emma made her way out of the dining room. As she did, the rest of the manor argued. They jumped on Robin's back and pestered him about his arrogance.

Friends and family began to slowly nibble at each other, but Madeline escaped. She bounded up next to Emma, carrying a saucer which held a candle to accompany them.

Madeline was just about the only person Emma trusted as she allowed her company. She needed someone by her side. She couldn't do it all by herself, not in a place she hadn't known and with people she knew less about.

Madeline sidled up next to her. She pointed the candle outwards as she showed the way with the light burning strong down the dark hall.

'Don't you think we need to gather everyone? A lot of people are scattered around the manor.'

Madeline was right. But Emma was going too fast. She couldn't stop on her way to the sitting room.

'Later. Perhaps after I speak to Mr Banks.' Emma advised. She wanted to keep things minimally complicated for now. Take one thing at a time, she had in her mind.

The two entered the sitting room. Emma sat down beside the fainting couch, bringing the candle closer towards her and Mr Banks to get a better look at the victim Madeline remained standing, waiting by the window and keeping tabs on how the storm was progressing.

Emma looked over the injured man. The blood was gone – Dr Gottfried had done an excellent job with the stitching. Even though Mr Banks was all cleaned up his face remained deathly pale with a blank expression. In fact, he hadn't even seemed to notice that Emma and Madeline were there. His eyes were shut, but he wasn't asleep.

He visibly shivered, both in fear of the memory that remained sharp behind his closed eyes and the cold which seeped into the castle-like manor.

Over his shoulders was an old rug, similar to ones they used in the army. It was thick and warm and even made of the same British green material, but still not enough to keep the poor man from shivering. Emma watched as his teeth jittered and noticed how his hair was still heavy with the storm's rain. She brought the candle closer to his face to try and provide some warmth. His eyes opened at the sudden heat, the dancing flame reflected in his eyes.

Emma looked at his collar, noticing the blood on it and wondering why the doctor hadn't removed it.

'It's dried on.' Mr Banks said as he noticed Emma's wandering gaze.

Mr Banks smiled. The old grandfather clock in the corner of the room chimed, marking nine-thirty. The sudden clangour of noise stirred Emma into action and she dredged up some confidence to finally say her first words to the man in front of her. Simultaneously, she turned to the water bowl on the table with an old rag draped in it. She took it, gently wringing the rag out and using it to dab at Mr Banks forehead.

'It has been a rough night.' Emma said soberly. The thunder pounded down, emphasising the truth in her words.

Mr Banks lay down on the fainting couch, about to reply when he heard the creaking of floorboards outside the door. Henry Smallhorn came into view, leaning against the doorframe. He said nothing, only eager to know what Emma had found out from Mr Banks that involved his brother in law.. He couldn't bear it if he had to find out any heavy news at the same moment his wife did. He would need to draw on his strength to be there for the family and the ordeal that would follow.

Although Emma would rather it was just her and Madeline, she saw all these emotions written on Mr Smallhorns' face. She saw the desperation converging upon him and threatening to swallow him whole, and knew that he needed to be here for what would follow. As long as he kept to himself in the shadows of the doorframe, she'd let his presence slide.

'Mr Banks -'

'Howard, please,' he interrupted her, casting a wide smile to add some familiarity between the two.

'Howard then.' Emma coughed a chuckle. 'You say you were attacked. Did you see a face or something… anything at all?'

His face went blank. He lifted his hands out from the warmth of his blanket, gazing to the ceiling and tracing the patterns of the plaster with his eyes. The same question kept replaying in his mind every time he slipped back into consciousness, searching through everything he remembered from tonight, trying to find the answer.

'I didn't see a thing. It was too chaotic and the weather was too violent to make anything out. The only thing I can say is that my attacker was cloaked in dark clothing with a hood over their head,' Howard sighed. He thought more about the hood. He wondered if it had just been used to keep warm and dry out of the storm, or if there was another purpose to it. Perhaps to shadow the attacker's face so that Howard couldn't tell who it was.

It was all too disturbing, so horrible that he didn't like playing it back in his head.

Howard stumbled over his next words, pausing to collect himself before he continued.

'I was chased across the river. The combination of the rain, the wailing winds and how much the river slowed me down… I didn't think I would get away in the end,' Howard stammered, shuddering at the very thought of it. He swallowed awkwardly, his lips dropping down to make a gloomy expression. 'The water bashed against me. It was rougher than normal due to the storm, of course. I remember trying to think of a rational explanation as to why the water was so brutal against my back, why it felt like it was maiming me. There were red drops flying past my eyes, coming from behind me. That's when I realised what was happening. A knife was repeatedly jabbing in and out of my body. It stabbed me in the back and then moved to start slashing my legs and my arms. It was like being attacked by a shark or some kind of sea monster. The blade just had a hold of me,' Howard explained. Emma could see the fear smeared across his face. His eyes were dark, reflecting Emma's reflection back to her like an empty pool.

'What happened then?' Emma encouraged

A cold sweat had manifested while Howard had slept. He swore that he was sure he was dying and the doctor's handy work hadn't cured him. He could feel it in his cold face and with every breath he shivered out from his mouth. He even swore he could taste the stainless steel of the knife with every inhale, as if the knife was now inside his body, infecting him. It went deep… bone deep. He felt the panic from reliving the memories rise up, threatening to drown him. He pushed them back down, trying to keep his composure. He owed it to Emma to tell her what happened.

'Well, I ran. I ran as fast as I could, even through the looming trees that tried to snatch parts of me as I ran past,' Howard said. Emma sensed a little dig at the Smallhorns for not trimming the trees by their pathway. It had become clear to her that Mr Banks wasn't a fan of the Smallhorns. His skin seemed to crawl just from being in their manor, in their territory.

Emma looked deep into Howard's eyes, asking him how he broke free at last.

'I saw the lights in the manor.' There was a little smile on Howard's face as he thought about the only happy part of the night.

'I was sure that the storm would have cut any electricity long ago. But seeing those lights burning bright gave me the last push of energy I needed, and I stumbled to safety. That was when I saw you,' he finished, looking up at Emma the same way he had when she pulled him up earlier that night. The look on his face told Emma he wouldn't forget it for the rest of his life.

Howard was thankful for that moment, that it was Emma who had found him. Emma had an aura about her which left Howard feeling comfort, like he could trust her to look out for him. He felt safe around her amongst everything and everyone else. To him, she was his ally and the only one that he could trust.

'Was there anything out of the ordinary, Howard? Or anything else that you had seen or heard?' Emma asked. She needed more if she wanted any chance of solving this case

At first, he thought he had lapsed into some sort of a delirium when it happened. What he had seen – or better yet hadn't – it was too bizarre to comprehend. Howard never thought in a million years that something like this could've happened to him. He was a lonely, old farmer. He had no family for miles and he never married or had children. It was just he, alone at the farm close by the Smallhorn manor. *Things like this never occurred in the country.* It was something of a story. A myth or a legend, only in story books written by writers that were alarmingly a little *too* into thrillers and crime fiction. *Did anybody ever keep an eye out on them?*

'No, nothing,' he said, crying and shaking. He stopped suddenly, as if he had just remembered a new detail. He readjusted himself, sitting up straighter and looking Emma in the eye. Emma watched him eagerly like he was a mummy awakening from a curse.

'Wait a minute. I do remember something. Yes, I remember…'

Emma leaned closer. Howard's words were on the tip of his tongue.

'I remember seeing smoke coming from across the river. It was rather strange, really. It was just there, floating in the air like magic. Now that I'm saying it out loud, I wonder if my head is still a little fuzzy,' Howard said, chuckling.

Smoke. Emma hung up on the word. She remembered seeing Frank separate from the stable hand, escaping for a smoke from his pipe.

'Smoke you say?' Emma reiterated. She thought about Frank and the last time she had seen him. He must have been there, that was the only explanation for this phantom-like smoke Howard had seen. She wondered briefly if Howard had made the claim up but she dismissed this theory when she looked into his fear-stricken eyes.

'What were you doing in the woods in the first place?' Madeline asked, stepping in but remaining at the window. She kept her arms crossed, giving the impression that she wasn't very impressed by the lack of information Howard had given.

Howard was frightened at the new voice and it took him a while to realise where it had come from. He turned to see the shadowy figure of Madeline at the window – a figure that blended with the darkness, just as his attacker had.

Howard turned back to Emma, taking her as his place of refuge once again.

'I was in my house by the fire when I noticed my cattle had escaped. The weather spooked them. Braving the storm, I went out after them. There was a damn hole in the gate you see, and that's how they all got out.' Howard shook his head. He knew it was something he should've mended weeks ago and well before the incoming storm.

'They had me out for a long time trying to round them up and all the while the storm got worse. I tried wrangling them up but they spread throughout the woods,' Howard sunk his head back into the pillow, staring up at the ceiling once more. He noticed that the flame died away as the warm colour left the plaster.

'The cattle took you all the way out to my woods?' Mr Smallhorn asked, unimpressed. He clearly didn't believe Mr Banks.

Emma turned to him, a little frustrated that he had chimed in like that. Emma also got the impression from Mr Smallhorn that if he hadn't been out in *his* woods, perhaps the attack wouldn't have happened.

'Why did you go out so far into the Smallhorn property?' Emma asked, showing Mr Smallhorn that she was on his side.

Howard's eyes glazed over as he came up with an answer.

'The storm blew me away. Blew my whole farm away, actually.'

Emma turned to Mr Smallhorn who sighed and shook his head. The excuse wasn't good enough for him. Nothing would be as long as his bitterness for Mr Banks remained.

'Before I knew it, I was out too far, but I needed to bring my cattle back in. The woods are not the place for those beasts,' Howard explained, but it hadn't seemed to win Mr Smallhorn over. He sighed a little and continued to cross his arms. He shook his head and leaned back into the doorway, blending back into the darkness beyond.

'The storm took you out?' Emma reiterated.

'It hit real bad and I was against the grain. Before I could even look up to see where I was, I knew I'd gone too far.'

'Why didn't you turn back and leave your cattle to see it out?' Emma asked.

'Trust me… I didn't want to go out but I didn't have a choice. It was either let my cattle die or try to save them. I did what any farmer would do.'

Emma didn't think the cattle would've die. The woods would've protected them from some of the storm

Emma let Howard's words digest. Howard had said all he could. Emma didn't want to push him more, knowing that too much may push him over the edge. He had still been a little inconsolable throughout his story, shivering and failing to regain any colour back into his complexion. The deep cuts of the knife and the wickedness of the untamed storm had got to him. Now he needed rest.

She dropped her gaze slowly to Howard's shivering hands which helped hold his sheet under his chin. She watched him as he closed his eyes. He concentrated hard on trying to go to sleep, thinking it was best to ride this one out. Hopefully by the time he awoke the power would be restored. At least asleep he could escape from his troubles.

Howard's jaw clamped shut, the muscles in his cheeks standing out. It was clear to Emma that she had to move on. She removed herself from her chair and looked to Mr Smallhorn. Again, Emma was lost. She couldn't just go out and investigate by herself. She needed the family and better yet, a man who knew his woods better than anyone else.

'Will you accompany me out to the woods?' Emma asked.

He nodded.

Chapter 6

Mr Smallhorn was the first to brave the storm again. On a night like this, he would've preferred to batten down the hatches with everyone inside and ride this one out. But he had a duty he couldn't back out of.

Leading the way, Emma came out of the door next. She stepped ahead of Madeline's father, wrapping her coat around her body to protect from the wind and rain whipping against her. She squeezed her arms around herself in an attempt to remain warm and dry.

She marched forwards, past Fillius' car and to the edge of the driveway. She peered down the valley of green grass, casting her torch light forward. Loud rumbles of thunder sounded like animals in the night. Spooky… Spine-trembling even, but nonetheless Emma pushed herself onwards.

She took a sharp left, using her body to slice through the heavy breeze now working against her. Nobody had checked the barn during the first search for Frank Lightfoot. Emma made a mental note to check it herself before making her way down into the woods towards the river's edge.

Before she could turn to get a look at the barn in the dark distance, a strange sense of mystery came over her. This was another place undiscovered, like much of the manor was for Emma. Even the best of detectives would have trouble in a place of such unfamiliarity.

The more she paced forwards, the more it became obvious to her that indeed she was out of her depths. She knew she had to be strong and put up a front of confidence to the Smallhorn family.

She looked over her shoulder at the brave folk who had decided to join her in her efforts to investigate. Behind her, wincing in the heavy rain and forceful wind, was Madeline and her father huddled close together. Battling behind them on their own was Alfred Lightfoot, the older of the Lightfoot brothers. He kept his head bowed and his hands pushed deep in his pockets. He looked like a man afraid to climb out of his jacket, like a tortoise which had buried itself into its shell.

The poor man had been looking down to his feet, watching where he was placing them on the stones so as to not roll his ankle. Now he looked up at her, startled by the wild weather which had been the worst he'd ever experienced. Upon seeing how composed Emma was, he made an effect to maintain his anxiety and fear.

'We should investigate the barn first. Frank may be taking refuge there,' Emma shouted.

'The barn?' Madeline shouted in return. She didn't like going into the barn, even as a kid. The smell of the hay trapped inside was a terrible one which always made her nose run. She didn't like how it was always dark inside and so far away from the manor. She liked it better in the protection of the trees, scared that at any moment the wind would tear the barn walls down and bring the roof off.

'It will keep us out of this ghastly weather. The barn is old, but strong-built,' Mr Smallhorn said, holding his lips close to Madeline's ears so she could hear him over the wind.

She smiled a little. Maybe it wouldn't be so bad. In fact, it would good to out of the weather she was sick of already. Even though she was better dressed than before, not even her thick raincoat and hefty stable boots could battle it for any longer.

Emma didn't like the plan as well as everyone else did. She did need to check the barn, but if the storm picked up she feared they could be stuck there for a while. She thought of being left alone with the family in the barn, or worse, finding Frank hidden in the rafters, huddled against the wooden beams and waiting to drop down to kill the rest of them like he tried to do with Howard. She felt panic flush over her skin, but just for a moment as she then realised that she had made a civilian mistake. She had assumed who the killer was, and detectives must never assume. That was just detective 101.

Once Emma swapped gravel and stone for grass, it went cold. A dip down the slopes had come with the cost of a change in temperature.

A smouldering fog reigned over the grass. The cold had turned the moisture in the air into ash-like mist which curled at her ankles.

Now, Emma had come within yards of the barn, the ground beneath her flattening out. The red of the barn doors appeared brighter in her flashlight, almost the same shade as the blood Howard had been covered in. She was getting closer.

Night was really dark down the East side of the manor. There were no lights on this end of the manor and yard, even when the lights were usually on. The night really did come to life on this end, reclaiming on the light and electricity's demise.

Emma's blood went cold as she neared the double doors of the barn and she felt a chill that she couldn't convince herself was from the weather alone. She stared at the doors as they shifted in the wind, pushing in and out as wide as they could before the latch stopped. With each shift, the doors banged and shuddered, the lock on the handle rattling each time and making it seem like something was trying to get out. She thought again about Frank and the possibility that he could be the killer hiding out in the barn. She bet he could smell her helplessness as she had never felt so small and timid before. 'If I had wanted to come down and see this place, Madeline, I would have, long before this moment,' Emma said as Madeline squeezed up beside her. Madeline sensed the fear which had stuck in Emma. She could see it running down her throat, clogging it and making her eyes glisten with fear of what lay before her.

Madeline couldn't argue with her. She also didn't like it. This time it wasn't so much the hay and how it made her nose run, but more a sense of fear. In fact, she had always contemplated getting locked in the barn late at night as a kid, imagining that a monster would be hiding in its dark corners, ready to spring out and eat her. Just before it did, a guttural groan would come from the pit of its stomach and the last she would see was the gaping jaws of its mouth and the rows of its shark-like teeth.

She hardly dared mention the times she imagined that *thing to anyone.* But facing the doors in the dark had caused that nightmare to come to light.

'I used to be scared of this place. But things were very different back then. We are on a mission now and that mission is more important than any irrational fears we may have.'

Emma looked at her.

She started at the doors, forcing herself to raise her hand over the handle.

As she took a hold the doors rocked her arm back and forth, temporarily pulling it almost out of her socket and then back in again.

Mr Smallhorn and Alfred Lightfoot came over to help. Madeline's father had experience handling his barn in any weather. Without saying anything, he leaned his hips against the door, and pulled the handle to level the doors out straight. They didn't sway anymore under his hold.

'Get that latch, will you?' Alfred looked to the latch. He realised what Henry had done to make it easier, meaning that all Alfred had to do was lift the metal latch with his finger. One flick did it and the doors came free. The two men took the brunt of the double doors as they flew open, whacking against their hardened bodies.

Before the doors could break free from their hold, Emma and Madeline rushed inside. Already the aroma of hay filled the air. It was overwhelming and Madeline was sent straight to her memories. She hadn't been inside the barn for years, but the smell never changed. The smell of the hay was mixed with old wood – wood from the barn that hadn't been changed since its restoration in the mid seventeenth century.

It was dark inside and Madeline didn't dare to step any closer in. She kept her eyes straight on the steps in front of her which lead up to the second floor.

There were noises in the barn, other than the crashing and croaking caused by the wind. A pitch fork dangled from a hook on the wall, swaying in an invisible breeze. It grinded among the iron plating of the wood.

Emma stepped a little deeper inside, the scent of the barn thickening.

Rain had gotten in and was dripping from the roof, piling into a puddle behind a cart at the back. The wind howled and moaned, its voice changing and narrowing as it swooped through the cracks and holes of the barn.

Emma studied the barn for a while, casting her eyes up the steps and looking to the second floor. There were tiny windows which let the darkness in, meaning she couldn't see anything up there without her torch. Her flashlight searched the barn, following the creaks and groans created by the wind. The walls seemed to rock sideways, like a pirate ship at sea. It felt turbulent and almost enough to make her sick.

The sound of metal clanking boomed behind her as Mr Smallhorn and Alfred pushed the doors in and linked them up to the hooks on the inner walls. Those little, iron hooks were just enough to hold them open, though the doors did try their best to come off loose again.

Henry Smallhorn took a match from one of the shelves, lighting it and carrying it over to one of the lamps. Once lit he carried it to the others, igniting them as well. Soon the barn was filled the ashy light of the barn lamps.

Emma could feel everyone relax a bit as the orange glow spread through the barn, banishing the darkness.

'That should do the trick,' Mr Smallhorn said as he blew the fire off the match, letting a trail of smoke blow away with the wind.

'If Frank Lightfoot had been caught out in this terrible storm, the chances are this would be his refuge. Someone please check the second level and around the haystacks at the –'

Emma's words paused.

A scuffle came from behind the rickety staircase at the centre of the barn.

Everyone was quiet. Emma's body froze as she waited for anything further. She cocked her head to one side, listening. She cautiously walked further into the barn, past the steps and towards the stack of hay at the back. She raised her flashlight, illuminating the stacked hay. *For once an assumption has paid off. It's rare, and goes against all my training, but this time it was actually helpful.*

Emma supposed the noise was Frank. It had to be.

She expected Frank to crawl from where he hid and come to them with welcoming arms. For too long he had been stuck inside the barn, without a coat or flashlight to attempt leaving with.

Emma called to the darkness. '*Frank?*' she asked. 'Frank Lightfoot, is that you?'

There was no response. He didn't seem willing to speak, indicating that maybe he was afraid - or, if he was the almost killer of Howard, that he was too ashamed to face everybody.

Emma prepared herself to have to go closer and investigate the haystack herself. She drew on all her available courage, reminding herself that she had some members of the Smallhorn family behind her. Just as she was inhaling to step forward, someone came out.

'Wait.' A young, skinny lad emerged from the shadows of the haystack. In his left hand he carried a block of wood that looked to have been shaped by the knife he held with his right.

The boy was Reggie. Not who they'd expected to see.

He was scared, wide-eyed and cornered like a startled animal. His alarmed nature didn't allow him to place down the knife. To him, someone had just barged into his safe place with unknown intentions. He wasn't going to do anything bad with the knife, it wasn't in his nature, but his instincts had kicked in to protect himself. So, he kept hold of the knife, thinking it was for the best.

'Drop the knife,' Emma demanded. How quickly did Reggie listen? The knife clumsily fell from his grip as soon as the words left her mouth. Luckily the blade stuck into the dirty, hay-strewn ground and not through his foot.

'Good god, son. What are you doing with that knife?' Mr Smallhorn demanded. Reggie was speechless, unable to speak. He was frightened, and all he could do was hold up the block of wood up, indicating that he was making something to pass the time.

Emma walked closer towards him, keeping Reggie in the glow of her flashlight. She got to the back of the barn where Reggie's informal little camp was pitched. It was a place where he usually came every night as the barn was safe and warm. He was out of sight and left alone. Rats were usually the biggest of his problems, but he had traps set up all over the place to keep his little patch of land clear.

'What are you doing here? Have you been here the whole time?' Emma asked, astonished.

Reggie nodded quickly. He squinted his eyes in response to the torch light that never left his face. It was only until Emma noticed his discomfort that she lowered it to his chest, but still high enough to see his eyes.

'This is where I sleep, miss. But I couldn't sleep so good with this storm, so I've been riding it out.'

In this time of anxiety, he had found a comfortable place of solitude. Emma lowered the torch to his feet and asked him to step out into the glow of the lamps. Reggie stepped forward, kicking up the dust with his bare feet. Once he got into the light, he felt safer.

His shabby clothes and frizzy hair were covered in hay and horsehair, sticking to him like a cat owner's worst nightmare.

He stood in front of everyone, them forming around him like a semi circle. The silence between them brewed as the storm reverberated, sounding louder and rattling the walls even harder this time.

'Reggie. We need to know that you are telling the truth.' This time it was Madeline who spoke. She held her hands out and looked at him with wide eyes. Reggie felt safer talking to Madeline - someone he knew, unlike the stranger who had lured him from his hiding place. Emma scared him a little, but he also felt aggravation and annoyance at this stranger who had come into his space and was now questioning his innocence, his very character.

'God's honest truth, I have been in this barn this whole time. Why… What is happening?' Reggie asked, looking back at Emma, his eyes searching her face for answers.

Her makeup dripped with the rain which beaded from her hood. She shivered and in their stare, lightning cracked once again. It always struck when something momentous happened. It was becoming quite the reoccurring thing, Emma thought.

'I'm going to trust you,' she said finally, looking tense but in control. She had remembered seeing Reggie before, with Frank when she had looked out her window. She also remembered seeing them go their separate ways. Mr Smallhorn and Alfred, however, hadn't seen what Emma had.

'You went with my father to the barn doors after fishing, remember?' Alfred prompted.

There was a little heat behind his voice. With it, his eyes welled as he focussed on the knife which Reggie dropped. He didn't believe Reggie one bit, but tried to keep a level head because he knew Emma did believe the young lad.

Emma turned on her heels, walking closer to Alfred. The smooth sound of the dirt crunching and sliding beneath her shoes sounded almost like sand on a beach, so unlike the situation they were actually in. She narrowed her eyes at Alfred. 'We don't assume,' Emma hissed quietly enough for only him to hear. She knew he was heated and that he had a right to be, considering the involvement of his father. But now was not the time. It was still very much a mystery as to where Frank had gotten to, and that is what they had to focus on.

'Can somebody tell me what is happening?' Reggie asked, exasperatingly. He had been clueless the entire time.

He noticed the panic look upon each of their faces. He knew something *bad* had happened, but he didn't know what.

'A man was attacked. The neighbour,' Emma said, putting Reggie out of his misery. He withdrew back inside himself, taken aback to the news. It dawned on him that his location was unaccounted for.

He knew how secluded the manor was, how far from civilisation they were. He was smart enough to realise what this meant. *It could only mean that one of them had done it.* The realisation struck him as he looked at each person present other than Emma.

'As well as that, Frank Lightfoot is missing.'

Reggie staggered a little closer, the news too much along with the attack. He looked to Emma, silently asking her involvement in all this.

'I am a friend of the family and – quite conveniently, a detective. However, I believe this *attacker* sees me as rather inconvenient, I would say.'

Reggie didn't want to stay in the barn any longer by himself. With a possible attacker on the loose and it potentially being Frank Lightfoot, he'd rather stay in the safety of other people in the meantime.

Reggie didn't want to, but he'd been forced to brave the storm with the others. He put on his flaky yet tough shoes and laced a thin jacket over his shoulders to try to keep dry. It was all that he had and he knew it wasn't enough to keep him warm, but he had to stay with the others knowing that there was an attacker and a missing person on the loose.

The party of five left the barn. The doors were kept open and the lamps had been left to burn in case Frank came for shelter.

Madeline's father led the charge along the outskirts of the woods.

The path opened up before them. They each stuck close by, going through the woods with great trepidation.

'So, you are a detective, huh?' Reggie asked in his charismatic way.

'Isn't it lucky?' Emma answered. She thought a little light-heartedness could do the trick. Everyone was a little on edge and alarmed by the whole ordeal.

'Indeed, we are,' Reggie agreed.

Emma worked her way out from under the lowered branches of the trees like an adventurer burrowing her way out of the Amazon. She did it with a strength which couldn't be matched out in the open. The trees had done their best to block the wind, but with it, a startling scream whispered from tree to tree, bending around the oak and piercing up to the lonely travellers.

Reggie walked silently, bunched up beside Emma. Reggie wondered if she really was a detective. She didn't fit the description in his head, not to mention she was well out of her place, being out in the country – not many detectives or people of that sort found their way out past Sherrington.

She must be one. But she's so young – not much older than me, in fact.

Reggie tried to figure it out, but there was a way about Emma. He'd never met her before, but there was an aura around her that was different. In her voice, he caught the Londoner accent. It was something that Madeline sometimes let slip from her years of schooling when Reggie would sometimes hear her speak. It was more sophisticated, different from what it sounded like out in the countryside.

The group had finally reached the river Emma trembled along the pebbled water's edge.

In the open area they faced the full brunt of the storm once more, and a collective shiver ran through the group.

What a storm it was. Just torrents of black sheets of rain.

Emma stood by the river's edge, gazing up to the sky. She noticed how the darkness consumed itself and how it had an almost supernatural feel to it. The thunder rolled from behind the menacing clouds and every so often, the sky cracked open with a burst of surging lightning. This indeed felt like it was a message for them.

Madeline walked out towards the river's edge to stand with Emma. Her eyes went from side to side, searching for something… anything, but there was nothing.

'So, if not Frank, then what are we looking for?' Madeline asked.

Emma couldn't think of anything in particular. Instead, she supposed they were looking for anything. 'Find any clues. Find anything that can corroborate Howard's story.'

'I guess that narrows it down a little.'

Ignoring her friend's sarcasm, Emma went down closer to the river, Madeline following behind. Her father decided to search down the other end, Alfred trailing after him.

'Wait. What is that over there?' Reggie said to Emma, having stuck loyal to her. He had spotted something across the river. He pointed his finger, flicking it past Emma's eye for her to follow its direction. At first, she hadn't a clue what he was talking about. She thought perhaps that he had seen something. But it wasn't Frank.

Emma then thought about the many hauntings of the manor and wondered if they reached the wooded area. She believed that maybe a ghost lingered among the trees and glowed at night, a travelling knight slaughtered in battle perhaps, howling eerily along with the wind. Madeline hadn't mentioned it, but Emma sure could imagine it.

Emma looked up, following where Reggie was pointing. She let out a breath, realising it hadn't been something supernatural.

Nestled in the trees on the other side of the river were cows. Half a dozen of them, hidden within pockets of the woods, behind the trees and out of the storm. Reggie had pointed out the glimmering glow of their eyes. Like villainous monsters converging around a lonely campfire, he found them shining in the background of the trees. As soon as she saw them, Emma could make out the sound of them mooing.

It wasn't the kind of mooing that she had thought a cow would made. It was more of a groan… a distressed one.

'Poor things. They really did get out,' Emma said. She felt guilty about just leaving them there. She supposed going over there to lead them back home did give her an excuse to cross the river and further her search in the end.

'What are you doing?' Reggie squealed as he felt Emma's hand wrap around his wrist. She lowered herself down, sticking her gumboots into the shallowness of the river's edge.

'What do you think I'm doing? I'm going to cross the river to the other side. I need a bit of a railing, if you don't mind,' Emma shouted back over the howling wind.

It was cold as the water swarmed her gumboots, her second step taking her much deeper into the water. Her skin was cooled by it and the waves of the raging river splashed tall, seeping over the edge of her boots and wetting her socks.

Reggie turned his attention to the others who soon noticed Emma braving it across the river. They had been alerted by the sounds of her splashes and trudging lunges like a shark sensing the vibration of a moving meal.

She hadn't asked Madeline or the others to join her, but they had gone in anyway, following after her to cross to the other side.

The might of the river was terrible. It was up to her hips in the deepest part of it. As she crossed the middle, it went only a couple inches past them, but she was still on edge. As she stepped, she used the pebbles and large rocks beneath to push off of, bobbing up and down rather sporadically.

The sheer power of the river carried by the wind was more than enough to knock Emma off her feet, but the determination of Madeline's family kept her strong. She felt the strong hand of Alfred's rest on her shoulder, helping to hold her up and force her forward.

She stood stiffly.

There was something amiss.

Under Emma's boot, she'd felt something other than a pebble. It was sharp and it dug into the side edge of the rubber. When she lowered her hand down to pull the strange object out she gasped with surprise at what was in her hand.

Emma had wrenched a knife from its resting place in the riverbed. She raised it to the moonlit sky, watching as the moonlight reflected off the sharp steep blade.

The water dripped from the tip of the blade and she watched as it cleansed what it had been used for.

As Emma studied the knife, she looked at Reggie. It looked exactly like the one he'd been holding in the barn.

No one had noticed Emma's find. She snuck it inside her coat before they could, slotting it into her breast pocket and making a mental note to analyse it closer when she got back.

Eventually, Emma was the first to make it out of the river. She climbed out, grasping the smoother rocks on the edge to pull herself up.

The mooing grew louder; this time it was more painful. It didn't sound like mooing anymore. It sounded like screams, helpless pleas. The cattle just wanted to get back to their home. They were sick of the storm and getting jabbed by sharp branches with no flat land nor grass for their hooves to settle.

Emma looked at one of the cattle in the eyes. They sparkled, just like how the absent stars should have in the sky. She could see the glittery wetness on the tip of its smudgy nose and the clumpy hair around its cheeks caused by the rain. It was safe in the woods amongst the others. But something about the trees seemed as though the woods wanted to keep them penned in. It was horrible, like a nightmare to Emma. She just wanted to help.

Before she could come forward, something caught her eye. She turned and froze at the sight of the bloody red splatters upon the rocks.

It looked fresh, almost glowing under the night sky. Horrified, the sight of blood was confronting, something Emma had never liked it.

She had to remember she was the professional one. She kept her cool and cautiously made her way towards it. At that moment, the crashing water signalled that the others had climbed up onto the river's edge.

Each sopping wet, Alfred, Mr Smallhorn, Madeline and Reggie came over. They were oblivious to what Emma had discovered. She decided to keep it a secret for now, knowing this didn't put Frank in the best of positions.

'What is it?' Alfred asked, noticing the obvious discomfort on Emma's face. He kneeled down next to her, Madeline doing the same on her left. They all saw it at the same time. Henry Smallhorn stood behind the three, peering down at the rocks splattered with blood.

'What. Let me see.' Reggie tried, seemingly taking the role of a little boy once again. But Mr Smallhorn didn't want him to know. He was too young to see such a ghastly thing. He did his best to block it out with his body, but the words couldn't help but escape his utterly shocked lips.

'Blood.'

'Indeed, it is,' Emma relayed.

With her flashlight she exposed the pool of it. Drenched with rain and the constant splashing of the river, the blood had become saturated. It was watery, never quite drying in time before Emma could investigate it for herself.

The rocks were formed in a structure similar to that of a bowl, helping to keep the blood trapped inside. Emma watched as blood dripped from the tips of the jagged pieces and drained back into the middle.

The blood trailed about four feet from the main source. Little specks flicked from rock to rock.

Emma looked on with grief and disgust. Though the sight had sickened her, she remained professional enough to hold in the contents in her stomach. She maintained a straight face as the flashlight dangled from her bent wrist.

'It looks fresh, Emma,' Madeline whispered. The wideness in her eyes hadn't left since they had begun their journey outside.

Restlessly, without thinking, Alfred came to Emma's aid.

'It couldn't be my father. Could it?' The blood was there. Frank Lightfoot was still missing and Howard Bank's story checked out. It was beginning to make a whole lot of sense that Frank could indeed be responsible. If he wasn't, then it was someone else...

Alfred didn't want to admit it. Hell, he hated to think what his brother would do when he had to break the news to him.

Miserably, Madeline supported the claim – a claim she reminded Emma of that was coming from the accused very own son.

'It is possible that Frank is the one responsible. However, no one knows the entire story yet. We cannot assume. Where there is crime, there is always more to uncover than just picking out culprits.' Emma spoke her wisdom, all the meanwhile never taking her eyes off the blood.

She sighed, lifting herself from her kneeled position and looking up to the storm.

The moon glowed behind the smoky clouds. If it weren't for all the mystery already, Emma would think that it was an eerie night.

'How far did you say Mr Bank's farm is away from these woods?' Emma asked, directing her question to the only man around her who knew.

'Not that far out. Walking distance from here,' Mr Smallhorn replied. No one knew what Emma had on her mind, but one thing was certain; she wanted to see the farm for herself. She would even wrangle in the cattle if she could. But with the fears of a crime and the display of blood to prove it once and for all, she needed to continue her work.

Emma readied herself to find her way towards the farm. The cries of the cows continued drifting throughout the woods, unsettling everyone nearby. It was scary to look out into the darkness of the woods, never seeing but hearing them call out.

Emma dusted her hands off on her sides and scaled the rocks to find a smoother place to stand.

Alfred stood up straight. He casted his eyes away from the blood, understanding what Emma wanted to do. He thought that Emma was crazy to continue with this journey instead of heading back inside.

'You're crazy. We're not going out even further, are we? Not in this storm.'

Emma continued to brush her hands upon her coat. She used the rain to wash them, using the crinkles in the coat as somewhat of a basin.

'Go back if you want to. Take Reggie with you and tell the others where we are going and what has been found.' Emma was ok with it. At least she knew that if anything were to happen to either of them, the other would be responsible. Besides, there was no way of communicating with the rest of the manor. Perhaps it was long overdue to send a man back to give a report of what was happening.

Alfred pulled Reggie in closer to him. He gave him the torch for him to lead the way. He nodded at Emma and told the others to come back soon.

They left and the three watched them jump back into the river. They crossed it, making a dash through the woods and up to the manor.

'What about the barn? The lamps are still burning,' Mr Smallhorn said. He wasn't the type of man to flee and abandon anyone, least of all his daughter. But he did need to deal with the lamps in the barn. 'There was a fire once from those lanterns,' he explained. 'Nearly burned the whole place down.'

Emma didn't think that it was right for him to leave and neither did Madeline.

'Only a silly person would go out on their own. Attacker or not, the weather is far too dangerous to go out alone,' she insisted, still falling to persuade her father. He was as stubborn as his daughter, even more so in fact. He didn't listen to her and with or without Emma's permission he had already made his mind up.

'I'll meet you back here. Go with Emma and stay with her. I'll be ok,' he spoke these last words with intense seriousness. It was like he was telling Madeline what to do again as a kid. After school, come straight home. You'll be safer then. She listened now like she had listened then, though it was with a little more reluctance this time.

Without a moment's more delay, Mr Smallhorn followed in the footsteps of Alfred and Reggie, hurling himself in the river.

Madeline watched her father struggle. She smiled at him, again with that empty smile which she always wore when she never got her way. She knew that her father was only doing what was best. He was brave to venture out into the storm alone and from then on, with Emma by her side, Madeline knew she needed to be brave too.

Madeline turned to Emma. Those stony eyes came alive with determination, her teeth clamping down to push through the storm. Emma saw her fierce nature – one that someone who lived out in the country would need to survive in moments like these.

After a while of walking past trees, dodging their branches and trying their best not to tumble over the pebbles, the two reached the end of the river system.

The river crossed the boundary between the land, the end part of it now in the Banks' side of the property, Madeline explained. There was an inexplicable feeling of being lost and living dangerously as they crossed the land. Madeline didn't want to go, but decided to join Emma rather than leaving her alone.

Emma was curious as to how Madeline felt about Mr Banks. She remembered the anger in Mr Smallhorn's voice as he spoke about Howard and their dispute over the land, and wondered if Madeline shared this same view.

'The farm is down there. Look, you can even see that the lights are still on,' Madeline pointed out. They were hardly lights. It was clear to Emma as she spied the lonely, small home that it was just dim light coming from oil lamps that were about to burn down.

Emma turned around. Madeline was still pointing to the home in the distance.

She then used her finger to swat her hair out of the way. The rain was still heavy and the wind hit her skin, drawing the wetness into her eyes.

'Madeline,' Her voice was flat.. She was tired but there was still a job to do. She had found a mound of pebbles to stand on. She looked like one of those highland walkers, someone who had stopped on their journey to check out the view. Though Howards barn wasn't anything to stop and gaze at for too long. Much of it had been destroyed. She could see the full scale of it. Things had been overturned – things that were hard to describe in the dark, but their notice was obvious.

'Have you been here before, Madeline?'

'Not really. Only as far out as we are now,' she called back.

Another step and Emma would have crossed the boundary between her family's land and the Banks'. She did stutter a little over the border. She knew it was wrong

There was a tremendous weight. Huge and unbearable. Breaking the laws of her family and Mr Banks' was something she never did as a child. She never expected that it would have to happen. It was ok, but there was still an odd feeling about it which she only understood.

Madeline had a brave face – a face which Emma couldn't read – as the two scurried along.

The rest of the way was downhill. Lumps of ground and small rocks trailed the path down from the end of the river..

Maybe it was the cattle or heavy rain which loosened them, Emma thought.

The skies trembled, the thunder crashing and the lightning exposing the lay of the land for the second it shuddered.

The ground was wet and muddy under her feet. It was deep like a Floridian swamp marsh. Thank Christ alligators in Northern England would be something from a fantasy novel. Something about the notion of alligators across the Atlantic in some swamp in Florida marsh lands made Emma tread even more carefully in the mush.

She looked to her feet only to not see them. They were buried, taken by the stanching mud, rainwater and straws of hay.

'Watch your step,' Emma said to Madeline.

She cocked her head sideways as she boldly leaped forward onto a dry patch of hay.

'Thank god for these ugly boots,' Madeline said.

A half-smile rose from her mouth, spreading onto her cheeks and turning them red.

She followed Emma's smudging prints the best she could until she made it to her.

Emma grabbed onto Madeline's hand to secure her safety. Her hand was cold and limp. *Madeline really was braving it out.*

Madeline had always been the pretty, un-messy girl. For a woman who grew up in the country-kind of life, the wealth of living in a manor evened her out. London did change her though. She liked the high life and dressing up fancy. But the country girl instincts she was born with kicked in when she needed it. She was always reliable to get stuck into something when she needed to be.

The first thing which struck Emma was not the minor wreckage of Howards farmhouse beside her, but the farm alongside it.

The spotty, orange glow of the house lamps shone a dim brightness beyond the wonky fencing.

The two hobbled their way towards the fencing, dodging the pot holes and fallen planks of wood and tin iron in their way.

Emma came within feet of the fence. The wood was old and knackered, chipped and un-straightened. It was obvious to both Emma and Madeline that it had been worse for wear before the storm.

She stepped closer, gliding the tip of her pointer finger along the middle beam. One end of the beam had come loose from its nail while the other was still tightly secured.

'This fencing is in bad shape,' Emma said.

A huge shotgun-like chunk had been taken out of the middle section of it. It swayed sideways in the whipping wind, moving so hard that Emma thought it would shoot up from the ground and blow away. She put her whole hand on it to hold it down. There she felt the whole force of it rock. She hoped that Mr Banks would come back when he was fit and ready to come and mend his fencing. That way he wouldn't have any troubles with his cattle anymore. But it was the gate she remembered he said he had trouble with.

Before she could move along the fence to investigate further, Emma noticed that Madeline was on the move.

She moved around to the front of the pen, scaling the side of it to keep out of the slush ringing it.

Emma quickened her place and joined Madeline.

The two stood at the front entrance of the pen, their flashlights blaring inside. The pen was vast and empty, as they expected it to be Inside the ground was just as bad as outside, made worse by the scent of cow excrement.

Emma could barely contain herself. She took her hand to her nose and pinched it to block the scent, at the same time thinking how terrible it would have been for the cattle to live in it. She supposed they had gotten used to it, as did Howard Banks. Time was indeed a healer as they said.

Emma stepped closer to the gate, out of the slop and onto a grassy mound. She fiddled with the gate latch. It was loose but not as broken as Mr Banks had claimed it was. Hanging from it was a tough piece of leather, a sort of back-up mechanism to tie the latch closed.

She heard Madeline approaching from behind, the sound of her boots sloshing through the mud intensified by the fact that Emma had already disturbed the ground. She came close to Emma and studied the latch for herself.

'It isn't so much broken as maybe in need of repairs,' Madeline announced.

She fiddled with the leathery strap, flicking it with her finger and letting it dangle.

'It looks like it has been left open,' Madeline said, turning to Emma – who thought very much the same thing – the gate had been *left* open.

Suddenly a flash of light caught their attention from the corner of their eyes. The two friends immediately turned towards it at the same time. Coming through the trees and over the river, a clear yet tiny light was shining from the manor.

A flashlight…? Emma guessed.

It flickered on and off a few times. Like a code.

'It looks like someone wants us back,' Emma said.

Emma and Madeline stood up from their half kneeled position. Emma cleaned her rough and dirtied hands with the wetness of her coat again. They decided to head back to the signal.

With the blood on the rocks, the cattle let free in the woods and the unbroken latch, there was much for Emma to investigate. But there still had been no sign of Frank Lightfoot.

Chapter 7

There was an urgent call from the manor.

It was Dr. Gottfried who made it. He stood at the dark steps of the Smallhorn manor, erratically pointing the flashlight down the green slopes of the yard and casting it out into the woods. He hadn't known if anyone had seen his distress signal until Alfred Lightfoot and Reggie returned. Mr Smallhorn wasn't far behind. He had begun walking back towards the woods after distinguishing the lamps in the barn as he'd promised, when he had seen the urgency of the Doctor.

Under the strobe of lightning and the crash of thunder, a rather abrupt quake of violence had been committed in the sitting room of the manor, only moments before Emma had been led into the woods to investigate.

Mrs Smallhorn and the kitchen hand had been busy looking for Frank in the upper section of the manor. Fillius Lightfoot had taken his leave to the basement, combing through the unwanted junk left in storage, thinking that his father could've been busy picking through his brother-in-law's unwanted treasures.

Robin Smallhorn had taken to floating around. He had joined Fillius in the basement for a while, but grew restless and left to the outside perimeter to search the grounds a little. He didn't care for the storm so much. In fact, he had gotten sick of it. After a while he began to feel like a caged animal and thought that searching outside for Frank would do him some good. But like the team who had gone to the woods, Frank hadn't been found by him either.

Doctor Gottfried, his wife Millicent Gottfried and Madeline's grandparents had made the dining room their base, neither of the couples leaving the table. They thought the best plan was to batten down the hatches and wait out the storm. They also thought the best room to do this in was the room with the most candles and where the coffee was still slightly warm. Every once in a while Doctor Gottfried would get up and check on Mr Banks, casting a quick glance into the room and then hurrying back down the dark halls to the dining room, where he thought it was safe.

Grandpa Smallhorn attempted to keep everyone busy with his tales of the war. Dr. Gottfried had been the only one who seemed to listen as their wives had drifted away. It was something to pass the time until the morning came.

For now, everyone was stuck. There were no services and only one vehicle had come to the manor. Henry Smallhorn did have his own, but it wouldn't arrive from London for another week, having been taken for a check up. Fillius wanted to drive back and had offered to take everyone that he could home, but it wasn't the brightest idea to drive out into the storm. He'd have to wait until the morning at least.

Everyone had kept busy the best they could and were under a collective false pretense that everything was normal, at least for the time Emma and the others were gone.

Howard Banks had been left alone. He tried to sleep, but the pain that spread over his body was overbearing. Over the pelting rain on the windows and rooftop, he could hear the voices of Grandpa Smallhorn and the doctor down the hall. It was more of a mumble and he couldn't pick out their words, but it was noisy nonetheless.

He twisted and turned on the narrow fainting couch. He let his hand droop to the ground, his fingers dusting the carpet atop the floorboards. He gazed up to the ceiling. Shadows of the storm continued to dance in bewitching patterns, distracting him. It was then that he remembered Emma. She really was quite a pretty woman. He blushed thinking about it, but it could've just been the normal colour coming back to his pale face.

Howard Bank's hadn't seen the doctor come by in a while. He was used to the routine where he came by every twenty minutes or so to poke his head through the door, but he hadn't been in thirty minutes now.

Howard was beginning to feel lonely. He didn't like being cooped up in the Smallhorn manor. He knew he wasn't well to leave, but he did want to leave the sofa at least.

With an attacker on the loose he began to feel as though he were a sitting duck. If the person who'd tried to hurt him before was still around, there was every chance they'd come back to finish the job.

Howard checked the grandfather clock in the corner of the room again. *It really had been thirty minutes since he came to check on him.* He thought he'd been abandoned.

The time was half-past twelve now. Midnight had come but no one planned on sleeping tonight. With all that had gone on, nobody could sleep even if they wanted to.

Howard sat up a little. He punched the pillow under his head to fluff it. He thought about the doctor and how he had never saw a black doctor before. Howard was still a young man, but he lived a rather old life. He hadn't left his farm since he bought it when he was only twenty. All he'd remembered outside of the country life was that people of colour in the major towns and cities didn't become doctors or anything as such. It was rather brutal and people looked down on those like Dr. Gottfried. He'd read in his morning paper that it was worse in the United States, but the doctor seemed to him a rather pleasant man.

He had a soothing voice which a doctor needed. It was a mixture of calm and professional, and something that he'd expect of a doctor, but Howard wouldn't know anyway. It had been a long time since he had left his farm to see the world outside of his very own. He only went into Sherrington once a fortnight to purchase food in the market which he otherwise couldn't grow. He'd also purchase hay bales for his cattle and pellets for the chickens.

While Howard had been deep in thoughts of his serenity, he heard footsteps.

He flattened himself back down a little and pulled his arm away from the floor, burying it back under the cover of his quilt. Without moving his head much, he looked out the corner of his eyes where he could see the entrance of the doorway.

Normally Dr. Gottfried would come in and stand by the fainting couch to check on him, but this time he hadn't. The footsteps stopped at the doorway, confusing him.

Howard turned in place and rolled his head away from the pillow. He looked at the doorway and saw someone who was not the doctor.

It was at this moment that it crossed Howard's mind that there was one person other than Frank who hadn't been accounted for. Whilst everyone was looking for Frank, one man had been left astray.

'Who are you?' Howard asked. There was a person cloaked in the darkness, their body outlined but unrecognisable to Howard. He knew for sure that it wasn't the doctor. The doctor was a chubbier man whose gut bloated out over his belt. He was also balding, but this person had long hair.

The person didn't answer.

'Tell me who you are,' Howard demanded.

Silence was returned once more.

Now Howard became nervous. An odd feeling came over him and as the figure stepped into the room, Howard became inconsolable.

He tucked himself under the quilt a little more, hiding his neck as he held the edges of it tight with his fingers.

At last, the unknown person had stepped into the light of the dim candle on the table.

It was Uncle Billy.

Uncle Billy cast himself into the light. He stood over the fainting couch, looking down at Howard with a menacing expression. The wrinkles on his forehead cut deep, his brow creased and furrowed. His eyes were wide and glowing, striking fear deep into the observing Howard.

He looked angrily at Howard, like he was a man who didn't belong in the manor but instead a monster who'd climbed down from a belltower.

'What are you, some kind of a mute?' Howard asked. He narrowed his eyes at the man. When he didn't respond and Howard saw the distinct anger sprout upon the man's face, he wondered if this was the person who'd attacked him in the woods. He wondered if he'd come back to finish the job.

Howard moved, shuffling awkwardly on the fainting couch. Something was off about Billy. Howard had never met uncle Billy but it was as if the storm had enraged him. He never knew of his past and the trial and prison time he had gone through.

To Howard, the man invading his space was a disturbed man. The fact that he didn't speak spoke volumes about him.

Billy's mind rushed and flooded with a convergence of anger and unsettlement. Displaced and changed by the course of his horrific life, he didn't see Mr Banks as the friendly type – nor did he with anyone he didn't know or had never seen before. He didn't trust him.

'You *bad* man,' Billy finally spoke.

"You bad man" The words ran through Howard. He didn't know what he was talking about.

'You bad man,' Billy said again.

'What?'

Billy grumbled and grizzled. His words sounded like a feisty pit-bull guarding his yard. Billy's raven black hair had fallen over his eyes, concealing the full moon of them, only showing a sharpness between the thread.

Uncle Billy then threw himself atop of Howard.

His hands spread, his fingers hooked and stiffened like a hawk's. He reached for Howard's neck and grabbed hold. He held on tight, tightening his grip like he had caught a slippery fish.

Howard thrashed his body around. He yelled through the suffocation Billy was causing, trying to shout. He could barely get the words *"Help"* out of his throat.

With one last struggle, Howard turned his body over, tipping Billy off of him.

Billy hit the ground hard. He rolled over the carpet and hit the edge of the table. He groaned and instantly got back up, making another attempt to tackle Howard. He bore down on Howard, standing over him whilst Howard suppressed his arms from closing around him.

'Where is it?' Billy struggled to speak.

He spoke in a delayed, mentally unstable voice. He was like a man child, someone that hadn't progressed into an adult and was still a child at heart, but it had been the *prison Billy* talking. Prison and the torture of serenity in his holding cell had done it too him. But Howard hadn't known.

'Get off me, you monster!' Howard struggled.

Soon he was off Howard, but not due to his own choice. The shouting and scuffle could be heard throughout the whole building, causing the manor to converge upon Billy.

Doctor Gottfried was the first to come. The older gentleman carefully grabbed Billy, hooking his hands around the curve of his shoulders and ripping him off Howard.

Billy reeled backwards. He barely missed hitting his head against the table.

Billy got up and walked around the table. He took the long way around as Doctor Gottfried blocked him from coming back around.

Fillius rushed in. He stood by the doorway and let Madeline's grandparents come through. Soon after, Mrs Smallhorn came down and entered the sitting room. She brightened the dark room with her lamp. Then she saw the face of her brother and the terrible grief-stricken fear in Howards.

'Billy. What has happened?' Mrs Smallhorn asked. She looked back at her brother again.

Her brother had been distraught. He breathed heavily with panic. His chest heaved and sweat dripped from his forehead. His hair dangled down to his earlobes and crossed over each eye. It was damp from the rain and his clothes were also drenched. It seemed he had been out in the storm before coming in.

She walked up to her brother who'd failed to answer. She came up to him but did not stop; she only slowed her walk down once she looked to the window to see Robin Smallhorn peering inside.

He had his hands up against the glass. He looked through and had heard the commotion over the whipping weather. He had seen the whole thing, yet he remained clueless as to what had happened.

All he did see was the thrashing movement, then the glow of a brighter lamp light soon after. That was all. Soon, he'd come inside to see what had happened.

Once Mrs Smallhorn attended to her brother and the situation had calmed a little, Robin Smallhorn had entered from the front doors.

The scuffle and the screaming of Howard Banks was enough to alert everyone who'd been outside.

'What is going on?' Robin asked as he joined.

'I don't know,' Mrs Smallhorn replied. 'Doctor, what did you see?'

'They were having a scuffle. Don't know what it was all about,' Dr. Gottfried replied. He scratched his head and studied the mess left behind from the fight. Papers, books and ornaments had fallen to the ground. A candle had been knocked from the side table by the fainting couch.

'I came in and found Billy atop of Howard. He was choking him.' The doctor stated.

Mrs Smallhorn turned to her brother. At that moment, the constriction of her hold of him had loosened. She stepped back from him a little, her mouth wide open. She couldn't believe that he had attacked him. It had been a long time since Billy had acted violently, in fact he hadn't since his trial. His streak had come to an end. Howard's wounds had been opened and new cuts had been added. But Billy was bleeding now too.

'Billy. What has gotten into you?'

Prudence forcefully turned her brother around to face her, looking him right in the face. He was inconsolable, refusing to meet her eyes.

Billy didn't reply. He sobbed a little like a man who wanted to speak but couldn't. He started to cling to his sister like a sloth to a tree.

Mrs Smallhorn looked down to his thigh. Blood soaked through his shabby clothing. Shocked by it, Mrs Smallhorn couldn't form any words to make the doctor aware of it. Dr Gottfried left the room, finding that the commotion had made him dizzy. He needed to get out of the crowded room in order to gather himself. As he did, he saw to himself to alarm Emma who he hoped was close by.

He had taken a flashlight and made a break for it outside of the manor. He braved it out in the weather, with flashlight in hand, he stood by Fillius's motor car. He began turning his flashlight on and off again to signal Emma. He stood out in the rain until he was certain that the others would see it as a distress call to bring her in.

All who'd continue the search had come back inside. The doctors ingenious distress call had worked.

Madeline's father, Henry Smallhorn soon entered the room to discover what had happened. With the absence of Emma, the man of the manor reigned some authority of himself back in to ask and sort out what had happened.

It was Henry's home after all. He was due a little control. It was off of his back that everyone had come out tonight, so it was his job to collect the calmness of his family.

Henry Smallhorn broke apart the quarrels inside the sitting room. He had his eyes directed on to one person – Howard Banks – who Henry knew still despised him from previous disputes. He knew that any trouble that was to come would come from him.

Henry looked at Howard's rattled face, then quickly turned to observe his brother-in-law who shivered in his wife's arms.

'What did you do to upset him?' Henry demanded to know.

'Nothing.' Howard couldn't believe it and was left feeling perplexed and defensive. He couldn't believe that Henry would think that it was his fault.

'Well, you must have done something. He just doesn't go off like that, you know.' Henry pressed his hands to his hips, stepping closer to the edge of the fainting couch and invading Howard's personal space. He had him confronted and Howard choked, awkwardly stammering and swallowing, he was right to feel rattled.

'He attacked me!' Howard shouted. 'I was resting here all by myself and next thing I know he comes in and tries to kill me!' Howard pointed to Billy, his finger looking to everyone else like a dagger. He swore with his index finger and the grit

in his teeth that if it ever happened again, he'd hurt Billy even more, injured or not.

'You know, you have some nerve pointing at my family like that, Banks,' Henry fizzled.

'Come on, Henry, ease off him. I saw the whole thing, he didn't start a goddamn thing,' Robin admitted.

Robin had seen it from the window from the moment Howard had shouted for help. He had seen the whole thing happen, even past the murkiness of the rain-pelted window.

Billy shied away from the situation. To add to the tension, Madeline's grandfather shouted in an unpredictable moment.

'Barbarians!' He grumbled, waving his cane in the air.

The old man never missed a beat with what the war had turned him into. He believed in a good fight, that it was something of a manly thing to settle disputes with a good wrestle between foes. But scratching and choking was a little left field in his eyes. He didn't like the way Billy and Howard had fought.

'Give it a rest, father,' Prudence said. George had been a little too excited and the might he could've used to reprimand her disrespectful daughter was instead used to hoister his cane.

He glazed over the situation and took a seat. 'Back in my day we used to punch and flatten, not fluff around like that,' he ranted, but no one listened anymore.

Soon Emma and Madeline had rushed inside. They had been alerted by the doctor's flashlight and each dripped wet with rain. Emma abandoned her coat, shrugging it to the floor. She looked inside the sitting room. It was filled with everyone at question for Frank's disappearance, if indeed he wasn't the one who hadn't attacked Howard. She knew that someone she was looking at was responsible. Someone in the family was a rat who'd committed something terrible and was hiding it from the rest of them.

She was suspended from her task as she walked into something else.

'What is going on?' Emma asked, sensing a heavy scent of commotion.

'Some detective,' George Smallhorn said, unimpressed as he continued to grumble on to himself.

Billy heard the word *"detective"* and as soon as he did immediately acted as if he were a horse reacting to the word *"Whoa"*.

Detectives and any person of the law caused him to bolt and that he did. His ears shot up and he broke free from his sister, dashing from the door in an attempt to abandon the room. Emma stood in his way, but couldn't stop him, instead she was hit hard by his passing shoulder and knocked to the side. He scurried away deep into the dark of the manor and his sister followed. She called his name, trying to bring him back, but he wouldn't stop. She could only follow him.

'I was attacked by that lunatic,' Howard wheezed. His throat was still hurting and there was a red handprint ringed around it. He returned to lying on his back, sore and discomforted by the random fight between the two.

'I bet he did it. I bet he was the one who attacked me at the river and now he wanted to finish the job,' Howard shouted.

Henry was just about to lean over Howard again and give him an earful for accusing his brother-in-law, and would've if his daughter hadn't stopped him.

'Dad, is uncle Billy ok?' Madeline asked.

He shook his head and gritted his teeth. His eyes floated over to his sweet daughter's face and he sighed.

'Uncle Billy is disturbed, you know that. From what uncle Robin says, Billy has seemingly lashed out at Mr Bank's,' Henry had changed his tune. His brother, Robin Smallhorn and Dr. Gottfried could vouch for him, though he hated to side with Howard.

Things had certainly changed since Emma went out to investigate. In the hour she left, another attack was set upon Howard Banks. It sounded very much like an opportunity when nobody was looking. With only what Robin swore he saw through the foggy sight of a rain-stained window to go on, there wasn't much Emma could do without just basking the questions herself.

Emma took a seat.

She peered down to the floorboards by Howard. His arm dangled and pointed to a patch of blood that had been dripping from his wrist. His wounds had come undone from the scrap, but he didn't seem to notice. He rugged himself back up in the blanket and focused on the ceiling.

He didn't dare to look at anyone and Emma could understand. Like herself, they were the outsiders. They were not a part of the family.

Howard gently closed his eyes after a while and Emma watched him. He breathed more calmly and his heart rate had seemed to slow down.

She didn't want to alarm the doctor that there was more blood and didn't want to disturb Howard anymore that he already was.

'I will speak to Billy if I can,' Emma decided.

There was an exchange of glances around the dark room.

No one quite liked that idea.

'Are you sure that's a good idea?' Henry asked.

His voice sounded to Emma like he was trying to hide something.

She looked back at him, her face confused from seconds before when it was much clearer and confident. *Why wouldn't I?* her face said.

'Like I said before, the man is not well. He is brutally disturbed after what has happened in his life. He tends to lash out, just like what we witnessed,' Henry said.

Emma turned to Madeline. She nodded to back up her father.

'It's true, Emma,' Madeline said. 'Uncle Billy won't even speak. It's a trauma he has from his past experiences.'

Emma didn't care. She needed to speak with the man. It was only him who could tell her what happened. She didn't get the sense that the people who were left in the room with her were telling her the whole truth.

'I am officially calling this a crime scene,' she announced to everyone in the room.

Emma had no other choice.

It had seemed that the family were telling her to back away, but she needed to speak with Billy.

'*Crime scene?* What… A man goes missing and you call it a crime scene?' Madeline's grandfather spat. He had seemed to forget that the man next to him, dripping with blood and turning even more pale by the second, had been attacked.

Emma looked to Madeline then turned to Henry Smallhorn. She proceeded to say that she'd found blood at the river's edge, just as Howard said. Reggie and Alfred who were standing by the door also chimed in.

'It's true. There was blood, still fresh and rained on by the rocks,' Alfred said.

Emma had left out one thing. The knife that was found half-buried in the riverbed that by luck she had stepped upon.

She sucked her teeth throughout the entire conversation, knowing what she had in her coat. She even ran her palm over the handle of the weapon as they talked.

She never wanted to tell everyone about the knife. She hoped that if she kept it a secret, perhaps someone would confess to losing one without knowing she had it.

But, in light of the attack and what was transpiring, she revealed the knife. She took it from out of her coat and unravelled the cloth tied over it. She lifted it and let it dangle by the handle for everyone to see.

There was no blood on it – the water had washed it away.

'What is that?' Dr. Gottfried asked. He asked, but he knew full well what it meant.

'Dear god. This poor man truly was attacked,' Millicent Gottfried said, sounding squeamish.

'I found it in the river. It had been dropped or tossed in the water, but with it and the blood, this confirms the attack,' Emma finished.

She wrapped the knife back up in her cloth. She never wanted anybody in the room to get a hold of it. As she gazed at it one last time before she covered it away, she thought to herself that it looked awfully like the one Reggie had – but that was impossible – *How could it get from his hands to the river where she saw it?*

She shook the thought, thinking that it was nothing. But they were almost identical.

'I was there too,' Reggie said as he found the courage to speak. He didn't seem to pick up on the knife again. He didn't at the river nor in the room, just as Emma was thinking about it. But his words had caused trouble.

Grandpa Smallhorn slowly peered up to Reggie. Before his eyes had landed on him, they were already squinting in disgust. He didn't like the tone of Reggie's voice and before he saw him, he knew who he was.

'You, *boy.'* Grandpa Smallhorn bellyached.

Reggie stepped deep into himself. He looked shot, eyes blared and he shivered at Madeline's grandfather's sharp turn on him. He pointed at Reggie with an intent of anger and suspicion.

'I haven't seen you at all. Where have you been all this time?' His words grumbled. His mind was focused on nothing but accusation. He didn't know that Reggie worked for Henry Smallhorn in the stables as he kept to himself most of the time.

'Me?' Reggie lifted his finger to his chest. He couldn't believe what Grandpa Smallhorn was alluding to.

'I was in the barn, battening down the hatches, and then them lot came and found me.'

Reggie looked to Henry, Madeline, Emma and Alfred for confirmation. Alfred stepped away a little from his place, separating himself from Reggie so as to not be associated with him any longer. He did rather think that it was certainly a possibility that the criminal could be him.

Reggie had found himself to be a coincidental young man all of a sudden. He knew it didn't look good for him once the others worked it out, but he hadn't let what just happened slide.

'Didn't we just witness Billy attack a man who someone previously attempted to murder?' Reggie asked. He hoped to reel everyone back in and get them to think about Billy's actions again, but no one took the bait. Billy was at least a damaged man and had an excuse for his outburst. For Reggie, he had the same knife and he'd been outside the whole time. He was also the last one to interact with Frank Lightfoot.

Reggie looked at everyone's blank expressions. He couldn't get the words that he wanted out. He wanted to tell them that it wasn't him, that he was innocent of any crime. He was astonished as to what they were all thinking of him, and it rendered him mute.

'You were in the barn all alone,' Henry stated. He hated to admit it as he liked Reggie and had always believed that he was a good worker. He looked after Reggie, but he couldn't glide over the facts in front of him.

'With a knife mind you. A knife which looks almost exactly like the one that the detective here has in her coat,' Alfred added.

Emma listened, remembering the knife that had been in Reggie's hands. It had been like catching a child with their hand in the cookie jar. It certainly had begun to look bleak for Reggie.

Reggie gulped. At once, he realised the correlation and now he knew what everyone thought of him. The only question was what they were going to *do* with him.

In his mind, he knew it was a different knife that he had used in the barn. But he couldn't deny the fact that they were identical. He even started to think that it could've been the same knife himself, that they were perfectly the same. He had to remind himself that he didn't do it. He didn't attack anyone.

'I swear… I swear I didn't do anything.'

'And you went with my father to close the barn doors before we came in,' Alfred said. His voice had gotten louder, much more confident and full of accusation this time.

'You killed Frank then attacked this man here?' Grandpa Smallhorn blustered, only adding to the scrutiny that Reggie was under.

Reggie looked to Howard but Howard couldn't do anything. He could barely roll over to show his face and whether he contested or agreed at all. Reggie stepped closer into the doorframe, now looking to Emma. He pleaded to her with his eyes. He didn't know her, but he needed her to save him.

Emma got up. She shouted, silencing the roll of chatter in the room looking to accuse Reggie so easily.

'Enough!'

Emma turned to face everyone. They all gazed at her and waited for her to speak.

'We cannot go around accusing everyone of a crime. Any one of us could be responsible and until I find out who, nobody is to accuse anyone.'

Emma was stern. She was just about the only person left who was logical enough to not become so primitive. How quickly they all turned on someone. It must be the storm and the sheer panic of the power outage which made them behave like animals.

'Mr Smallhorn.' Emma looked to Henry with dire urgency.'Please keep everyone in order.'

He nodded.

Emma then turned to Madeline. She asked her to take her to Billy. Whilst the commotion was still fresh in his wild mind, she'd like to hear what uncle Billy had to say.

****

Chapter 8

A MAN SUSPECTED OF MURDER;
A CRIME INVESTIGATION OF '1906

Nothing definitive was ever found, but there was one man at the crime scene who had been detained hours after it happened. Time will tell if he speaks in his cell.

FRONT PAGE OF THE LONDON SCOPE.

KILLER CAUGHT RED-HANDED AT THE CRIME SCENE.

Marabelle Bogsworth and her husband, Hamish Bogsworth, were found murdered on the corner of Juniper street, London. The two were reported by their neighbours to have had a confrontation with each other earlier that evening. The argument between the two was undetermined and it is unclear if it had anything to do with the murder. The two were later found dead outside their London home.

Blood hasn't stained the pavement of London since the infamous Whitechapel murders some twenty years ago. Not since Charles Finch's 1863 novel of the demon barber on Fleet street had a neck been slashed so severely.

The Bogsworth couple were recently married. They were both twenty-six years of age. Their horrific death has sparked fears of a killer which London knows best. Could it be a revival of the Whitechapel murderer – one which we had not yet put away, or could it be another reaping murderer on the streets of London again?

The neighbour to the Bogsworths had heard the couple arguing next door. *"The walls in London are thin between residents,"* she mentioned, but again, it was hard to understand what it was about. Most of the time it was nothing, but something about their last argument sounded malicious to their neighbours. When it was asked of the Bogsworth's neighbour as to why she never called upon the police – or at least some other assistance – she merely muttered that it wasn't her place.

The young couple used to argue all the time, even before they were married. Sometimes the whole street would know about it, as most of the time it would happen when it was very late and quiet. It would seem that there was no shame between the Bogsworth's. Yelling matches were a constant.

Such news had been kept away in recent interviews and newspapers, but the police department has since leaked these details before the upcoming trial of the suspect.

A source has provided the detailing's that many of the arguments between the married couple came from the subject of money and infidelity.

The young couple were in love, but some who knew them would say that their love had died before they married.

Hamish Bogsworth would play his part of becoming a doubtful husband when it came to his loyalty. He would routinely drink and gamble and was said to frequent the late night bars and chase the young females.

Marabelle Bogsworth would later find out about her husband's antics, as well as releasing that the money had been drained to the point where one more month of it and their house would foreclose.

'He would roll in late most nights and talk ever so much about how he hated his wife. I hoped he would leave it at that and spend his money at least for the time being,' The barmaid, Sarah Whittaker said the night after the murder. *'I didn't think someone else would kill him once his wife found out. I had my money on her to do it herself.'*

This was no murder-suicide. The way the knife slashed both of their necks was consistent to each other, quite the way Charles Finch would describe it in one of his novels. The murders almost seemed *inspired* by these infamous novels. Perhaps it was found to be the perfect way to assure a quick and bloody death in quick concession. "It was risky to kill out in the open. It must've been a swift act," said an on-duty police officer.

There was no backwards motion of the blade, but rather one that had been pressed into the throat from the front, then dragged across to open the main artery. It was done in such a way that it was possible that the two victims had never seen their attacker coming – no one had in fact.

The chief of police who had arrived first on the scene remarked the following:

'The streets of London are an unease once again. An identical case to the Whitechapel murders has come back to haunt us, but I vow that we have the right man in custody and the streets shall rest easy once more,' Chief Maston promised.

Chief Maston reminisced the Whitechapel murders. He had been a young officer some twenty years ago when they happened and he did not think that they were the work of "Jack the Ripper".

People of London have grown fearful, many believing that it is the coming of a second act. Strangely, a rather sort of obscure folk have relished the idea and have felt a little nostalgia of the famous murders. It would seem that many people are glad to be living through a possible Jack the Ripper return.

Chief Maston had been quick to shut the speculation down. Although people still believed, it was clear what had been discovered at the crime scene.

'Jack the Ripper is not the culprit responsible. We have the man which we found at the crime scene in custody. He is

young and couldn't possibly have been a grown man during Jacks' terrible reign.'

It wasn't Jack the Ripper, albeit the crimes had been quite similar. Over the next week, the people of London had been left to wonder if this *"killer"* had used the Whitechapel murders as somewhat of an inspiration.

The slash of a knife to the neck and leaving the bodies in the street for the police to find was similar to the historic crimes of Jack himself in the past. But it was all just speculation and a rumour "*feed-frenzy"* on the street's, the Chief did emphasise.

When the reporter working for the London press asked if the police did indeed have their man, Chief Maston replied: *'It is very likely. He was there on the night when we came. He was by the bodies, looking through them for valuables of any kind.'*

'What will you imagine the suspect's sentence to be?'

The chief had been hesitant to answer, but it was appropriate to settle fears on the night it occurred. By the time the trial loomed closer, he responded with a less speculative turn.

'I would expect for Billy Javers to be buried under the prison.'

From the London Scope, January 8th, 1906 (page 1)

The commotion of the courtroom.

A week after the murders of the Bogsworths murders

Billy Javers stood chained to a podium as the defendant. Faced with an uproar of people on either side of him and a begrudging, but experienced judge before him, he was welded to his place.

The judge had to ask for silence more than once. That number had surpassed the dozen mark by now. People did not like Billy Javers and saw him as the monster he'd become.

The courtroom felt sorry for the Bogsworths. They fought and they each went astray from their relationship, but they never deserved what Billy Javers had done to them. No one did.

Billy looked like a wrecked man. He gave the appearance of a man who'd been ridden hard and put away wet. His face became scared and he'd complain about a constant ringing from the times he'd banged his head repeatedly against the cement of his cell wall.

He was tired, he didn't sleep in the week he'd been kept at the local detaining office. His hair had become all greasy and he ate as little as possible as the reality of what he was confronted with burned within him.

Billy had very much become a shell of his old self. He was once a jolly fella and an adventurous person in his youth.

Something had to have changed him and his way to become the man he stood as today. Nobody, not even his family knew.

In a bizarre twist of events, when Billy was asked if he was guilty, he confessed.

Through the commotion of the jury, the relatives, the crowd and the judge, no one noticed anything strange about the way Billy had acted.

He had given in. A week's worth of solitary confinement, a lack of eating and drinking, rotting in the shade where no sunlight could touch his cold walls, and having to deal with the demons of his mind for so long, Billy had become insane.

There was no way out for Billy. He knew the circumstances never looked good, him being found over the bodies and searching through their belongings. He knew where he was heading and no amount of pleading could save him otherwise.

Moments before, the courtroom doctor pointed out a change in Billy's behaviour. He'd tracked and logged him in his holding cell and when he came in for fifteen minutes of each day, he had seen that Billy had violently bashed his head against the wall, leaving a new layer of blood each day as he did so.

It was the first that the judge had heard about Billy's self-inflicted violence. The judge knew fairly well that in any cell in London, it was rare that self-violence was an occurrence. More times than most, prison guards and officers would beat the accused into submission. The judge rather believed that the same thing had happened to Billy Javers, but he never pursued it.

People who committed murder and crimes of a similar calibre never deserved the decency of a *look into.*

'The man went in psychotic and nothing has since changed,' the lawyers of the murdered couple said.

Mr Bogsworth and his wife, Hamish's parents - stared daggers at Billy. They shared the same shark-like intent of their lawyers. It was a done and dusted case for them and they wanted the better chunk of justice for their son and his wife.

The judge had no problem with disregarding the comment of the doctor. He saw Billy as a man who had always been how he stood in the chains before him today.

He didn't look like a man who was capable of looking after himself. By the judge's eye, he did look to be in a bit of a mental state, but he hadn't known what kind of man Billy was throughout his life. He didn't care to look past any further considering what he'd done.

He looked homeless, like a drifter who had come off the street to murder and rob a wealthy couple for everything that they had.

Billy hadn't contested anything.

He had his head dropped forwards for the most part, feeling his wrists swell from the cuffs and the bruising of police fists who had beaten him into submission in his cell all week. He could still hear the deafening squeal in his right ear go off to his beatings and his head split almost constantly.

He never seemed to listen to the judge and the vicious lawyers on the other side, just the hissing of the crowd behind him and the jury gasping in pure shock.

Behind him, seated in the front row, was his sister and his parents.

Prudence Javers, who would be married to Henry Smallhorn in four short months, looked on in anguish.

She couldn't believe what her brother had become. She hadn't seen him for months as he moved to London to find work in an old bakery.

In the space of half a year, life had turned out quite differently for Billy. From what Prudence had heard, he was doing well with his new job, but since the time she'd last heard from him he was now being tried for murder.

Billy never moved nor twitched. He turned his back to his family and never looked at their grieving faces. Though she couldn't see his face, Prudence didn't take her eyes off him.

She could barely see the side of his face and the hair which dangled over his left eye. His looks had changed as well as his demeanour. He was less the talkative man he once was and was now more submissive. She couldn't help but think that he must've been under some spell to make him act in such a way, nevertheless, commit such a dreadful crime. It was the old Billy which she clung onto and as she silently watched, sat by her husband to be alongside her parents, it was those memories of her brother that convinced her that he wasn't the murderer.

The court and the police were so quick to jump at Billy. He was found at the scene of course, but he didn't have the chance to be heard. He was beaten and enclosed to forget himself that he was innocent. As well as the force, the people of London had been sucked into the local papers, believing that it was Billy from the very moment they read his name.

By some miracle, some believed he still was the Whitechapel murderer. They believed Billy to be older than what he was, thus starting a new conspiracy which hadn't yet travelled throughout London. Some liked the hysteria of another era of murderers. People were starting to collect the papers and even visit the courtroom outside just to get a glimpse of the man. Billy had indeed been sent many letters from fans who wanted to speak to him and tell him what they thought of him. It wasn't a simpler time as it once was, instead it was quite *"delusional and anti-law"* .

Prudence couldn't stand it any longer. She cried. She didn't know what was worse, if her brother hadn't done it but would be locked away forever, or the fact that he had indeed murdered that couple. She obviously knew which one she'd rather, but it was tough to think about. Everything had collapsed around her.

'Billy Javers was found hovering over the bodies. A nightly patrol had come from the junction of Spartan and Juniper Street to see him looting over their corpses. He had blood all over his clothes and when they saw him, he tried to run away,' Chief Maston got up and proudly relayed.

'The medical examiner and his reporter profoundly lack any explicit in this case. Every inch of the examination was clear as crystal," the chief said. He turned to the medical examiner and cocked his brow.

'The reports show that the couple had their throats slashed and their heads were almost sawn off. There are no signs of a murder-suicide, as Mr Javers lawyers suggest. It would be completely impossible with the way the knife went in. They would've died in seconds, leaving no time for that possibility.'

The judge listened to what Chief Maston had to say.

Everything had been rather conclusive for him to make his mind up days in advance. The trial had been something of a *page cover* for the past week and much was expected of the judge to make the *right* decision.

The chief of police was given great leisure for his fortitude of recent time. He had helped put away some of the more dangerous crooks and bastards in London, before then handling the tougher jobs in Birmingham with the gang resurgence. But even before then, he was a young officer who was close to the Whitechapel murders, but he hadn't been able to put the killer away. There had been names and beliefs, but nothing came of any of them.

This time, Chief Maston was nothing short of stubborn to put a murderer away. He was young then, but he wasn't about to make the same mistakes that his chiefs made.

'And what do you make of the beatings during his confinement?' The judge asked.

Heads turned throughout the courtroom. The judge didn't intend to bring up the beatings of Billy at all. It was likely that it had happened, but nothing was ever said nor proven. For a moment, everyone believed that the judge was beginning to side with Billy.

When asked about them, Chief Maston seemed to retreat slightly. It was obvious by now to the judge, as he could see how torn Billy's face had become and the purple bruising up his arms and down his legs.

His sense was beaten out of him, as well as his authority to assert his mind.

When asked about Mr Javers' handling in detention and the obvious severity, Chief Maston said, *'Mr Javers acted up during his time in our care. He threatened to harm officers and fellow inmates when he got his hour out of confinement. His doctor couldn't even go in without half a dozen officers at the door. After a while, he'd begin to do it to himself. Constantly he would be taken into care once we found blood all over the walls due to the numerous times he'd bash his head against it. He became worse off than his usual self. Animals quite like himself do not like to be caged.'*

When asked if he thought the prisoner tried to kill himself by his means, Chief Maston nodded and spoke with a straight *'Yes.'*

It was nothing but the chief and his word. He could've said anything about the accused. Billy hadn't really tried to kill himself. He knew it, but the chief had fabricated the idea to make it seem as if Billy wanted an out for what he'd done. It was a clever trick and Billy refused to confront and deny the notion. To him, it wouldn't matter what he said.

Chief Maston went on, *'Since the Whitechapel murders, we no longer do things without caution. We are always sure of how to handle the accused and we do it assertively. Once we catch the criminal, we make sure that they can't get away, which is why Billy was given the lengthy time in solitary confinement. Neither of us want a killer on the loose.'*

By the way Chief Maston spoke and sweated under the heat of the courtroom, it would seem long ago that he already had his mind made up. When he would glance at Billy Javers from time to time he always looked to Chief Maston like a killer. He looked at him like he knew who he was from what he saw. Billy Javers was a guilty man.

'And do you believe that Mr Javers should be hanged by the neck until death for his actions?' The judge asked.

Chief Maston didn't give it a second thought. The only delay he had in answering was to clear his nagging throat. His hands folded over the table as he leaned over. With a clear intent on his face, he steered from his notes and turned to the judge to look him in the eye.

'I would much rather the evil go straight to where they came, rather have the right to live amongst us, your honour.'

He received an uproar of applause from the crowd. The spectators hung on the edge of their benches. They cheered and smiled ripely at what the chief said. They were very much in favour of seeing Billy dead, much opposed to the middle-class who bundled outside the courtroom.

The chief's time was up. He stepped down from the stand and Billy's parents were asked to come up.

Mr and Mrs Javers continued to deny that their son had any part in the murder. They knew he was a good boy.

The judge had it on the record that there was a chance of a mental disorder – something which wasn't conclusive or thought as much to be an excuse for ending the lives of others.

It was immediately refused. The notion barely lasted and the papers had painted Billy as somewhat of a monster with a good heart, but was easily set off to go crazy.

Mr and Mrs Javers insisted that a mental disorder had never touched their son.

'He was a great child and we were very loving to him,' the mother said.

'We used to take him and his sister out when they were younger. We used to come to town and visit the zoo and the Tower of London. We would go on picnics on the weekend and his father would take Billy out fishing on our property. He was a very happy, charming young boy. When he got older, he came to London to make a life out of himself away from the country. Before he became a baker along the Shepperton ally in London, he helped look after farms in Sherrington. He was always determined and he would write to us often. He wanted to find a lady to marry and start a family. He also wanted to purchase the bakery he worked at after some time. He always told us that he would come back to the country with his family in retirement and station a farm close to our manor. He would never do something like this. It is not like him,' Mrs Javers finished.

Billy's poor father was almost overwhelmed with tears after what his wife said. It brought back memories of a happier time, a time that hadn't felt real anymore with what had come to override it. He did his best to contain himself. He stood a tall man. He was very well representative of himself, rather like the nice suit he wore to work and the courtroom.

The poor lady was full of tears when she left the stand. She did all the pleading she could and she tried her very best to convince the judge, but even she knew that she couldn't get her beloved son out of this.

Billy's poor mother tried to show the judge just how sweet of a man Billy was. She could never understand how he'd ever commit murder. She faced the fact, though she didn't want to believe it. The least she could try to do was get him a lighter sentence, no matter how set the rest of the courtroom was upon their stance on the matter of Billy's guilt.

When Billy's father came to the stand, he stood a stern but very sombre man. He came to court wearing his best suit and combed hair, but even during the longevity of the trial, he had begun to sweat through it.

'Billy was a strong child growing up. I taught him everything he knew. I taught him how to fish, I also taught him how to set up a campfire using rocks. All you had to do was whack them together and create a spark. I also showed him how to steady the flame on the straw when the first sign of smoke came. I think he even got it the first time, that's how good of a learner he was. But I know what you are going to ask me. Yes, Billy was born with a problem. He has an anger issue and it is something that he has learned to contain for most of his life. We don't know what it is, but we hear it's becoming more common now.'

He looked to his son, but Billy didn't look back.

'Please continue,' the judge said.

'Billy wouldn't hurt anyone. He was kind to everyone – he didn't even like to harm the animals on my property when we'd hunt or fish. He wanted to make a life for himself. As my wife said, he wanted to start a family and move back out with us up north to the country. He always did love the fire in our home and we kept it burning for him.'

Mr Javers wiped a tear from his face as it rolled down his wrinkled cheek. The stern father seemed to have crumbled, but as soon as he mopped up the tear, he had regained himself.

The judge sighed. He shuffled his papers and rearranged them to focus on Billy's early prognosis as a child. The doctor had indeed listed that Billy had anger problems which had later been updated in his file to autism and an intermittent explosive disorder. It was quite severe at that and it did cause him to sometimes lash out at his family – even as a young boy. He lacked occasional emotion. His mental deficiency was something which the judge observed to come back even greater during the process of Billy's entire trial. Perhaps it was something that Billy would have let go of if his life in London had prospered.

'Did you ever beat him as a boy?'

The judge asked, the room falling silent.

It seemed unnecessary at first to ask, but the judge perhaps thought that his anger had been suppressed by pain.

At last, it all came out, ending in a gruesome murder on Billy's part. Now it looked like the parents were to blame.

Mr Javers looked to the ground. His mind searched for an appropriate answer, but he knew what he'd done and it didn't look good.

'I did, your honour,' Mr Javers said, his voice heavy with regret. At that moment, he too seemed to know that perhaps his son's murders was something of an outburst built up from suppression.

'I own a manor, quite like my daughter's fiancé – the Smallhorn manor.

In my manor, he used to play with the antiques. if he broke one of them or dented some very valuable armour, I did beat him, with a stick. It was the kind of stick a teacher from the Victorian era would use to reprimand their students. I think it was that exact stick. It was found in my office, so I used it for the children whenever they needed reprimanding.'

Mr Javers was a kind and loving father, but *"reprimanding"* his children wasn't something out of the ordinary for most families. The judge knew this. He tried to correlate the actions of trauma that could've been caused when Billy was a child to how he acted out now. Perhaps it was something that always happened with troubled people on the wrong side of the law.

'Did he ever ask you to stop?' The judge asked.

'He used to,' he said. *"Please stop daddy, I didn't mean to break anything".*

'He always hated the stick. I remember him saying "Oh no, not the stick. Please don't use the stick". Multiple times, your honour. But he never resented me long after it. He understood why I had to do it… why we all do it.' Mr Javers looked around the jury and the crowd. He even looked to the prosecution. When he did, blank faces were painted on just about everyone. Mr Javers was right.

Prudence Javers, soon to be Prudence Smallhorn, was the last to come to the stand. When she got up, a heavy silence steadied the crowd and the jury. She was a young female. She looked scared and frail as to what her life and her brothers had become now. She looked so pale that at any moment the judge would call a recess to let her vomit in discretion.

'The defendant's sister is at the stand,' the clerk announced.

'Do you recall the beatings of your brother?' The judge asked.

'Yes I do, your honour.'

'Did it stay with him? Do you think such actions were carried out for his victims last week?'

'No, I think not, your honour.'

Prudence cleared her throat. She turned to her brother, her eyes twinkling with unshed wells of tears. She remembered how well her brother had been doing over the last year or so. She didn't hear much from him as she never went to London, but she knew that he was starting a new life with a new job. He did say he wanted to start a family the last time they spoke in person. Billy seemed very normal. He didn't care that their father beat him. It was something of a normality for each family. Prudence indeed learned her lessons when she saw the stick. She didn't get it very much after that first time.

'I love my brother and cherish everything I had growing up with him. He was the kindest, sweetest man a sister could have. He looked after me and made sure I was ok all the time. He got along well with my fiancé and his part in our growing family is even more important as it ever was.'

Thoughts on the matter did not outweigh the words from the family. The crowd randomly spat out at a frenzy and the prosecution team thrived from it.

The case had not been decided, but from the moment the police team spattered their flashlights over Billy Javers, it was already over.

Prudence looked to her brother one last time. He never looked back. He never looked at anyone. She screamed at him. 'Billy, say something,' but there was no reply. He didn't look like he wanted to get out of his mess. He looked conformed to it. When he stood on the stand, half-filled bottles and scraps of trash were thrown at him, some hitting the man in the cheek. He didn't feel a thing.

After the prosecution gifted the family of the victims the chance to speak, all was said and done. The judge did however make one decision of the case that gave Billy's family some relief. Instead of being hanged until death, Billy Javers would remain incarcerated for two life sentences, unable to have the chance of parole until the ripe old age of seventy.

It would seem that the words of the family did play a pivotal part in Billy's sentence. The fact that he had mental problems since birth and the lack of any evidence but a sighting from the routine officers at the crime had been the one distinction.

The judge's conviction of Billy wasn't fair for everyone in the room. Although the sentence was high and it was likely Billy would never see the light of day again, almost everyone wanted the man to die.

They lusted for blood like barbarians. It would seem the only way to calm the crowds' fear-riddled souls was to take a life for a life. But it wasn't the case.

The parents of Hamish Bogsworth dropped their heads. It wasn't the result they wanted. But there was nothing more which could be said. The judge had made his decision, both to appease the two parties of the court and the people who'd bombarded the walls outside the courthouse.

Billy was taken down from his stand. The court-guard unhooked the chains tied to his cuffs to hold him down and took him on his way.

Billy beat the crowd to the side of him as he was taken out of the court. Rancid fruit and vegetables were pelted at his face, most of it splattering the shoulders of the officers who were taking him on his way. He never looked back to his family.

It was somewhat of a relief for the Javers family. Mr and Mrs Javers didn't want to have to go through seeing their son hanged. Seeing him die and having to listen to the crowd cheer for him to choke under the crack of his broken neck and cheer until the last twitch of his toes came wouldn't be fair. It would be like all the hate in the world seemed right for the moment, like everyone before them would suddenly turn to fight for something terrible. But in a weird turn of events, it would also seem right. It was so confusing for the family, but Prudence didn't think so.

Prudence watched the back of her brother right until he turned the corner and vanished into the patrol vehicle that would take him to live out his sentence. She was glad that death wouldn't come. But living in prison would make him think of it. After a year or two, death would start to sound like a dear old friend, one that you'd want to visit after a tough time.

Even after the conviction had been decided, even after her parents had given up, Prudence still had hope. His sister vowed to get him out.

Years had passed and Billy Javers was doing surprisingly ok in prison.

Indeed, he would never leave his solitary cell, but it was due to his choice. To his luck, he'd been placed in a cell with a narrow little window which almost always faced the sunrise each day. When the sun had come through, his entire cell was lit up, but he'd always have his back facing it.

Billy cried most days, tucking himself into the corner by his bed and curling in a fetal position. The prison guards always found him like that. He had turned into some kind of a caveman, or a hermit. *"The man was no longer a monster, but now a bat."*

Some guards even referred to him as being somewhat of a cave bear or a titanoboa hiding in its cave towards the end of its existence, awaiting death. But with each day that he passed Billy's cell, he began to feel more and more sorry for him.

It's funny what prison makes of people. Inside, there are both imprisoned and free men often sharing the same place, yet there are still boundaries. When the free birds see those who are caged, they instinctively know they are two of the same kind but with separate flight paths. One cannot help but feel bad for the other.

When the prison guard became fed up with finding Billy curled away from the sunlight, he dragged him out.

Billy had refused to eat and drink. His skin had turned a slimy, pale white and the man had become hunched over with his hair having grown down past his shoulders.

The prison guard was rough with him, but he had to be to get Billy out of his cave. Once he had dusted him off and taken him out of the dark, he granted Billy Javers a job in the prison workshop.

He was sent to the wood shop and given the opportunity to work on sanding the wood. Once he grew comfortable and the guards began trusting him, Billy would begin to build anything from bird houses to tables. He had been given a hammer to work with – they even let him carry a belt with nails and a drawknife to shave the wood down. The prison guards had kept a close eye on him but found that the man had become quite responsible in his new environment. He was quite good at his job and even built some needed resources for the prison.

Billy was quite proud of his work and for it, he was given allocated time to come out of his confinement and extra treats at mealtime.

For eight years Billy continued his work. He got up at seven sharp and worked for eight hours without a break, heading back to his cell before his afternoon meal.

It was a time where Billy could evade his routine beatings in the bathrooms. There was a gang of inmates who took a liking to him. Once Billy had lost all the weight from his trial and his confinement, he was an easy target, but his time in the woodshop had bulked him up again.

Billy accepted that this was now his world. There was nothing more outside of what he was already doing. Though the life never came with the chance of freedom, though he knew nobody inside would ever let him walk out those doors to taste freedom, it was the best he could get. And yet, he still never spoke. He never got to know anyone, never speaking to anyone or making any friends. He kept to himself with the exception of the doctor who routinely checked on him from the prison infirmary.

Billy had indeed accepted his fate and didn't see the point in speaking anymore. The ordeal of his wrongful term and the tight, enclosed walls of the prison had changed him for good.

But, one day, his life changed.

Billy Javers was to be set free.

After eight years of prison, thinking that it would be the place he would be until the day of his death, new evidence had come in to save him.

Fingerprints had been taken at the crime scene from a knife that was later found hidden in the trunk of a nearby tree.

It had been lodged and hidden away for many years until it was found, the trace still intact on the handle as it was kept out of the elements. Billy did think it was weird when he was called away from his cell for further testing. He left his fingerprints with the examiner, having no clue what was happening and why they were doing it. That night was just about a week ago now and since, the examiners had come back to show that the fingerprints of Billy Javers did not in fact match the ones on the knife found by the crime scene.

Billy was shown the knife. He could not see the blood as it had been removed from the blade previously and tested to show a match of Mr and Mrs Bogsworth's blood. When they saw Billy's face when confronted with the knife, and the blatant confusion expressed, they knew that they had the wrong man.

Chief Maston died some years earlier, laid to rest thinking that he'd put away the right man to finish his career, but in fact he'd imprisoned someone completely innocent. The chief's name had been widely stripped of any accolades. As it turned out, the chief had been a part of many fabrications. He hadn't found a name for any investigation he'd carried out. He thought Billy Javers would be his redemption, and subsequently made things up to get his man in prison.

As it turns out, Chief Maston was much more of a crook than the people he had put away. Such information had of course sparked speculation throughout London that perhaps Chief Maston had been the Whitechapel murderer all along. But it had only been the words of those still obsessed.

The only trouble that Billy Javers had got himself into was the fact that he was in the wrong place at the wrong time. He had been walking to his work in the late hours of the night. With it being past midnight, he hadn't expected to run into anyone, let alone two dead bodies on the corner of Juniper street. He didn't know what he was thinking. It was a rash moment of judgement, and before he could even think about what he was doing, he was sat hunched over the two bodies, pickpocketing them.

He saw the nice clothes that they were wearing. He saw the gold watch that was around Mr Bogsworth's wrist. He saw the sparkling, diamond necklace laced around Mrs Bogsworth's neck and he just couldn't resist. He knew it was wrong. He should have never looted the dead bodies, but it was too tempting. He picked a fair amount of cash stashed in the depths of Mr Bogsworth's pockets, not caring that he was now soaked in blood. He figured he'd walk the one hundred yards back home to change, thinking that nobody would be out late at night to see him.

To him, it was a victimless crime and an opportunity that he couldn't refuse. But as soon as he felt the glow of the police flashlights land upon him, he knew then and there that he should have gone to the police first. He knew he shouldn't have looted the Bogsworths.

He knew what the situation looked like. He knew that it didn't look good for him once the police found him standing over two recently murdered bodies. It looked like he'd done it. Knowing what was coming, Billy had run from the police – apparently making the situation worse.

It didn't take him long to be caught. The underside of his shoe was coated in blood, causing him to slip as he turned the corner of Juniper and Vincent Street.

Once the police patrol caught him, he tried to express what had happened and why he was there. But it was no use. Even he could understand why they'd think he had just murdered the married couple.

The police whistle screamed in his ear as loud now as it did then, taking him back to the night. He was reminded further of it as he saw the knife in the new chief's hand.

'You are free to go, Mr Javers. You are not the man who murdered the Bogsworths,' the chief said. He was a northern man, from Newcastle maybe. The voice sounded comfortable to Billy. It reminded him of his sister's fiances' home and his new family in Sherrington. He did like Henry Smallhorn and he did like to visit the manor up past Sherrington. The Smallhorn manor was very similar to the manor that Billy grew up in. Billy missed his parents' manor after it was sold and liked the nostalgia the Smallhorn manor gave him.

An inch of Billy's old, sweet and loving self came back to him. Once the bells of freedom rang in his ears, he didn't quite understand it at first – and he never would.

How could the system put away an innocent man for eight years. If there was a God, how could there be this unjust situation?

Billy was a victim too. It wasn't just the Bogsworth's lives that had ended that night, but Billy's too. He wasn't the man who he used to be anymore and nor would he ever return to be.

He cried in the warden's office. It was all he could do. He'd fallen to the ground and curled into the safety of a ball, pressing his sweating body against the cold walls.

The warden called upon four guards to airlift Billy out of his office. The warden grunted in displeasure as he did so, never liking to see freedom come to any man who had entered his domain. If it were up to the warden, he'd keep Billy inside for good. The man seemed dangerous more than he ever was. Releasing anything like that back into society would be fatal, he thought. 'If he didn't kill then, a man like that would certainly kill now,' the warden stated to the papers when the story hit the next day.

Billy Javers sought exile. Though he was an innocent man, the public took on a firm belief that the warden's words printed in the papers would come true. A warped man's mind would want to come out and take vengeance on a city that had wanted him dead. Many people believed he'd kill for real from what he'd been put through. He had lived like a killer in prison, so who's to say that he won't act like one now?

Once the news was told to the family, they came to bring Billy home. Mr and Mrs Javers' lived in London now, a place where Billy no longer wanted to be. Instead, his sister took him in, her and her husband Henry not minding if Billy came to live with them. And so he did, for years. He floated around the manor, hardly ever seen by its occupants. He chose a room on the bottom floor by the dungeons. It was what he'd been used to, and he quite liked it.

The Smallhorns had their first daughter, Madeline, shortly after Billy's arrival. He liked to look after her. Seeing his sister's child reminded him of the time he wanted to begin a family. He became very attached to her. As Madeline grew older, she had fond memories of uncle Billy, but he still hadn't changed. Prison moulded him into something of a mysterious, mentally unhinged person for the rest of time.

Now Uncle Billy walked the manor alone. No one could come for him out in the lonely country, nor could he have the desire to fulfil what he'd been made out to be. He kept to the shadows and frequented outside, no matter how bad the storm was this night or any other.

Chapter 9

'What happened Billy… Why don't you tell me what upset you?'

It was getting late now. The storm had come to its peak. It had grown louder to the point where Emma believed she could hear rain dripping on the ceiling above her.

Emma sat in front of Billy, peering at him. Billy's face appeared from behind his dangling hair, wet from the rain he'd been in before his confrontation with Howard. Billy's clothes clung wetly to his thin body, his skin sunken to the point it barely covered his veins and muscles.

Emma looked at his hands. They were resting on top of the dining table, shaking.

Bold black pupils gleamed in his sunken eyes. Emma could say that she'd been staring into the eyes of a demon all this time, but it was really a man with great pain.

Madeline had barely enough time to tell her about his story. 'There was a paper about it. I think my mother has it kept upstairs somewhere,' she had said before finding Billy.

Emma looked at Billy's hair again. It was wet and plastered to his patchy face. There was mud on his skin and clothes, smeared in some areas where it had dried.

Billy had been outside for some time. He hadn't known what had happened, and that Frank Lightfoot was missing. He didn't know about the blood by the river's edge and the knife found in the stream. Like before, his solitude had protected him from having to deal with confrontation.

Billy drew in a shaky breath. At long last, the man spoke.

He mumbled something – something which Emma had to lean closer in to hear. 'Intruder. That man. He is an intruder,' Billy said.

He closed his mouth.

With every word he spoke he trembled. He had spoken as if he were cold, like the storm wasn't really doing him any good.

His head was horribly slumped to one side. He looked towards Emma's direction, but never actually at her.

The rain lapped and splattered upon the roof above. It hit the narrow concrete path off the manor and before the pebbled drive. It filled the silence, but Emma needed to keep the conversation going.

'Thank you, Billy.'

She looked to Prudence Smallhorn who sat beside her brother. She rubbed his shoulder. She did it to keep him calm, like a dog afraid of a little thunder.

'Billy has never met Howard Banks before. He must've come in without seeing him and thought that he had snuck in. He doesn't take well to people who he has never met.'

Emma knew it all too well. Heck, this was the first time she'd ever heard Billy speak to her.

'Why did you fight with him, Billy? What caused you to attack him?' Emma asked in her desperation to get Billy to talk, but he was stuck.

He rocked backwards and forwards by only an inch or two in his seat. She could see that he wanted to get the words out, but his brain wouldn't allow him. She had never seen a man so bent with trauma before in her life. It was frightening.

'I'm afraid the answer we gave would be very much the same,' Madeline stepped in. 'Call it a reflex, perhaps. It's just some primal instinct that kicks in when something isn't quite right. He *even* attacked the farmhand, Reggie on his first day, then scurried off to his bedroom for half a week.'

Madeline had no problems speaking out about her uncle right in front of him. He didn't even seem to hear it, just the powerful voices screaming in his head as he still bobbed backwards, then forwards.

'I'm sorry. I will try to talk with him and get something. I think he trusts me the most.'

Emma agreed with Madeline's mother. Perhaps she was right and it was the only way to get Billy to speak.

Emma got up from her chair. She walked the length of the dining table. Her wet feet smudged the carpet, leaving brown smears of mud along the edges which no one seemed to care about anymore. She gazed to the window where Fillius Lightfoot's vehicle was parked.

The oil lamps hanging either side of the front entrance to the manor were lit once again. Doctor Gottfried must've redone them once he went out with the signal.

She looked to the halo of bugs which swarmed the lights. The candle flames were enclosed with glass to protect them, but even with the heavy rain and wind, they looked fragile, as if one gust could blow them out.

She thought about using the motor car to get everyone home one by one, but there was still a crime to be solved which any one of the inhabitants of the manor could be responsible for. No, they would have to stick it out.

An hour went by. Everyone had retired to different rooms to get some rest for the night. Dr. Gottfried, Henry Smallhorn, Alfred Lightfoot and the detective were the only ones who stayed up.

Emma wandered the lower section of the manor. She figured that the doctor and Henry were in the dining room, keeping a close eye on the injured Howard.

It was foolish for Emma to go to sleep. To help pass the time until morning would come and the storm would let up, she decided to search the manor. There wasn't any particular reason for searching the manor, but she used the opportunity to take a look at the antiques lining the corridors.

Before heading to bed, Madeline had advised her to take a look at the dungeon downstairs – adding that sometimes she could hear the trails of screams and groans when she went to bed. Emma knew she said it only to frighten her, but now she wasn't so sure.

Emma looked through the dungeon, carrying only an oil lamp as her source of light.

It was known as the most haunted room in the manor, and she believed it. She couldn't imagine what kind of people were brought to the dungeon hundreds of years ago.

It was perhaps the darkest place in the manor. It was eerily quiet; the kind of quiet where the tiniest of noises were louder than ever before. Only this time there were groans and tremors coming from the walls.

Emma stopped and listened to them. It was so quiet inside that she couldn't hear the rain and thunder anymore. The cement walls were thick enough to drown it out. For once, Emma found some serenity and it was even better that it was silent. She had her own peace and quiet and enough time to sort through her case.

The thought about Reggie's knife had stewed in her mind for quite some time and when she found an identical knife in the riverbed, she couldn't help but think that Reggie had something to do with it. She did remember seeing Reggie with Frank at the barns. They had looked like they went their separate ways, but she hadn't been entirely sure. She thought about the way the family were so quick to turn on him, seeing what she'd be thinking to call him responsible That wasn't how it worked though, there was much more to discover, and it wasn't right to turn on one another.

Emma put the knife out of her mind, right after she tugged at it through her coat to make sure that it was still there. Now she concentrated on Billy.

While she was giving Emma the rundown, Madeline had seemed upset by what she was saying. Emma could tell that she didn't want to be explaining it. It was something of a personal matter, but when the two were alone, it was a chance to tell Emma what anybody in the family wouldn't.

She thought about Billy's story. It was sad but also helpful to Emma in figuring out if Billy was responsible. Billy was nowhere to be seen when Frank went missing, and then there was the commotion with Howard Banks. Something about Billy and his mysterious behaviour had struck her.

Emma waddled towards something that had caught her attention. In front of her was a glass case that had been smashed.

She dragged the oil lamp towards it and moved between the rubble at her feet. Surrounding the case was old furniture and a pile of antiques. They had been clustered together as the dungeon had become somewhat of a storage for the Smallhorns, but this particular case intrigued her.

She peered down and gazed at the broken glass. She set her lamp beside the razor shards. She reached in her hand and carefully skated past the pieces. Inside the waist height cabinet were an assortment of antique blades. They looked Eastern European, Arabian maybe, or perhaps ancient Persian.

She didn't know, but she quite liked the inlaying of the handles. Each was a blunt red with undetectable patterns which flowed well onto the face of the blade.

The knives hadn't been correctly placed. When Emma noticed that each had been left off-tilted, she couldn't help but think that someone had broken the glass to take one. It was rather brazen to do so, but whoever did must've been in a rush.

A knock at the open door behind her alarmed her.

She jumped right out of skin, a little scream belting from her throat.

She turned to face the open door. In the light stood a figure. The front of the figure was cloaked in darkness, aided by the backlit light behind them.

'You startled me,' Emma shivered. She still didn't quite know who was at the entrance. She peered back down at her hand. With her surprise she had come within half an inch of pricking the sharpest end of a glass shard she'd ever seen.

Still shocked, she carefully withdrew her hand from the shattered case. She brought it back to the handle of her oil lamp, picking it up and shining its light towards the unknown figure. She'd been surprised to see that it was Fillius Lightfoot.

'Sorry. Did I startle you there?'

The light showed his fine white teeth. Fillius stepped closer in, leading with his legs in an arrogant way. He had his hands in his pockets, and he still carried that pearly smile.

'No. Not really. I mean... It's not you, it's just this place.'

Emma glanced around the dungeon. She looked wall to wall and Fillius followed her gaze. He understood what she meant. He had always been a little afraid of it himself. He didn't want to admit it, but with only Emma in the room, he saw it as a chance to get to know her a little better.

'Believe me, I know. I was terrified of this place when I used to visit with my family. The rats, I tell you. They are the worst of the worst. The ghosts I can deal with.'

Fillius chuckled. He stopped by a dirty puddle of water. Something had been dripping, a pipe from the ceiling perhaps. It brought with it a musty, antique smell which leached into the room.

'It's not really haunted though, is it?' Emma couldn't believe what she was asking. She was a detective, she wasn't supposed to believe in those kinds of things, not to mention entertain them.

'I think so.'

Fillius got closer. He fiddled with a banner which hung loosely over a cabinet. He fiddled with the fabric between his fingers, collecting the dust from it.

'So, detective... What do you make of what happened upstairs?' Fillius asked.

Emma pulled a face. It was the kind of face which told him that she couldn't speak to him about it.

'I can't disclose anything with you, I'm afraid to say. But the truth is, I'm a little puzzled to say the least,' Emma had to admit. Fillius was the son of Frank – she thought she did owe him something after his father still hadn't turned up. Frank Lightfoot was also the cousin of Henry Smallhorn. In some respects, there had been a piece in the will in place to inherit the Smallhorn manor if something dreadful would happen to the Smallhorn family.

The way that Fillius had brought himself to Emma let her know that he did.

Emma backed up until the broken glass cabinet behind her pinched into her back. She didn't think that Fillius was a bad person, but she didn't like the situation she had found herself in. Alone in the dungeons with someone who could be responsible for Frank Lightfoot's absence, she didn't want to risk it.

His eyes locked on to the shivers which had come over her. He could see that he had frightened her.

Fillius heard Emma gasp. At the same time the ill thought of something bad happening to Frank crossed Emma's mind, Emma pricked herself against the glass.

'Ouch.' She stepped forward and immediately grabbed her finger with her other hand.

'Are you ok?' Fillius asked.

'Fine. I'm fine.'

Emma turned back to the cabinet. Pain which left her finger spilling with blood had clouded the rest of her thoughts. She quickly took a tissue from her pocket and wrapped it around her finger to suppress the bleeding.

'Ironic, huh?' Fillius leaned over. 'A glass cabinet holding knives and you get cut by the barrier.' He couldn't help but chuckle and didn't seem to notice how it was odd that it was broken to begin with.

Emma's mouth shut hard and she looked away from the cabinet. She threw an angry look at Fillius, a look which was pinched with pain as well. She'd forgotten about the incident with Fillius before, but his poor humour brought it back crystal clear.

'You nearly killed me before,' she wheezed. 'With your motor car,' Emma added.

The confusion had left his face.

'Oh… Please forgive me,' Fillius said.

His stiffened posture was let go of, his head slouched down and an even wider grin then spread upon his face. 'Believe me, I didn't mean to. I get a bit careless turning up the drive. The slopes make the driveway a little hard to see over the bonnet.'

The excuse was pathetic. Emma didn't believe it, but what else could she do?

Emma came forward, grabbing him by the arm and dragging herself into him. Fillius's half-hearted apology did not sit well with Emma. Not one bit.

'You do know that I will be keeping a closer eye on you from now on, right?' Emma spat her words out like acid. Her eyes even seemed to tremble and quake, quite like the noiseless thunder undoubtedly still beating the manor and its grounds to death.

'How could you keep all your focus on me when a criminal lurks free in the house?'

The words surged through Emma's mind. She took it as a threat, but a different kind of threat. With it, she no longer knew just what side Fillius was on and whether he wanted Emma to succeed under this challenge.

It was getting late for the residents of the manor who had chosen to stay awake until the morning came. Emma had been tired until her newfound shock from the conversation with Fillius Lightfoot.

In the awkward silence, the two broke apart, Emma and Fillius each gazed up to the ceiling. They heard feet and a smothered bump hit what was the ground on the second floor above them. The two stared at the dungeons beams and watched the dust fall from the ceiling from the disturbance. The way the dust had fallen from between the beams, it was beautiful, almost substantial like a waterfall. It slipped between them and formed a small pile in front of each of their feet.

Fillius looked down, kicky at the cloudy dust at his feet. It was old, with little chunks of the wall having come down with it. The thuds overhead had stopped. Emma looked to meet Fillius's gaze. Their mouths were left open in wonder to what had happened.

When Fillius tried to speak and ask what Emma thought happened, they heard a scream coming from where the thud chad originated.

It was a terrible, blood curdling scream. The scream ran through every nook and cranny of the manor, blowing harder than any rain and sounding louder than all the thunder in this year's storms combined.

The scream was panicked, one of a woman.

'My god, its aunt Prudence,' Fillius said.

There was another crash, then another wail. As it happened, the two leaped from the dungeon and ran upstairs to join the commotion.

When Emma galloped up the stairs – with Fillius tailing behind her – the screams had grown louder. They were so loud that she could feel them in her bones. It bounced off the walls as she burst from the steps and down the narrow hall towards the sound.

'In there,' Fillius shouted, as he pointed at the kitchen doors.

Emma forced her elbow against the door. It swung open and when it did, uncle Billy's body came into view.

He lay on his front, slumped onto the kitchen tiling. His arms and legs were sprawled out and blood leaked from his body, drowning him in a pool of his own blood.

There was a knife in his back – a knife identical to the ones Emma had found in the smashed case. She recognised it immediately.

'Keep away,' Emma demanded. She threw her hand out to the side of her and blocked Fillius from coming any closer.

There was no denying it. Someone had stolen the knife and stabbed Billy with it.

Emma kneeled to the ground. She got close to look at the carnage left of uncle Billy. He'd been dead for less than a minute; the killer had been quick to get away. There was blood everywhere, all over the ground and travelling fast. It ran like a river and seeped between the sealed lines of the patterned tiling. Emma shuffled her knees further back as she noticed it getting closer. She gazed up to the kitchen cabinets where Billy's handprints tattooed the white paint with blood.

Prudence Smallhorn continued to scream. Her hands were bloodied and her clothes were also soaked. She held them to her cheeks, her eyes wild. Emma had never seen someone so terrified and upset at the same time.

Prudence's brother was murdered and she'd been the one to stumble in and find him.

She screamed so loud that the colour began to drain from her face. At any moment she could pass out from the terror, but an unknown person came to gather her up and take her away.

Emma looked up to see that it was Doctor Gottfried. He picked her up and dragged her out of the kitchen. It was unbearable for her to have to witness the death of her brother any longer.

'No. Billy, no!' She screamed and kicked. She didn't want to leave.

The commotion and discovery of the murder had summoned the rest of the household. The residents who had been fast asleep came crashing down from their rooms to the kitchen.

'What is all this. What is going on?' Emma could hear grandpa Smallhorn caterwauling from outside the kitchen.

Madeline had come down from her bedroom. She witnessed the doctor carrying her mother away. She was screaming and crying. She was helpless. It frightened Madeline. She'd never seen her mother in such a way before.

Tired-eyed, she rubbed them and tightened the rope around her gown. She groaned in a scratchy voice – a voice which could tell anybody that she had not fallen asleep, no matter how hard she tried.

'What is going on?'

When she pushed the kitchen door open to find out for herself, she could hardly peek an inch inside before her father blocked her.

'You do not want to go in there.' She looked at his stern face. It was a face that had seen it all and then some. Again, she'd never seen her father look so terrified before in her life. Both her parents were sore at the heart. It was a truly unsettling feeling.

Madeline trembled. Her eyes pooled as she knew that something terrible had happened. She didn't know what it was, but the look n her father's eyes with her mother screaming behind her told her that whatever it was, it was deeply unpleasant and upsetting. But she still wanted to know.

'It is your uncle Billy. He has been murdered.'

Madeline's heart pounded. She stepped away, taken aback by what she had heard.

'Uncle Billy… dead?' Madeline couldn't believe it. When her father rushed back inside the kitchen to help, it was then that Madeline turned to her mother. Now she saw the blood stained on her clothes and her hands. It was up to her cheeks. The doctor had sat her down in the dining room and stayed with her to calm her down, but she was only getting worse.

Shock had turned to realisation. Once she had been taken away from the scene and left to think, it had gotten worse for Madeline's mother.

Madeline cried for uncle Billy and her mother. She wanted to go and be with her, but she needed to be there for Billy also.

Madeline broke into the kitchen. As soon as she entered, her presence was met with the bitter disgust of her father.

'What are you doing?' He groaned. 'I didn't want you to see this. It's bad enough that your mother had to endure it.'

'I needed to see it for myself,' Madeline said. She came in a little closer. She stayed close to the French ovens, now she could see Billy in full view. The blood poured from his lifeless body. It slowly streamed across to her, spreading like a vein in different directions across the kitchen tiling.

She covered her mouth where a gasp hid behind. She looked at the knife in Billy's back. The blade was covered in specks of blood; it was better labelled a dagger by the way the blade curved how large it was to remain half-stuck in Billy's back.

Madeline looked to Emma. She had her hand wrapped in a cloth which had been taken from the kitchen bench. She kept it professional so as to not wipe away any fingerprints or indeed touch the blood herself.

'When did this happen?' Madeline managed to ask.

'Literally minutes ago. I heard the thud from the dungeons, then your mother began screaming,' Emma announced. She carefully took the knife from Billy's body. She pulled it out and nothing had ever felt so squeamish and *different* before in her life.

'I was there with her… Emma, that is. We heard the thud then the screams soon after,' Fillius said. He had cleared himself from the crime by saying so, making sure that was the first thing he said.

'Someone murdered uncle Billy… How could anyone do this?' Henry Smallhorn said grimly.

'I don't know. But certainly someone amongst us did.' Emma took the blade and wrapped it with the cloth. She set it aside on the kitchen table. She told nobody to touch it. When she told everyone in the kitchen to clear out, the others joined the rest in the dining room.

For those who hadn't known or seen what had happened, they were immediately told by the steady voice of Henry Smallhorn.

Alfred Lightfoot and Madeline's grandparents were told, as was the maid and Reggie who'd rushed down from the third floor.

Emma had asked Madeline to stay behind to help her in the kitchen. 'In all honesty, I don't know what to do with the body,' Emma confessed. She stood over Billy – rather sinisterly in the dark of the kitchen. She hadn't had experience with murder before. It was something which she'd never learnt firsthand, only in books and study and with the occasional practice of a specimen in the local morgue close by the university in London.

This was much more devastating. It really was. Billy had been murdered and worse, it was of a personal connection to her best friend and her family.

Emma didn't know whether to move the body or to leave it. It seemed wrong of her to leave it in the kitchen, but she didn't want to disrupt the crime scene.

'There isn't much we can do. We can't move it,' Madeline advised. She had no idea what to do, but she knew as much as anyone that it was never a good idea to move a body.

Emma knew what she could and couldn't do, but deep down, she still felt it wrong to leave Billy in the kitchen how he was.

Madeline had a sudden urge to vomit. Blood was everywhere and enough had found its way down the side of her hand once she turned it over. She hadn't known how the blood smeared her skin. She'd been so careful not to touch anything. With great effort, she forced the urge to throw up out of her mind.

She hurriedly washed her hands and wiped them with a paper towel, but they didn't make water hot enough to get rid of the thought of it.

It all happened away from Emma's eye. She'd been too fixated on the body to notice.

'Go bring me something to put over him,' Emma ordered.

Madeline rushed out of the kitchen without an idea of where she was going. She escaped the mayhem of the dining room and took the back passage to end up in the hall. She'd hoped to find an idea or come across something she could use.

She ran down the dark hall, her heart beating hard and with every breath a grunt escaped her mouth. It was then that she remembered Howard.

She walked on a little further and entered the open door of the sitting room. She peeped into the sitting room next to it and saw that he was asleep. His body was awkward on the fainting couch. His arm had fallen and his fingers hovered over the carpet. The wind and rain had lulled him back to sleep and had beaten the shrill cries of her mother – at least she thought.

Like magic, Howard rolled over and looked at Madeline from the corner of his eye. In a sluggish voice, he spoke.

'What is happening?' Howard asked. He looked up and barely got his head around the cushion to see Madeline in the doorway.

'It's nothing. Just sit tight there, please,' Madeline pleaded.

Part of her felt a little embarrassed. She hated to think that Howard was now thinking that she'd been watching him sleep, but her mind was too messy. The less Howard knew, the better, Madeline gathered.

She entered the bathroom and went to the only thing she could think of to put over Billy.

The bath curtain.

It hung from a silver frame over the bathtub, half drawn and crinkled.

She went to the bathtub and ripped the curtain off its rings. She thought it was a little unorthodox, but there was little time to think in her raced mind.

She carried the bathroom curtain in her arms and hurriedly turned back down the hall to meet with Emma again.

There was blood everywhere. They had to move uncle Billy and when they did, the blood had slid across the tiles, wetting most of the floor. They wrapped him in the bathroom curtains and watched as the blood seeped through it immediately. What was once a white cloth that had only been touched by bathwater was now soaked in blood.

Emma and Madeline wrapped Billy Javers cocoon-like. They left him in the kitchen, alone in the dark with as much dignity as they could give. It wasn't the best, but it was all that they could do.

Emma had found her best friend's resourcefulness rather impressive.

She washed herself in the sink. She looked down at her hands and watched the blood flow off them and roll between her fingers into the basin. The bright red blood had turned an orange colour when it came into contact with the water. It wasn't like the blood she'd found at the river's edge, instead more diluted than what rain could ever do.

Emma had seen too much blood in her lifetime to ever be fazed by it. She had come across many dead bodies in the London morgue in her days of schooling. It was all part of the job to become desensitised to it. But she'd never forget her first dead body.

Mark it down, Billy Javers would be Emma Squier's first dead body.

Emma came out of the kitchen and settled into the dining room. Madeline's mother had calmed down for now, but she still shivered with the thought of her brother's death. Madeline's father took the doctor's place once he'd found out what had happened. He sat beside his wife, taking her into his arms and comforting her as best he could. She sobbed into the fold of his armpit and Madeline began to cry too. She had to stay strong with Emma in the clean-up, but once it was over, she found the time to cry and grieve.

Emma hated to see her friend break down – and her family also. It hadn't been often that she'd see Madeline cry, maybe once or twice in their childhood.

The family consoled each other, as did the doctor and his wife with Reggie also. Fillius and Alfred Lightfoot were already taken back by their father's disappearance, but the body of a different victim had sent them rushing into a new kind of fear... a new fear that their father could be dead or perhaps even responsible for Billy's death.

Howard Banks had by now awoken from the commotion. He had stumbled into the kitchen once Madeline had passed him with the bath curtain. He wanted to know what had happened, having heard screams and cries which he'd never heard before.

The screams had been brutal, ripping the fabric of everything around him and Howard couldn't help but come to investigate.

Howard wore his blanket around his shoulders, trying to keep himself warm but still shivering. Reggie was seated beside him at the end of the dining table. The two were silent – being just about the only people in the manor whose place wasn't to go asking questions. They felt wrong for being there. It wasn't their family and it was something rather personal to be a part of. The doctor and his wife felt that way too, but at least they had a job to do.

Emma turned her direction to Doctor Gottfried.

'Dr. Gottfried.' It was the first time she had called him by his name.

'Yes?' He matched her whisper with one of his own.

'Please... Can you inspect the body?' Emma asked. She kept her voice down as the two spoke in private. It wasn't something Emma wanted to involve the family with. It was a very gruesome and invading part of finding a body.

'I will do all I can,' Dr Gottfried insisted, wanting to help Emma.

Emma leapt to her feet. She and the doctor headed back into the kitchen alone.

When Emma pulled the bath curtain over to reveal Billy's body, the doctor shied away.

The smell of the blood and the already turning foulness of death wafted up his nostrils, but it was the sight of Billy that mainly caused to doctor to recoil.

Billy's skin had turned a pale white already, his skin warped close to his muscles and bones, showing every lifeless vein and indent of his body.

When Emma had revealed the body again, the cocoon that Billy had been wrapped in was filled with blood. It stuck to the fabric and oozed like fresh sap from a tree.

The blood gushed like water from a sewer pipe unloading into a river system.

The body had been turned over and the stab wound in Billy's back was revealed.

'He would've been stabbed once at most. The blade could've pierced his heart with one hit from the back,' the doctor observed.

The two leaned over the body. The gash to the left of the centre of his spine was thick and deep. The doctor took his spectacles from his front pocket and placed them on the bridge of his nose to gett a better look at Billy's neck. Around the skin of his Adams' apple was a huge mark. He touched the bare skin with his finger to feel around the bruise. He took his glasses back off and turned to Emma.

'He has some angry red marks around the neck. It is very minimal, but I see it as clear as day.'

'So, he was grabbed from behind and then stabbed?' Emma concluded.

'It is possible. Whoever did this snuck up on Billy, brought their arm around him to control him then stabbed him in the back.'

Beside her, the doctor got closer to the body and when he did, he pulled an instrument out of his pocket. Emma wasn't sure what it was, but when the doctor studied the body, he asked to see the knife.

Emma stood up from her kneel. She reached up to the kitchen counter to grab the towel which the knife had been wrapped in. As she brought the knife out of its hiding, she looked at the long ash-coloured hair which looked wet across Billy's forehead.

The doctor stated that Billy had indeed been murdered very recently. Ten minutes ago, to be precise.

He looked at the knife when Emma pulled it out. 'Ah… as I suspect,' Dr. Gottfried said, now sounding like the detective himself. 'A long blade. Sharp and curved also.'

'To go deep enough through his back to pierce his heart,' Emma finished.

Dr Gottfried did not speak, but allowed Emma to think through the situation. She recounted what she had heard and who she'd seen. As far as she knew, Fillius was safe as he'd been there in the dungeon with her, unless he'd systematically placed the body where it would fall moments later to cause the thud when he knew he'd be seen far from it. Howard had been sleeping and his body was still worn and injured and the doctor himself had been making his routine checks on him. They were the only people Emma could account for, yet still she couldn't be sure.

The doctor glared into Emma's green eyes. He asked what she'd been thinking, supposing that she was running through everyone in the manor.

'I need to get a check on everyone's whereabouts. Somebody had found a small window of time to commit this murder. Whoever did this could be responsible for Howard's attack and possibly Frank Lightfoot's disappearance,' Emma said.

'Do you think Frank is dead?' The doctor asked.

Emma shook her head and looked to the ground where a little bit of blood had slipped out of the curtains. She wasn't sure. For all she knew, Frank could be alive and well and he could be responsible for everything.

'One thing is curious though. This weapon had come from the dungeon. I have seen the broken case where it has been snatched from. Someone has moved amongst us to find it and used it to murder Billy.'

Doctor Gottfried looked at Emma in awe. He then turned to the blade, seeing how far the blood was stained to the handle.

Emma laid her hand to her temple. 'This night has turned into much more. I now have a murder investigation,' she said.

Emma left the kitchen.

The doctor was just about the only person that she could trust. He was a doctor and she needed one tonight.

She entered the dining room with a look of dread that covered her entire face. Her hands slipped down to her hips and her head was kept bowed. She let out a deep exhale then looked up to the entirety of the dining table. They all looked back at her. They all knew what she had to say before she could get her words out. Emma sensed this, but her words still needed to be let out. She needed to confirm what had happened, and from the doctor's short appraisal, there was no longer any doubt as to what that was.

'Billy Javers has been murdered. I am calling this investigation as this night has become much more than what it already has. Someone here is responsible,' Emma said, steadyingher words.

Instantly, the people at the table fell under an onslaught of fear and mistrust. Everyone turned to each other. Some exchanged looks, but all had taken turns looking at each other... deciding who was amongst them was the killer.

Everyone looked for a flicker in expressions, waiting for someone to slip up. Everyone looked for something in someone that spoke of murder, but no one had budged. Emma hadn't seen a single slip of anyone's mask. The camouflage of a murder was still being worn.

Emma pressed her hands upon the table. The whip of the storm continued to hit the walls and the rain torrents which pelted the roof and the windows revived the feeling that everyone was indeed stuck.

'One of you is responsible for murdering Billy Javers and I don't think it will stop there. On this night, no one is safe. We are stuck by the storm and this killer has already told me how opportunistic they are.' Emma swivelled her stare to each person down the table, from Madeline's grieving parents in front of her, all the way down to Reggie and Howard at the very end of the table.

She had everyone where she wanted, except for the maid and the still missing Frank Lightfoot. But for the most part, she had everyone in her sights.

'We have to go look for our father. We have to make sure that he is ok,' Alfred cried. In his voice, he hinted that he feared he'd end up like Billy, or perhaps he already was.

Down the end of the table, Howard's eyes creased. He shook his head and spoke.

'For all we know, Frank could be the person who attacked me at the river then murdered Billy. Perhaps he is the one *we* may have to look out for instead.'

Howard's words didn't get much praise from the rest of the table, but they were all thinking it. Nobody else had the guts to even promote the thought that Frank could be the killer, but it certainly was possible.

'We have to do something. We all have to suit up and prepare ourselves,' Madeline's grandfather said. George rather clumsily slammed his fists against the table and the empty plates and cutlery rattled.

The old man hadn't seemed to know the entirety of what was going on. His mind had drifted a little over the years and bombs and gunfire from the war was all he heard in the back of his mind most of the time.

As he spoke, Mary drifted from her place of hiding.

She came from her nook, tired-eyed and re-dressed in her apron.

Mary, the kitchen hand was spooked by the sudden outburst as she stood with her back to the shade of the wall. The rattle of the instruments she cleaned reminded her of the time she feared what would happen to her if she ever dropped them.

Everyone had forgotten that she was there. She was only just outside of the kitchen when the murder occurred. She couldn't sleep in the storm and decided to go out for a smoke, but only briefly. She went out to the bins outside to clean away the leftovers of dinner that she'd accidentally left behind in the kitchen sink when the murder occurred.

'No.' Robin Smallhorn replied to George's comments. 'We cannot trust anyone. We can't start giving out weapons to everyone just in case we hand them to the *wrong* person,' Robin advised.

Emma looked to Fillius. She noticed something about him during the table's conversation. He had become unsettled, looking as if he'd been locked up tight and he wanted to get away. He shivered and grit his teeth. Suddenly he shot up from the table.

'I can't stay here and wait for the killer to strike next. We have to get out of here,' Fillius shouted. He looked up and down at the table. No one answered him. Everyone looked at him in a state of shock. The once reserved and strong man he was had now become a frightened young boy.

'If anyone else wants to leave now, be my guest.' Fillius hooked his coat around his shoulders, taking it from the back of his chair. He walked out of the dining room and into the hall.

'Wait, Fillius. No one can leave,' Emma shouted, but he didn't listen. Fillius continued on his way down the hall and out the front door of the manor. In a hurry, Emma, Alfred, Madeline and Henry pursued him.

The party stepped out under the raging storm. The moon hung over the hedge of the woods in the near distance, casting an eerie glow causing the smoky clouds to brighten in the sky. The rain pelted down hard like bullets. Emma did not care, even though she didn't have a coat over her body as she stood bare in the rain.

She called out to Fillius who'd made it to the driver's door of his motor car.

'Fillius. You cannot leave.' She tried and tried, but Fillius just wanted to get away.

'I'll go and get help and come back with a dozen officers. I'll be back shortly,' Fillius said, but Emma didn't believe it. She knew that he was frightened and that he just wanted to get away. It was more shocking to her that a fragile man like himself didn't tear in the rain.

Fillius opened the door and jumped into his vehicle. Before he could start the engine, he noticed something in the passenger seat. He had left a crowbar at the floormat – something he'd used days before and left in his vehicle. He picked it up and placed it on the seat next to him, thinking he could use it as a weapon like George suggested.

Without wasting another moment, he turned the ignition. The engine turned but just as quickly it spluttered out. Fillius did a double take. He studied the dashboard and tried again, but nothing had moved. The second time, the motor car didn't even turn over. It did nothing but choke on an empty tank.

It was then that the oily scent which Emma could smell before became apparent. As the motor car had its troubles, Emma followed the exhaust pipe of the car where the fuel pump was closely in front of it. She peered down at the pebbles, now seeing a dried pool of fuel.

When she hovered her flashlight under the frame of the motor car, the thud of Fillius's door came. He hurried towards where Emma was kneeled to find out what was wrong.

'It's the fuel line. It's been cut,'

The evidence was clear by the distinct smell coming from the oily pit below. It was something that both Emma and Madeline noticed before but never acted upon. The fuel line had been cut for some time.

'God dammit!' Fillius exclaimed. He ran his fingers through his hair and paced in circles.

He was angry, but less so compared to the fear which grew now knowing that his only ticket out had been cut… *purposely.*

Emma stumbled to her feet. She rested her hand upon the back panel.

'Someone has cut it on purpose,' she gasped to those gathered on the front step.

Someone had deliberately cut the fuel line to Fillius's vehicle, making sure that their only way to get help in the storm had been eliminated.

Chapter 10

He was burning. He peered down at his hands and saw the grease turning his skin black. The cuts that his handy work had caused and where he liked to chew the corner of his nails when he was bored began to itch from the grease.

Under the flash of the unbearable lightning and the orange glow of a lamp by his shoulder, Robin Smallhorn tried his best to patch up Fillius's motor car.

Robin knew what he was doing. He had been a mechanic in the army in his early twenties. It was a skill that he'd always wanted to learn once motor cars became a little more advanced. In the army he'd work on Jeeps, the kind of vehicles which soldiers could fold up into and could endure any terrain. American vehicles he had a grasp on, but European ones were built differently.

Fillius Lightfoot's car was built a little different to Robin's expertise. He didn't like sports cars. It wasn't as simplistic as what he'd been used to, neither did he have all the right tools to work on it.

Fillius leaned closely over Robin's hunched body. The lamp dangled in his hand and he held onto it strongly so it wouldn't be caught in the wind. Ironically, the oil in the lamp had died down. Only flickers lived on for them to see for a few moments longer.

Fillius was wet. His back was drenched from shielding Robin from the rain. If it wasn't for the sake of his vehicle, he wouldn't stay out a second longer in this weather.

'There isn't much I can do without my garage, son.' Robin pulled himself away from the fuel pump, dusting his hands off as best he could and accidently smudging grease on his chin in the process.

Fillius drew a ragged breath as someone came up behind him with a newly lit oil lamp. It was the doctor.

'You two best come back in now,' Doctor Gottfried said over the howling wind.

Fillius had to give up. There was nothing he or Robin could do to mend his vehicle. He dropped his head, but the doctor caused it to come straight back up by placing his hand on his shoulder.

'It'll be ok, Fillius. In the morning we will sort something out. Besides, the detective would like to speak to each of us.'

Doctor Gottfried hurried back inside. Fillius and Robin scrambled after him as the thunder clambered and the wind picked up behind them with a howl. The door clanged open and Madeline was visible standing under the frame. Her hand hooked around the doorknob, waiting to close it back up as soon as the others came in.

Robin had had just about enough of being outside. Once he came in he still shivered, keeping his coat on. He made a dash for the bathroom as the others returned to the dining room.

Emma had talked to Madeline's grandparents while Fillius and Robin had been out fiddling with the car. She had also had a word with Alfred, whom she hadn't quite gotten to know until then.

It was an interrogation, but Emma didn't like to call it that. She could see that the family was hurt. In their separate conversations about what had transpired, neither of her first few had said very much. Fillius had only talked about how he grew up close to the Smallhorns. He visited on occasion and didn't know about uncle Billy's prior conviction when they were children. Madeline's grandparents were of course shocked. Their son in law had been murdered. It was a terrible thing, even though Billy Javers was a man they had barely known themselves. They did know of his time in prison and for years they believed that he had committed the crime he was accused of. It was so obvious that he'd done it, based on what the papers wrote.

Madeline's grandfather was still a dotty, old man. He half-knew what had happened.

When he spoke, he often gave Emma the impression that he didn't know that Billy Javers had even been murdered. It was either that, or he took the loss of a life as something of a normality as he'd been used to death for the majority of his adult life. He was a little desensitised by it, but his wife managed to bring him back in. She fixed him up when he needed to be and she swore that the two had barely drifted off to sleep when the commotion occurred.

"Whoever it is, I hope they know who I am. I killed people at Somme, you know,' he mused.

Madeline's grandfather's short outbursts didn't mean much to Emma. It was innocent enough since he was closing in on the ripe old age of ninety. He was a dotty man and out of everyone in the manor, he was the one with the longest life and the most experience. He never remembered things from a week ago or fully sensed what was happening in the moment, but he remembered the war like it was yesterday. His adventures and battles in the first world war were etched in his memory. It was bloody and it was God-forsaken, but he loved every moment of it.

Emma let the old man slide, but she had been glad to know that George Smallhorn had her back. Behind his weakened body and the twigginess of his slender arms, she saw the warrior in his eye.

Madeline had to apologise for her grandfather. She had sat at the other side of the table next to her, joining the conversation. It was a little strange to her that she had suddenly been a part of interrogating each of her family members over the murder of her uncle, but she wanted to help Emma out as much as possible. She was only a young detective; someone who had never been on the job and didn't have any experience to help with this terrible night. But Emma was strong. She was determined to follow what she had learned. It was about time that she stopped thinking about how tough of a situation she'd been put in, and instead how lucky she was for the opportunity to solve the crime.

Next to be interviewed by Emma was the doctor.

Dr. Gottfried seemed an innocent man on the outside. He was yet another asset that could help the family at this time. He had helped to mend Howard Banks and had helped determine what had happened to Billy Javers. He was a nice person – and his wife too – yet Emma still had the power to ask him the questions she needed to.

'What brought you to the manor on this night?' Emma asked.

Dr. Gottfried frowned. He thought she'd remember what he told her when they first met at the dinner table.

'My wife and I are friends of the family. We have been for many years, in fact.'

The Doctor drew in a full breath. His belly oozed out over his belt as he sat comfortably in the chair. He scratched his shortly shaved balding hair to jog his memory when Emma asked how he met the Smallhorns.

'It was quite some time ago now. I believe it was overseas, actually. My wife and I had planned a Nile cruise in Egypt. The Smallhorns were there at the same time as us,' Doctor Gottfried explained, smiling at the memory. He looked to the wall beside him, spotting the Smallhorn crest hung on the wall

'We were just as young as they were back then. Turns out we both held a residency in Sherrington, the Smallhorns just outside of the town – well… here I suppose,' Dr. Gottfried chuckled. 'I think it was just before you were born that we met them,' he said, looking over the table to Madeline and smiling.

'Oh yes,' he sighed, his eyes glazing as he became lost in the memory. His face became blank as he remembered that very day when the sun burned brightly down onto a cool, calm I river, the old pyramids beside them and the crocodiles tanning by the riverbank. He had never felt so old as he did when he remembered that day was almost forty years ago.

'Dr. Gottfried, do you have anything against the Smallhorn family?' Emma asked, plunging straight into the deep end of her questioning.

He struggled to comprehend it. For a moment, the features in his face contracted into a knot of disgust as he snapped back to the moment. He breathed heavily and after all the effort, he finally said the words *"not on your life,"* jabbing his fingers towards Emma with each word.

'And what about Billy Javers... Why might you or anyone else want to murder him?' Emma was persistent. It was of great distaste for the doctor to think that anyone would think he'd be responsible for murder, but he understood why he was asked. All he needed to do was to give his straight, honest answer.

'I would never hurt Billy. I barely knew him, in fact.'

'But you knew of his prior convictions?'

'If anything, I felt even more sad for the poor man once they were proven to be false. After that, I didn't hear much of Billy when he came to stay here. You knew as much about him on this night as I always did. He was a hermit. He kept to himself, dwelling in the dark. He was sick.'

Doctor Gottfried retreated into his seat. He curled his arms up, crossed them and held them over his chest. He explained himself the best he could, but there was more for Emma to ask.

'Is it true that you were one of the few who stayed up? Did you remain in the dining room all this time?' Emma queried.

Before Dr. Gottfried answered with a definitive *yes,* he hesitated. The saliva in his mouth swirled restlessly then awkwardly slid down his throat. He bowed down to his hands as he released his crossed arms. The backs of his hands were firm and his palms were rough from scrubbing them of blood and carrying the heavy oil lamp.

'I did get up from the dining room from time to time. I made my rounds to the sitting room to check on Mr Banks.'

'And what did you see?' Emma asked.

Dr. Gottfried shook his head. There was nothing much to say about what he *saw*.

'Mr Banks. He was fast asleep. His body needs mending and sleep will do him all the good in the world,' he said.

Emma turned to Madeline. His story seemed to check out. He was merely getting up and doing his checks on his patient as he did when Howard was first brought in. She didn't see anything suspicious about the doctor.

'Look, I'm a doctor. I help people. I try to make people better. It's been my career and passion for more than forty years. Why would I ever turn to harming anyone when healing is all I do?' Dr. Gottfried said, stabbing to make his point clear. He never evaded an answer, nor did he resist saying anything. Emma looked at Madeline and nodded. It was good enough for her. She went to ask Dr. Gottfried to leave and send in the next person, but before she did, he stalled.

In the corner of Mr Smallhorn's office was something of great use, something that the doctor had just realised could be of use.

The doctor jumped to his feet. 'Is that a telegram?' 'Yes.

It looks like it,' Emma turned and said. She didn't think much of it until Dr. Gottfried made his way towards it. It was there in the corner of Mr Smallhorn's office. It was alone on a table, covered in the nightly shade. If it weren't for the sparkling brass which reflected off the glowing candle, he wouldn't have seen it.

Doctor Gottfried ran his fingers over the brass. With his other hand he caressed the wooden panel of the fancy – more expensive than most – case that it had been set in.

'This may be our ticket out of here,' Dr. Gottfried said in a daze.

He ran his hands along it for a little while longer, wondering if what he said could be true. When he turned to face Emma and Madeline, a look of triumph had sprung onto his face.

The wise and trustful doctor had a plan.

'I can send a telegram to my practice in Sherrington. I know there is a nightly guard taking care of the place tonight. He can read my distress call.'

Emma leapt from her chair at the news. 'Are you sure?' she asked.

'Quite.' He paused. 'Our only hope is that my guard will come across it.'

Dr. Gottfried was excited. A wave of relief had come over Emma and Madeline to the news. At last, it would seem that this terrible night would be over. He hurried to the door to grab his things to make a formal report. On his way, he let in the next person who Emma wanted to speak to.

In came Reggie Jackson. His face blushed, turning red. He grew warm under pressure and suddenly felt faint, his heart palpitating with a nervous beat.

He didn't like the situation he'd been placed in. As he stood before Emma, he wondered if she thought he'd done something. Furthermore, the awakening of a murderer wandering loose about the manor did not bode well with him.

Sitting in front of a detective was bad enough, but he knew that the odds were against him. He knew what they saw of him in the barn. He had his knife – the exact same knife found at the river – and he was there with Frank Lightfoot at the end. He was the last person to have seen him.

Reggie knew that he was an innocent man, but he could only begin to imagine what everyone was thinking of him. He did nothing wrong and he was a good person right to the bone. But he was just a farmhand after all. He had no authority and the respect towards him was little to none.

They'd all rather he be in the spotlight than themselves after all.

He was a young, black teenager and someone whom anyone else could so easily blame. He knew that his luck of landing a swell job for the Smallhorns would only run out too soon, but he hadn't counted on Emma Squier. She had far exceeded his expectations.

There was no blame from Emma, just questions. She wasn't one to assume of anyone and her mind was always one to dissect upon someone or something to find the answer.

She made sure to keep Reggie comfortable. She didn't want to call him a guilty man unless she knew for sure. Everyone was just as innocent as each other in her proceedings.

When Emma asked how long he'd been working for the Smallhorn family, Reggie was so shocked that she hadn't accused him like the others were so quick to that he stumbled over his words, taking a moment to answer.

'Only a year or so, miss.' Reggie gulped, and Emma could see right through just how frightened he was. He was only a young lad, afterall. He wasn't a day over sixteen and he was rather sweet. Reggie loved nature and taking care of the barn animals, mostly the Smallhorn's horses. He was a quiet soul who liked to read and fish. Yet, Emma couldn't rely on how he appeared. She had to ask him some questions to do with both Frank's disappearance and Billy's murder.

'Have you ever run into any problems with the Smallhorns? Billy in particular.'

Billy wasn't a Smallhorn, but he practically was as he'd been living in the manor for some time. Reggie must've seen something, she imagined.

Reggie eyed Madeline who lingered in the background. He thought it wrong to say anything *hurtful* towards her family with her in the room. A flood of awkwardness delayed him from speaking what was on his mind.

Madeline nodded. 'It's ok, Reggie. Say what you please,' she advised.

'Well, if you insist, miss.' Reggie gulped again. He turned away from Madeline and looked at no one but Emma. He couldn't bear to look Madeline's way when speaking harshly about her family.

'I've had run-ins with Mr Smallhorn – Henry that is,' Reggie said as he stammered and squinted his eyes as he corrected himself.

'What sort of run-ins?' Emma encouraged.

'Nothing big. Just disputes over pay and such. He hasn't paid me for my work in a few months. I think he forgets sometimes, but I remind him all the time and I still haven't seen anything yet.' Reggie lowered his eyes to his lap. He felt embarrassed talking about it. It was so insignificant to him, considering what'd happened.

'And what about Billy Javers... Have you had any run-ins with him in the past?' Emma persisted.

Reggie sighed. He grew anxious on the chair. His skin began to crawl and his fingers started to press into the ends of both armrests. He rolled his tongue around in his mouth and puffed his cheeks out. Emma watched his discomfort, knowing that he was hiding something which she knew she had to get out of him.

'When I first started working here, I had some trouble with the man. Hell, I was only fifteen and he was in his early forties. I couldn't really say anything until now.' Reggie thought about his next words before he stumbled again. As he recounted the incident with Billy Javers, he felt upset, just as he had when it happened.

'What trouble? Tell me, Reggie,' Emma pressed.

'When I got here there was a dog. It was an old dog, mind you, but I loved him.' Reggie looked away from Emma's glare. His eyes glossed over and soon after, a tear rolled down his cheek. His eyes welled with the memory of something *bad* and now his cheeks turned even more red, a fierce red.

'One day I was in the barn and the dog was there too, eating. Billy came in – someone who I'd only met once or twice. He held a shotgun and without warning, he shot the dog right in front of me.' Reggie sobbed. It was an awful thing which happened. The thunder outside rocketed like the blast of the pellet on that terrible day. Reggie choked, but he was still able to speak.

'That damn bastard cleared that poor creature's head right off its shoulders. Right in front of me. I screamed at him, I asked him why. But he never answered me. He never spoke or gave any reason to why he did it,. The dog was old, sure, but it didn't deserve it. From that day on, I hated Billy Javers in secret.'

Emma felt the pain. Reggie had been traumatized. As she watched him flood with tears, she really wondered if such an impact on his life could force him to one day seek revenge. *Did Reggie Jackson have the vengeance of a tiger within him all this time for him to then murder Billy Javers?*

'I hoped I'd never see him lurking around the manor and until tonight, I never really did.'

Reggie dropped his head. He let the tears pour until his eyes turned dry. He wiped his face with his arm and snorted. He looked to Emma who'd welled at the eyes too, but not like him. She was sad to hear his story. In some way she could sympathise as she had been through something similar as a little girl with her pet cat. It was different, but almost the same.

'It was Moritz. That was the dog's name,' Madeline said as she sniffed and wiped a tear. She remembered the dog too. As she grew older and left to London for schooling, her home and her pets were almost forgotten, but she remembered Moritz. He was a lovely golden retriever, mostly splotched with specks of mud from running about the grounds most of his life.

Madeline was sad but happy to remember her childhood pet, but she didn't know that what Reggie had said was what happened. It sounded awful.

'Well, is it reason enough to get your long-awaited revenge?' Emma asked.

He sat on the edge of the chair, the sound of Emma's voice flowing over him in waves, but he wasn't really listening to her words. Still, he was numbed by the horrors of his memories and what had happened tonight.

At last, he shook his head clear. He caught a grasp of what Emma had asked and denied it at once.

'And what of the knife we saw you with in the barn?' Emma asked.

'It just so happens that an identical knife was found in the river as you said. But it wasn't mine. I was happily minding my own business before you came in. If you didn't, I'd probably still be there, fast asleep by now,' Reggie said as he slightly raised his voice.

The only conclusion was that there'd been two knives, both of similar liking. But of course, it wasn't a likely story. To anyone's mind, it would have to be Reggie just by the knife alone.

'I am just looking at the facts and the circumstances, Reggie,' Emma said as she unlaced her fingers and crossed her hands, laying them over Henry Smallhorn's desk.

She noticed his anger. The night had been cold, but he'd sweated like he'd been working in a factory all day in the middle of summer.

When Emma explained what she was trying to do, it seemed to calm Reggie down as he sunk into the back of his chair once again. He took in a deep breath. He never suspected that he'd be pouring with tears tonight. If the storm hadn't harmed a sweet night of sleep in the hay of his barn, the interrogation of a missing person and a murder would.

'You think I killed Frank Lightfoot then Billy Javers next?' Reggie alluded to in a frightened, sombre tone.

'I don't know, Reggie,' Emma sighed.

'Someone who had murdered Billy Javers could've murdered Frank Lightfoot too, unless he killed Billy and Frank is still missing to this second,' Madeline intervened.

Emma turned away from her. She nodded, but there wasn't something quite right. It was hard to tell if Reggie could have done it. It seemed unlikely that he would attack Frank and murder Billy with two separate knives. It felt a little disorganised, yet many times, murders were built on inconvenience and improvisation.

'And then there was that moment with you and Mr Lightfoot. The pair of you went to the barn to close the doors before the weather got worse. I know because I saw it first hand from my window,' Emma mentioned.

Reggie shrugged his shoulders. He couldn't see where she was heading. Before he could mention that the man had only come to help him, Emma carried on with her description.

'But I saw you peel away towards the manor after the job was complete. I saw Frank Lightfoot depart in a different direction to smoke his pipe. And that was the end of it. I was called to dinner before I could see where he went from there. It was dark as well, mind you.' Emma's eyes trailed off to the tabletop of the desk. She wished she stayed long enough to see where Frank had gone. The way he vanished so quickly and the fact that he hadn't appeared yet made her indecisive as to if he was a victim or an attacker turned killer.

Emma indeed had her suspects lined up. Some were higher on her danger list than others. The missing person and the murdered victim of the Smallhorn manor would prove to be a great mystery.

'So, I have you as an alibi?' Reggie insisted. 'You saw me tail off back inside when Frank went for a smoke?' Reggie asked. He had heard Emma say it earlier before for the rest of the manor to hear, but he needed her to say it again, just so he was clear that he was safe from her suspicion.

'I did, but I cannot provide an alibi to what could've occurred afterwards when I turned away. I didn't see what happened after, Reggie.'

Reggie gulped. He searched his memory and retraced his steps after affixing the barn doors. He was so out of breath then. Closing the barn doors had been a difficult task, with or without the might of the storm.

'I came inside for a drink. I went to the kitchen then went to the study for a while to find a book for tonight. I must've been inside for almost an hour,' Reggie said in a pleading tone.

If the murder of Billy Javers wasn't real enough for Emma, interviewing her suspects had released the adrenaline. She had put the works to them each and Reggie had sweated the most out of all of them. It was a situation that he had never dreamed possible and for Emma, being a detective had suddenly become *very* real.

'Did Frank Lightfoot say anything to you when you departed?' Emma asked.

Reggie thought for a minute.

Emma watched as Reggie's eyes rolled towards his eyelids, thinking. He stretched his tongue and pressed it out against his inner cheek until his words broke free.

'He said he'd like to go for a smoke, and that was all. For as long as I've known Frank – which hasn't been long at all – he'd always sneak away for a smoke. He didn't want his sons to see him. He thought they didn't know that he'd returned to the habit, but they knew,' Reggie confirmed. It was cagey at first, and Emma thought as much. But when Reggie elaborated, it was something which she'd already heard. It was truthful at least.

She thought about Reggie's last sighting of Mr Lightfoot. By what she had known, he'd been the last person to see him without a *bad* intent. It was curious to think if anything had happened between the two at the barn. If anything had, Reggie wasn't going to tell.

His face was blank. There was no telling if he had something to hide. Emma wasn't experienced enough to be able to tell, but being placed in the shock of everything that had happened, she was learning. She'd adapted quickly – quickly enough to look as if she'd been a detective for years.

'It doesn't look good for you, Reggie, I'm afraid,' Emma admitted. Her face creased uncomfortably and Reggie mimicked it.

Reggie looked up, startled, unfocused.

Now Madeline was standing up over the desk, looking like Emma's henchman. Her fists were balled against the oak and her hair dangled down both sides of her face. 'I think we need to keep you somewhere until the morning. If not to keep an eye on you, but to keep you safe if otherwise,' she said.

Reggie didn't have a choice in the matter. He looked to Emma and she was no longer an ally. He understood that nobody could be trusted. He had pleaded his innocence, but if it were he sitting in Emma's place, he'd be suspicious of his actions too. The knife and the inconvenience of Reggie's whereabouts were too far against him.

Reggie was escorted to the room next to Mr Smallhorn's office. Madeline locked him inside.

It was an adjacent study, but not as nice of a one as Mr Smallhorns. The room was tastefully furnished still, with a large chesterfield sofa inside placed before a similar but smaller oak desk to the main office. The room was once an office, but was now filled with clutter and unwanted items, yet still expensive books and ornaments which had lost their standing in Mr Smallhorn's favor.

'This is just until the morning,' Madeline assured Reggie with a soothing smile.

Reggie took a seat on the sofa. He turned back to her in the dark, his eyes welling with the fear of being imprisoned. It just looked too bleak for Reggie. There was too much going against him though, and he realised that it was only the right thing to do.

Madeline looked into his eyes, seeing the fearful look of a caged animal. She resisted the urge to forget everything and let him out, and instead locked the door behind her.

She hated doing it, but it was the right thing to do.

The light of the candle-lit hall had left and Reggie had only the dull moonlight which crept through his curtains. For the rest of the night, he'd wait the remaining four hours in darkness until the morning light would come. For at least with a killer lurking about the manor, he would be safe behind a locked door.

The last to be interviewed was Howard Banks.

He had waddled up the staircase and into the office. The man was tired and injured. He took his time and when he was asked to appear, Dr Gottfried mentioned that 'He wouldn't like it. The man had just about lost all the strength he'd gathered back up fighting off Billy Javer's.'

Emma was curious as to what Howard would have to say about the fight.

Seeing that his murder had occurred soon after the fight, it might have been Howard's motive.

'I didn't fight Billy Javers. He came and fought me.' When Howard was asked the question, he insisted that he hadn't started anything.

'Why would he want to fight you?' Emma asked.

Howard shrugged his shoulders, pulling a disgruntled face. It hurt to move, even so little. 'I couldn't really tell you,' he said, stooping back down. 'It was random. I opened my eyes and looked up and he was there trying to strangle me.'

Emma looked at Madeline quizzically for some insight.

'He did lash out here and there. He never liked visitors or people he had never met after the incident,' Madeline provided. But there was still something missing. Emma concentrated on the thought in her mind. It was something that Billy had said when she came in. It was something which Billy had demanded to know from Howard in their tussle. When he was torn away from him, Billy had been fixated on something.

"Where is it?" Emma recounted. *"Where is it?"*

Howard looked confused for a moment and then he realised what Emma had meant.

He nodded. He remembered what Billy was asking about – at least he thought he did.

'Why did Billy ask you that question during the scuffle… What did he mean by it?' Emma queried.

Howard sighed. He pulled his arm up to his head and scratched an itchy spot. The movement showed off the nasty blood stains up around the edge of his wrist which had seeped through the bandages tightly woven around his skin.

'I wasn't sure myself at first. But then I thought about it afterwards. I think it had something to do with part of the land on the estate.' Howard clenched his jaw tight. The wrinkles in the corner of his eyes deepened and he scratched the back of his head. He never thought he'd have to give up his secret, but there was no time like now to lie.

'Do you mind if Miss Smallhorn would leave for the moment?' Howard asked.

That wasn't the right thing to say to get Madeline to leave. Now that he said it, there was nothing more she wanted to do but stay and hear what he had to say.

Madeline crossed her arms arrogantly. 'Anything you have to say, you can say it in front of me,' Madeline said crossly.

Emma wouldn't side with Howard. He shook his head and now regretted saying anything. He didn't want them to think that he was hiding anything worse when Madeline pressed him to speak, so he just came out with it.

'Some years ago I cut a couple of tree's down on your family's side of the property. I did it and expanded the fencing to give myself some more land.'

Madeline could only cross her arms and shake her head. Her reaction was plain with a sly scowl. Though to Emma it sounded as if the warmth had been let out of a room to turn it cold again, it wasn't so revolutionary to her in her inquisition to finding the murderer, but to Madeline it was devastating.

'You bastard,' Madeline bit back.

'I only did it for my cattle. I get all the runoff from the river and it turns my land to mush. I needed part of the hill to recover, so I did what was necessary.' To Madeline, there was no excuse great enough and she couldn't wait to tell her father the news. She knew that he'd feel the same way, if not much angrier.

Howard gave Madeline the kind of look which said *your family could cope with it.*

She smouldered at him with anger. Now she knew as to why her father had such ill feelings towards Howard Banks.

Emma directed the conversation away from the problem which fanned this feud. It was less important for now and there was more to discuss. Before she and Madeline had been called in from Howard's farm, she'd remember spotting the fencing of his pen.

'Mr Bank's, why did you tell me that your latch was broken when it wasn't?' Emma asked.

The question left Howard a little gun-shy to speak. He looked like a man caught off guard until he remembered what she meant. Indeed, it had been broken, but later fixed, rather scruffily.

'No, it had been broken, but I replaced the metal latches with some leather bounding. As for the rest of the fencing, it doesn't look so great and a sturdy storm could set it free, as it did.'

Howard explained the problem and it was good enough for Emma not to argue. The leather was there and as she recalled, she remembered she'd clunked the mouth of her mud-boots in chunks of metal close by the gate which could've been the original latch.

Howard was free to go. Painstakingly he raised himself up from his seat and walked out. When he got to the door, he turned back to face Emma. He remembered that something had happened downstairs during Reggie's interrogation.

'There was just one more thing.' Emma withdrew from her notes, flicking her hair out of her eyes and looking up to Howard as he spoke.

'What is it?'

'I am not sure if it is of any relevance, but downstairs, just now, Mrs Smallhorn was complaining about the disappearance of her diamond necklace. She is under the impression that someone has stolen it.' Howard shrugged his shoulders. After he'd delivered the message he meandered back down the dark hall to return to the sitting room to rest.

'Not my mother's diamond necklace. Hasn't she been through enough already tonight?' Madeline said with grief.

To her, Howard had said it with some satisfaction. He said it like he was promised to be the one to drag down more sorrow for the family. Madeline turned to her friend. The look of worry and dread – if it wasn't apparent before – was painfully clear now.

'Do you know how much that necklace is worth? Father got it for her on their tenth anniversary,' Madeline said.

Emma remembered the necklace at the dinner table. It was a beautiful piece. Its bedazzling, sparkling gems could never be forgotten as Emma pictured it perfectly. She knew that she had them at dinner and she remembered she had the necklace on during Howard's arrival, but not after.

'When do you remember your mother not wearing the necklace?' Emma asked.

Madeline looked at her blankly. She drew herself away from the table and looked into the darkness away from the candlelight. 'I don't remember her wearing it before Uncle Billy was murdered. At least I think I remember not seeing it,' she said, confirming Emma's suspicion.

'Me too. I don't remember her wearing them when she came down. She must have set them aside when she went up to her room to sleep. If someone has indeed taken it, it was more than likely in that time frame.'

Chapter 11

It was only a matter of time before something would come up stolen. Murder's evil burned, one crime coming after the other, out of the frying pan and into the fire.

Emma wasn't only dealing with a missing person and a murder, but now a thief had been thrown in the mix. She did think it possible that perhaps all three crimes were committed by the same person. The unholy trinity, she thought of calling it. If it were true, she was truly dealing with a cunning assailant.

The fact that it was indeed the most expensive item in the manor could only mean that someone had been out to get it for a long time. It was a robbery with a message. It had almost been daring to take it, a risk to toy with how much leniency the criminal was getting.

Emma had become embarrassed.

Mrs Smallhorn had been left flummoxed. Her mouth fell open again once the realisation had hit.

'When I find who has taken it, I'll throttle them, I will,' Grandpa Smallhorn said.

His eyes went down to narrow slits when his words left his lips. Even he thought it wasn't a good idea to mess with a potential murderer. Grandpa Smallhorn did raise a curious question to his exclamation.

'Do you think whoever stole it murdered my brother also?' Mrs Smallhorn sobbed. She carried a thin cloth between her fingers. She dabbed the corners of her eyes with it, holding it the fancy way like she would with a tiny afternoon tea sandwich.

'I would say so, unless someone amongst us is an opportunist,' Emma said.

When she spoke, she looked around the dining room. Everyone was there but Howard Banks who'd retreated back to his sofa in the sitting room.

'Well, we must search one another. We could prick the thief right here, right in this very place,' Robin Smallhorn said.

He pulled himself up and made his way towards the doctor and his wife. But before he could pat Doctor Gottfried down, he was stopped.

'It is not up to anyone to go searching one another willy-nilly. Even as a detective, I have no right to do so, let alone anyone else in this manor.' Emma tore her words at the silent crowd before her. Her breathing was more forceful than the swooping wind outside and louder than the thunder at one moment.

They each looked at each other, undecided of what to do.

'Some bastard thief has not only murdered my wife's brother but stolen her most prized possession. They probably had a mind to kill Frank too while we're at it.' Mr Smallhorn summoned himself. His face went a pale white. His whole body jerked as he whipped his body around to stand by Emma. He got a good look at everyone. They were all dim yet unreadable for him to detect a lie.

'I let you in my home. I welcomed you with food, shelter and hospitality. But one of you has had the nerve to disrupt our sacred peace.' Mr Smallhorn paused. He allowed himself to breathe and then he began again.

In a softer, somehow more startling tone, he calmly asked, 'So which one of you is it, *huh?'*

The rebound of silence hit back at him like an electric shock. He shivered quietly and stiffened his shoulders. The tension in the room could be sliced with a knife.

'Whoever you are, you're just as cowardly as I suspected.' The insolence had him barking at the dark. Mr

Smallhorn gritted his teeth and looked to each of his guests. With each glance, he warned them. He returned to his wife and comforted her. He sat next to her at the table and placed his hand over hers to soothe her.

Just when Emma began to take back charge of the situation, Dr. Gottfried sidled up beside her. He spoke softly and quietly into her ear to keep their conversation private.

'Do I have your permission to return to the office?' He asked. 'I believe I can send that message and get us some help down here. The later I leave it, I'm afraid the less time we'll have.'

Emma nodded. She kept quiet too. She didn't want anyone else to know what the Doctor was planning.

Emma decided that she'd see if she could trust the Doctor. She didn't want anyone else to know; alerting the mysterious killer to an out could panic them, causing them to strike again. Emma thought it best to keep the doctor's ideas private.

It wasn't so often that a detective would trust a suspect, but her plate was full. In the doctor, she could trust. *Why else would he want to signal his office for help?*

'Make your way up to the office. Nothing more,' Emma warned.

Doctor Gottfried nodded. He lowered his body down and picked up his briefcase. Inside were more bandages that he'd intended to re-affix Howard's wounds.

'Let me attend to young Howard first, then I'll be right up,' Dr. Gottfried said.

The Doctor vanished back down the dark hall on his way to the sitting room as he had done many times.

Emma turned to the rest of the dining room. There was Robin Smallhorn, Madeline, her parents and her grandparents and of course, the Lightfoot brothers.

'Where is Reggie?' Fillius Lightfoot asked.

His question rang alarm bells around the rest of the room, but Emma assured them that he'd been locked in the second office upstairs. She didn't say why, but everyone knew. He would seem a likely suspect out of everyone so far due to what he'd been found with and his whereabouts at all the wrong times.

'You are just going to lock him up there?' Henry asked. There had been concern in his voice, but he truly and gladly embraced the idea. Now that things had gotten heated, he had begun to suspect Reggie heavily.

'It is for his safety too. If I had a good enough reason for each of you, I'd do the same to everyone,' Emma replied.

When the candlelight at the table burned out, the smell of Billy's body decomposing in the kitchen just a few feet away had become apparent. His body had been rotting, his limbs turning sunken and purple, and blood leaking from the knife wound in his back. The rancid smell had only gotten worse in the condensed, darkened room. There was no way for it to escape and everyone else could start to smell it again now.

Luckily, Robin relit the candle before Prudence Smallhorn could smell the stench of her brother again.

Henry continued to hold his wife. He promised her that her necklace would be found and with it, her brother's murderer also. She was delirious by now – and not in a good way.

She couldn't speak... She didn't want to speak. She looked deflated as she sunk into her husband's lap like a boneless body. She had been hurt and the pain caused from her terror had taken a physical effect.

Emma knew that her time was running out. As she looked at Madeline's mother as a living example, she knew that soon the confrontation of murder would become too much for everyone. By sunrise, there may be another. She knew she needed to act fast, starting with the missing necklace.

'Everyone is to stay down here while I go upstairs to look for clues. If anyone but the doctor leaves this room, you should consider them suspicious.'

Emma kept everyone put. There was no more moving throughout the manor without her authority anymore. Before she could leave for the staircase, a strange thud from upstairs sounded.

Emma was spooked. Her complexion turned a pale white and she stood staring up at the ceiling with her mouth gaped open.

She searched hard, almost as if she could see through the paint of the ceiling to see the movement which she could hear.

There it was again. Another, *bang!* – then a dragging like a heavy duffle bag being moved along the floor.

'Someone is upstairs,' Madeline's grandfather whispered.

'Oh, it's the murderer. It's Reggie moving about up there,' Madeline's grandmother claimed.

Emma very quietly tipped-toed away from the dining table. She placed her finger up to her lips, wanting quiet. She never took her eyes off the ceiling as she used her hand to feel the wall behind her to move.

'I'm going up,' she whispered. She was going to investigate alone.

Emma edged her way up the staircase. She stood halfway up, her head inclined towards the top of the landing. Darkness sweltered upstairs. It invaded her vision like a black cloud of smoke and it was impossible to see.

She kept her flashlight lowered to her hip and pointed it to the ground. She didn't want anyone to see her coming. It hovered over the scratchy wood that hadn't been covered by the red carpet.

She tried her best to move silently, but each step she took led to another creak on the steps.

Emma stood still for a moment, listening. There were no voices coming from the dining room and nothing coming from upstairs. The feeling of being alone in the manor began to press in on her, overwhelming her. But she composed herself, finding the courage to take another step up when she heard a distant thud. It sounded like someone knocking their knee upon the side of a bed or a drawer of some kind.

Knowing that she was close to her target, Emma pressed on.

Her hand gripped the railing to her left as she made her way up the staircase, the creaks which rattled throughout the manor fading behind her. She realised how long she'd taken to climb the staircase as she peered down it again. Emma thought she was likely to be climbing it until dawn came if she hadn't hurried on the second summit.

An eerie breeze bellowed down the lonely hall. She turned to her side and gazed down the longer end of it. She felt the breeze prickle her soft skin. It had to have come from somewhere, but somewhere unknown. A crack in the wall or an open window perhaps, but there was only one window that she could see down the very end of the narrow hall, past all the closed rooms, and it was closed.

She felt the goosebumps bubble up on her skin and the hairs on the back of her neck stand to attention.

She didn't need her torch light as much anymore. Her eyes had become well-adjusted to the darkness, and the moonlight which came out of the window helped as well, white as bone.

Rather beautifully, she could see a small amount of ruby red passing over the thunderclouds to signal that morning was coming.

To disrupt the beautiful setting, the wind still pounded the glass and blew with a roar of fury with every second it came. The rain sprayed and splashed, wetting the window with a sound which mimicked thousands of stale rice grains pelting it.

Lightning flashed again. It brightened the hallway before her in a great display, although the darkness below still hovered behind her, waiting.

The last door down the hall was Henry Smallhorn's office – the office which Emma had just left.

Over the last hour, everyone had been inside to meet her with her questions. By now she thought that everyone had gotten used to the manor and its eternal darkness if they hadn't already. She in fact had started to get used to it herself. She knew most of the rooms by now, but it didn't stop her from being uncertain.

She couldn't help but feel there were eyes upon her. She felt as though someone was standing behind her always, cloaked in the shade – a ghostly figure – one that Madeline had always spooked her with as torment.

Emma had always been a person of logic, always had a sound reason as to why things happened and how the mind was capable of playing tricks on the body. She remembered reading somewhere that thinking that somebody was watching you had something to do with how humans had evolved. From thousands of years ago, it was a response for humans to keep their wits about themselves from wandering predators. Some nasty person had turned those instincts into something else now, using ghosts and other unworldly creatures to turn it into a fear rather than a useful instinct.

For as long as she knew the trick cast upon all the population and for as long as she had a job to do, she stood strong. *It was only a sensory thing. That was all. It was a good thing, actually,* Emma cited to herself.

Emma stepped forwards and shined her torch down the hall where Henry Smallhorn's office was. She supposed she should check there first.

It was much quieter now.

Maybe the sneaky assailant has caught up to me. Maybe they knew that I'd come up to investigate and they've run off or hidden away, waiting for me, Emma thought loudly to herself as she cautiously moved down the hall.

Her torch was pointed out to the carpet a few feet in front of her.

She watched the shadows of the rain pelts fade away from the torch light, surrounding the horizon of it like bark at a tree stump.

The groans of the manor grumbled behind her, groaning up the walls. She began to wonder if she'd been transported into the hull of a croaking ship. She didn't know if she should think it was the old sounds of the manor or somebody making them.

She shined her torch light up to the wall to reveal a painting. It was one out of the hundreds she'd already seen on her tour, but she hadn't remembered seeing this painting.

It was an old man dressed in all black, from the clothes he wore under his black cloak and the thimble-like hat which rested upon his head. He had a grey beard, cut straight, and it dangled right down to his sternum.

He stood out in front of a barn with a clean field in the distance. He carried a book in his left hand and a cane in his other, stabbing into the ground.

He looked like a lord of some sort, someone who'd perhaps made a journey from London to visit the Smallhorn manor in the sixteenth century, Emma guessed. He looked like he was from that time anyway.

Emma abandoned the painting.

She went along her way towards the office in the last room of the hall. She passed the office that Reggie was locked in and thought she'd come back to it, to check on him.

Once she landed in front of Henry's office, she jiggled the doorknob and turned it open. The door came free and the wood shook. Emma let go of the brass handle, hating the vibration which came from it.

She looked inside and pinned her flashlight deep into the room.

At first glance there was no one inside. It had been left as she had. The candle had still to be blown out and the vanilla scent wafted from the new burn.

Emma wandered inside a little further. She walked upon the creaky floorboards until she landed in the centre of the room where a soft carpet cushioned her noisy feet.

At the centre of the room, she turned around and did a full circle. She looked upon all the walls where the books had been stacked in their cases. She looked at all of Henry's favourite paintings, ornaments and antique medieval armour and weaponry.

She turned to find his desk. She darted her flashlight towards it and looked behind it. There was no one hiding. She made sure of it, leaning over the edge of the desk and poking her head under it where the chair slid inside. No one was hiding under it.

Emma was left satisfied.

She left the room, but not before she moved the telegram machine off Henry's back shelf to place it on his desk for the doctor to come in and use after he'd seen to Howard.

When Emma left the office for good, she made sure to close the door tightly. She turned the handle as she did it, making sure that the metal wouldn't make a sound against the bracket when she did. When it slipped into place, she turned the handle the other way, allowing the mechanism to slide in to her manual operation.

She stepped aside and wandered back down the hall. She followed the carpet and passed the paintings upon the wall again until she made it to the second office.

Reggie had been locked inside for about an hour now.

Emma stood tall on her toes. She pressed herself forwards to look into the reverse peephole.

She steadied her breathing, making sure her body didn't lean against the door, instead using the prints of her fingers to cushion herself quietly among it. She didn't want Reggie to know that she was there so she could catch him in the act doing something out of the ordinary.

As she peaked inside, she could see that Reggie had found his comfort on the sofa. Emma could see that he'd curled up on it and gone to sleep.

He snored quietly, his knees were tucked to his stomach and his arm cushioned his head to fall asleep.

Emma watched him for a little while longer to make sure that indeed he was asleep.

She felt sorry for the poor teenager. The room was decorated with cobwebs and it was dark, with little light coming from the window where the curtains had been left half-drawn.

The room was overflowing with forgotten relics that had fallen second place in being displayed throughout the manor, most of which tainted the room with a musty, dust-riddled scent which was hard to breathe in.

Paintings littered the walls, licking that dusty scent with a slap of volatile organic compounds to make the room smell chemical-like. Reggie could cope. He had opened the window a little, the only downside being that the rain did come in a little.

Reggie's space had been invaded, but it was nothing that he had never beaten before. Reggie was used to living in a place like this. He would sleep in the barn with stacks of hay, old farming instruments and barn animals crowding.

It wasn't that he'd been invaded with a lack of space. He was very much used to it for most of his life. When Emma remembered how Reggie would spend most of his time in the barn, she didn't feel so bad anymore.

He went to sleep finding his way to a safe place like a cat who'd curled in a ball behind a mass of junk in a spare room. He was fine.

Emma stepped away from the peephole. She was satisfied with leaving Reggie be.

She climbed back down from her toes and landed softly back onto the carpet. She cautiously backed down the narrow hall. She came to a stop by an old traditional buffet by the edge of the staircase.

Displayed upon it was a bouquet of fake flowers stuffed down a cream porcelain vase. Next to the vase was a torch which had been toppled over to its side with fresh batteries leaning against it. Someone had left it behind after scrambling for batteries, Emma gathered.

Emma slithered her hand along the Italian marbling. She picked up the flashlight and stuffed a battery down in her coat pocket for later.

She handled her new torch, feeling the cold brass inlaying around the globe end of it. It wasn't warm, so it hadn't been used recently. Emma tucked her flashlight in her pocket as a spare and kept a hold of her new one.

As she fiddled with her new flashlight, she glanced down the bottom of the staircase from where she stood. She only looked when her senses took over.

It was dark – darker than what she remembered. She didn't glare for too long, but coming from down the bottom of the stairs, she saw a shadowy figure dart from end to end. They zoomed down the hall, heading towards the sitting room, coming from the dining room.

Emma gasped. The flash of movement happened so quickly that she hadn't the time to call out to whoever it was, then she remembered she wanted to be quiet in case the assailant was still upstairs with her.

Thankfully, the shudder of thunder which crashed from outside shrouded the breath she let loose. It was about the only time she was thankful for the poor weather.

'But, darling, there is a killer in the house. You cannot go up there on your own.' Emma listened to the voice of a woman that had drifted from the dining room.

It was muffled and she didn't know who it was at first, but the person was pleading.

'Millicent, I have to. The detective has allowed me and me only to use the telegram. I could get us some help.'

It was the doctor talking to his wife. It was coming from the dining room – the doctor had not yet left for the main office.

Emma listened as Millicent pleaded for her husband to find another way. She wanted to accompany him, just so at least he wasn't left alone. She worried too much about him and the doctor pointed this out.

Their voices from the dining room had sounded as though they were talking from within the walls. It was so muffled to Emma's ears, like they were talking under water. She wasn't sure if the conversation trailed off a little. The constant breathing of the old manor down every hall had confused Emma's ears.

Emma thought she'd heard Millicent reply, saying that *"I could go up with you",* but she wasn't sure if she had said that to him. The roll of thunder introduced itself as Emma's bane once again as it drowned out the voices for her to hear. The eerie groans and creaks of the manor were drowned away also.

Emma could hear a creak spring from behind her. It came from the other end of the hall; the hall which she had not yet ventured down.

It had groaned louder than any of the other times.

Emma slowly turned her head. She expected to see someone standing there by how loud it was. The turn was agonising. Emma lowered her flashlight and pressed it upon her coat to block it out. She didn't want anyone to see her. As she faced the darkness of the back wall to the hall, Emma couldn't make her mind up if she would be surprised to see someone standing there or not.

Someone had been hiding in the back of the hall, shrouded by the darkness. At first, she thought it was a display of knight armour, quite like the one a few feet in front of her on the other end of the staircase. But it wasn't.

The knights armour displayed along the hall's wall was thicker in her view and much bolder in the dark. The mystery hiding in the dark wasn't. The figure was paper thin and it shimmered, like a reflection over water.

There was a silvery, scintillating shine to the figure, which is why it was easy to mistake for another knight's armour on display, but this figure moved.

'Hello Emma. I've come to use the telegram.'

It was Dr. Gottfried.

He climbed out from his hiding spot and walked towards Emma. His feet never made a sound as he walked with an almost *glide.* Emma hadn't remembered him coming up the stairs. She wondered how he'd come up to the second level without her noticing. And then she remembered that she only just heard him speaking to his wife, Millicent from downstairs in the dining room.

Emma did a double take. She shook her head as if to dust the confusion away.

'Did I startle you? I'm sorry if I did,' the doctor apologised.

'No… Not at all, Dr,' Emma replied.

She stepped aside, her back hugging the wall.

She watched as Dr. Gottfried left his place and walked the rest of the hall. His feet were nimble. He didn't make a sound.

Emma watched him. His figure became a lot clearer and the way the moonlight was cast over his body for the hall window shone a milky glow over his skin and clothes. He carried his briefcase – the one that she'd seen him with downstairs. It was all so very strange.

As Emma tried to think of a way that he could get upstairs without her seeing him, Dr. Gottfried entered Henry's office. He seemed to vanish as suddenly as he'd come. The swelling darkness took him and then he was gone and out of sight when he closed the door.

Emma shrugged to herself. She was completely freaked out but she didn't know why. Doctor Gottfried was a calm and gentle man; he had no reason to scare her. Emma figured it was just the circumstance that she had been in which spooked her.

She hadn't expected him so *quickly*, that was all. Even still, she couldn't figure out how he came up to the second level without her seeing him.

Emma still had a job to do. She was itching to join the doctor in the main office, but she carried on to find the Smallhorn's bedroom.

In the glow of her flashlight, a shining statue of knight's armour appeared before her. Her body shivered. It spooked her a little.

She turned her nerves into courage as she wandered towards the Smallhorn's bedroom.

She pressed her body into the wood of the door. It was thick and stocky. She couldn't hear anything on the other side. She could swear that the thuds and banging had come from their bedroom.

Without another moment to waste, Emma wriggled her hand around the doorknob. With a leisured twist and tug, the door came free. Emma poked her head inside. She followed the spray of her flashlight. It sprinkled to the side of the Smallhorn's bed and trickled along the carpet.

Briefly, Emma got a look at their bed. It was large – a king sized bed. It had fancy brass banisters with curtains which rolled closed. The way the sheets fell over the top of the mattress and loosely bunched over the sides made it look like the waves of a desert.

The rest of the room was large. It was dark inside and she could barely see the paintings on the walls and the oak closet to the side. But Emma could only notice the room briefly.

She centred her eyes to the brighter section of her light. It hovered over a person.

Standing before the side dresser was the maid, Mary.

Mary was hunched over the dresser, her back turned to Emma. When Mary noticed the warmth of Emma's flashlight, she turned to face her.

Her eyes squinted at the harshness of the light. Mary couldn't tell who it was. She was scared… She thought the killer had come for her and at the same time, Emma had believed that the sneakiness of Mary could dig her up to become something more than just a thief, all by the way she'd found her.

Stunned and scared at the same time, Mary waited for the mystery person to speak.

'Mary?' Emma asked.

Her voice relaxed Mary. Now that she knew who it was, the fear had died that she had come for the *wrong* reason. It was the detective. She was safe from harm, but now, she'd been caught.

'Miss Squier?' She asked. She was nervous. Stuck in the light, Emma could see that she was hiding something. Mary was up to no good.

'What are you doing here?' Emma asked. She knew full well already.

She didn't receive an answer. Emma encroached upon Mary. She stepped closer in hopes of discovering what she had been doing. When Emma came too close, it was then that Mary gave up.

She moved aside. When she revealed what she'd been hiding behind her slouched body, it was then that Emma's mind had clicked. She saw the necklace that had gone missing. There it was... Mrs Smallhorn's diamond necklace with the spectacular ruby placed in the middle.

It sparkled as greatly as ever . Mary set it back upon a mannequin neck which Prudence Smallhorn had kept on her bedside table.

She never took it off its display, only to wear it.

'That's the necklace. That's Mrs Smallhorn's necklace that had gone missing.'

Emma cocked her head sideways. She paused and looked at the disgrace upon Mary's face.

'How could you steal it, Mary?'

Mary shook her head. She began sobbing about what she had done.

'I know it was wrong of me, Miss Squier. I don't know what came over me, I just saw an opportunity.'

Mary bowed her head in shame. She flattened her hands upon her clean apron as if to wipe them clean. She didn't know what spell had come over her. She'd been a maid for the Smallhorn family for years. Not once had she thought to steal. But this night was full of omens and cruel temptations.

'This family is so rich that I didn't even think that it'd get noticed,' Mary tried to explain. Mary's stomach was in knots and she looked like a mess.. The beauty and the promise of the necklace had power over her.

Emma took pity on Mary. She knew that Mary had made a mistake and she wasn't the crook she'd acted as. Emma stared at the necklace. She knew full well what it did to her.

She seemed like a woman who'd been starved and forced to watch those impossibly full everyday at the manor. As the Smallhorn's kitchen hand, she must've seen the diamond necklace ten times a day, being lured to it more and more. Emma understood. The necklace was breathtaking. It almost dared one to try and take it. It had caught Mary in a moment of weakness.

'But Mary -' Emma was stopped.

'I know what you are about to say, Miss Squier.'

Mary wiped her tears. She brought her apron up to her cheeks and dried them.

'I must look awful being here, Miss Squier. I know someone has been murdered and I'm strutting about the manor and stealing this precious jewellery. It sure doesn't make me look good. I know what you must be thinking of me.'

Mary bowed her head in shame. She stepped away from the necklace even further, as if not to be swayed by its temptation for even longer. She looked at it one last time and this time, she saw the poison within the jewels.

'Honest, I'm here to return it. You've only stumbled in to find me returning it,' Mary pleaded.

'Why did you return it?' Emma asked.

'Well, I felt so bad you see. With everything going on and whatnot. The guilt of me and the poor family with what happened to Billy and the Lightfoots, also. It didn't feel right to steal with their troubles.'

Mary sighed. She brought herself back to the moment when Prudence first noticed it had turned up lost. It did take her a long time to notice, but she couldn't blame her or anyone with what was going on.

'When Mrs Smallhorn declared that it had been lost, I knew I had to come back and return it. Then things will go back to normal, I thought.'

Emma stepped closer towards Mary. She stopped before the necklace and gazed down at it. The light neither shined through or on it. Instead, it orbited its own in a magical kind of way. Emma knew what Mary had meant about it. It was tempting.

Emma turned to Mary. She smiled and when she did, she let Mary know that it was alright. Emma wasn't going to do anything. She wasn't going to take Mary away. Indeed, Mary had intended to take the necklace back. In the eye of the law, the person who could do anything to take it all back and did was alright for Emma.

'It's ok Mary. I understand. At least you did the right thing to bring it back,' Emma reassured.

'You won't tell, Mrs Smallhorn, will you?' Mary asked.

Under normal circumstances, any detective would say they weren't done hashing it through, but Emma was certain of Mary's innocence.

'No. I won't,' Emma assured. 'I was wondering though, if perhaps you could tell me something?'

Mary nodded her head. "Anything." That nod had said.

'What have you seen around the manor tonight... *Who* have you seen?' Emma paused. She felt it strange to ask the maid for her help, but this was an opportunity to ask, as long as they were sharing each other's secrets.

Mary looked a little puzzled. She wasn't sure what Emma had meant. Of course, she'd stayed up at all hours and made sure to clean up after the guests at dinner. Mary had mostly been alone at all times and that was the kind of insight that Emma was after.

'Nothing in particular,' was all Mary could say.

'Have you seen anyone enter a room alone or have you heard or seen anything suspicious throughout the night, even just once?' Emma continued to persist until Mary's mind closed in on something in particular. It hadn't seemed important until now.

'Now that you mention it, Mr Smallhorn did come into the kitchen after dinner a few times. He went out through the kitchen door for a smoke and to look for Mr Lightfoot, I suppose.'

'Henry Smallhorn?' Emma confirmed.

'No.' Mary shook her head. 'Robin Smallhorn. I must have seen him go in and out of the kitchen half a dozen times after dinner,' she said.

Emma did think this was strange. She never remembered Robin Smallhorn mentioning it when she interrogated him. She knew he'd scaled the manor walls to search for Frank, but she never knew he'd gone through the kitchen.

'I did see him, I'm sure. When I was washing dishes,' Mary said once more.

'Did you see anything else?' Emma asked.

'Nothing else unusual, really. Mr Banks did come into the kitchen. He only came in to get a glass of water and reaffix his bandages. He even said he went through the doctor's briefcase to find some more bandages to patch them up,' Mary said.

'Did Howard do this often?' Emma asked. Now she took the time to sit on the bed. Mary sat next to her. She looked to her lap to search for an answer which she was quick to find.

'No, it was only the once. I said hello to him. He looked all sick and pale and he said he'd go back to the sitting room to rest. He honoured his word when I returned to the hall bathroom to replace the towels.' Mary was convinced of Howard's movements, though Frank's had been a bit of a mystery.

'I don't know, miss. I'm afraid I've been unable to focus properly tonight. From now on I'll be sure to keep a lookout for anything else,' Mary assured Emma.

Emma took the time to think about what Mary said. It'd been added to her mental notes, but she was afraid she was running out of time. She would need Mary to keep an eye out as best she could. The more help she could get, the better.

Certainly, the killer had run free throughout the manor for too long. They had evaded the eyes of everyone to move about. With the might of the storm to shroud their footing and the darkness to keep them hidden, the killer thrived off opportunity. Emma only knew so much, yet it hadn't correlated to anyone thus far.

Emma was prepared to forget everything that Mary had done. She saw the good in Mary when she came back to fix things before they had gotten worse. With a little information rewarded her way, she allowed Mary to be excused.

The plan being hatched downstairs was out of Emma's hands. She hadn't an inkling of the plot which had come about to overthrow her authority.

From the sitting room, the manor's guest had collated together in a matter of panic and urgency.

With Emma gone, each guest compiled together, led by Henry Smallhorn. They began to talk. Looking like a band of rebellious misfits, they huddled around each other, sat around the centre table, each face glowing by the candlelight.

'What do we do first?' Alfred whispered.

He bowed his head over the table. His knees shook anxiously, and his elbows rested on his knees as he awaited an answer.

'I say we go up there now. Before the detective even knows we are coming,' Fillius wheezed.

'Strike now while the iron is hot,' George Smallhorn agreed. He liked to go full throttle and he waved his cane up in the air like a swordsman leading the charge. He leaned forwards to the candle, his deep wrinkles creasing and the horror in his face glowing like a jack o'lantern. He lowered his flat cap down to his brow. When he did, a smile cracked and his jaw clicked. The old man looked evil in the moment, like a leader of a cult who didnt mind getting close to the flames.

'Yes, but how?' Henry Smallhorn chimed in.

It had been a question which all of them had been pondering since Billy's murder. They had banded together all at once, each thinking that Emma hadn't done enough to stop it. Everyone had turned to only one conclusion, that it had been Reggie all along. Reggie Jackson was the man who murdered Billy Javers and along with his crime, he'd attacked Frank Lightfoot and injured Howard Banks. Fear had banded the manor to one conclusion. It was the only way they felt settled. Now that he'd been locked upstairs, it was due time for them to face him.

'I don't know. But don't you think we should tell Emma all about this?' Madeline chimed in, hovering in the background. She had been seated next to Howard who'd found the strength to sit up for the secret meeting. He wore his blanket over his shoulders and he did shiver. The fierce brutality of the manor's intentions to get Reggie was what warmed him. It was him or them.

'No. Emma hasn't done enough. It is clear as day that Reggie is responsible for everything. Afterall, he had the knife and he was the last one to be with Frank. He is a guilty man walking. This is my manor and I am reclaiming control. We are the law now,' Henry declared.

Henry slammed his fist upon the table to emphasise his point.

'The only good thing that detective has done is trap that murderer in that room for us. We must take control of things now,' Fillius said.

He spoke with a punch of spite in his words. He had been angered that his vehicle had been tampered with, on top of everything else. He hated the thought that Reggie had even touched his motor car.

The manor had turned on their fellow man. They sat around the candle like it was the fire before a ritual. They lusted for blood as the fear of another dead body overtook their circle.

Henry Smallhorn didn't want to wait any longer. It was his manor and his place to rule. He didn't care about Emma's jurisdiction anymore. It was clear in his mind and everyone else's who he'd banded together that Reggie was the culprit they were after. Even Madeline had been drawn in. She hated to admit it, but she had been left with no other choice. She had to side with her family and under every circumstance, there had been too many problems going Reggie's way.

'Whatever we do, we cannot hurt Reggie. We have to get him and make sure that he cannot get away until help can come,' Madeline advised.

Everyone in the room agreed. Prudence nodded with a fierce energy. She wanted vengeance on her brother's death and she was determined to do what she could to contain Reggie.

'That room isn't going to be enough. We have to bring him down here. We will seal off the windows and the doors. We will each take a weapon to defend ourselves and to make sure that he cannot get away,' Alfred said.

'Is the doctor with us?' Henry muttered.

He turned to Dr. Gottfried's wife. Under the spotlight, she stammered to answer. In fact, she had forgotten to inform him about their plan.

The plan of the manor to revolt against Emma's lagging investigation was not known to the doctor.

'I forgot to inform him. He is upstairs in the office right now. He is trying to contact his practice with the telegram,' she said.

'Help will soon be on its way and we'll have Reggie waiting for them,' Madeline's grandmother said with a happy grin.Robin lingered at the back of everyone else with a grimacing face.

He didn't like the idea so much.

He liked Reggie and couldn't possibly believe it. He wondered which window the family's sense had drifted out of. His family were lusting for blood like barbarians, and he knew what they'd do when they got a hold of him. They said they wouldn't hurt him, but he knew that passions were high.

Robin was afraid to say something. His often-silent manner worked with him this once, but he still didn't like how the rest of the manor had unfolded before him. It was clear to see that the panic and fear of another murder had turned them to make a hasty decision.

He thought for as long as he remained in the shadows that he wouldn't be called upon and if he did and they caught him fighting for Reggie, he couldn't begin to think what they'd think of him.

Yes, it was true that Reggie had everything going against him. It didn't look good. Robin did suspect him, of course, but he hadn't come across anyone in the manor to believe that they could be responsible.

It irked him to put up and listen to what his own family had become. The bone-chilling wake of murder under a stormy night sky had his family clutching at straws to bring their fears to an end.

'I say we just go up there right now and surprise him before he even gets the chance to do anything. When we do, we'll get the doctor to give him something to relax,' Howard Banks recommended.

For a rare moment, Henry agreed with Howard. It wasn't so often that he did, if ever, but vengeance had put even the greatest conflict on the backburner.

Madeline couldn't help but notice the sudden bond between the two. As well as Robin, she had a conflict with the plan and she hadn't liked how Howard began feeding upon her father – a man he'd hated for years. All she did do was smile like something was wrong between it all.

'Come on. Let's go before Emma comes back down.'

Henry Smallhorn directed his legions up the staircase. With an assortment of weapons for their defence, they rallied up the stairs and busted down the upstairs hall.

Henry headed to the second office. He stood at the door and waited for a moment. The rest of the manor gathered behind to back him up.

Henry raised his hand to the door and with a hard fist, he knocked at the wood.

'Reggie. Are you in there?'

Henry's words drifted into thin air, dissipating before the cool smoke of his breath. He received nothing but a chilling silence. It spoke volumes from the other side. By the demanding tone in Henry's voice, anybody could figure that something was terribly wrong.

Reggie stayed silent. He feared why Henry had come.

'Please, if you can, open the door, Reggie. We wish to speak with you.' Henry sweetened his voice. He shaded his intent to lure Reggie to open the door and let him in.

When Henry was delivered silence once more, it was then that he turned to Alfred.

When Henry nodded at him, it was his signal to use his shovel – which he'd found in the dungeon. He lifted the shovel and moved it in a downward stab. He aimed the hard metal at the lock of the door which Emma had the only key of.

Reggie hadn't a choice. The door was locked from the outside and within, which Henry had seemingly forgotten. But to him, it looked like Reggie wouldn't obey his command. Alfred began bludgeoning the lock even more.

While Alfred repeatedly stabbed the lock, harder and harder with each time, Henry spoke between each blow.

'You are only making it harder for yourself, Reggie.'

Smash… Smash.

'If you won't open up, we'll open it for you.'

Smash… smash.

At last, the door lock broke free and Emma's defence was infiltrated.

The room had been opened, like a tomb of an ancient Egyptian burial. The moonlight glowed through. The team gazed at the shine upon the wooden floorboards. Henry stuck his flashlight into the room. The light invaded the darkness, exposing the dark corners and the shade among the stuffed rubble along the walls.

Amongst the piles and piles of leftover assortments which Henry had stored in his second office, there was no sign of Reggie.

'Where is he?' Alfred asked as he and Fillius hurried in. They each took a side by Henry. They searched behind the

Chester draws and between all the cracks in the abandoned furniture and relics.

George Smallhorn and his wife hobbled in. They looked up to the ceiling and gazed at the drooping cobwebs which were strewn in every nook of the small room.

'I don't see him,' Robin Smallhorn said. There was a little hope in his voice which he tried to hide. He hoped that Reggie wouldn't be found.

Henry asserted himself to the front of his desk. He looked over it to check underneath and behind it. He flashed his light under the small crawl space where a chair would settle. There was still no Reggie.

'He was in here, right? The detective didn't trick us, did she?' Alfred said with the shovel in hand. He raised it with a huff then dug the blunt metal into the floorboards by his feet.

'Wait.'

Madeline paused. While everyone stood still in their places, Madeline made her way towards the only window in the study. The curtains had been drawn half open, moving a little. The material flapped and whacked against the inner wall, but only lightly. Madeline slipped her hands between the curtain and drew it back. Now she could see that the window was slightly open.

'What is it?' Madeline's mother asked.

Madeline turned to her. With a heavy breath, she now knew where Reggie had gone.

'He has climbed out the window.'

Madeline looked to her father. The look he wore was one of shock. He had to jump two stories and brave a storm to get out.

'He jumped out of the window? He must've escaped when he heard us coming,' Howard said.

Madeline peered out the window. The moon was still out, but the sun was just peaking over the horizon. It was barely half past five in the morning and light would come soon. She gazed out to the horizon and there she saw the barn in the distance.

There was no light in the barn, but the way the sunlight needled through the back windows and shined out the front, it made it look as though the barn was occupied. That was when Madeline got her idea.

She looked at the barn, thinking that it was the only place where Reggie could be.

'What is it, Madeline?' Howard asked.

Her father managed to get a look over her shoulder to see where she was gazing. It was then when he noticed the barn too.

'It's the barn. That's where Reggie has escaped to,' Henry exclaimed.

It was brave for Reggie to jump to begin with, but to enter the storm again all alone to find a new refuge was something else.

Emma stormed down the hallway. She had heard the slamming of the shovel against the lock. When she came down the hall she noticed the office door was open, she saw the damaged lock that had fallen to the carpet.

Emma showed herself. She stood tight in the doorframe with her hands on her hips. She looked inside the room to see the entirety of the manor's guests. She stood wide-eyed and her mouth gawked open in shock.

'What is everyone doing in here? Why has the lock been broken?' Emma asked.

She was a little infuriated. Her tone was met by Henry Smallhorns who dished out the same back at her.

'We are sick and tired of waiting, *detective.* We have decided to take actions into our own hands, whether you like it or not.'

Emma listened and at the same time, she noticed the nods which agreed around the room. She turned to Madeline who hadn't said anything and didn't nod. Instead, she stood on the fence so as to not disobey her family nor Emma.

'This is mayhem. You cannot take matters into your own hands. There is a murderer amongst us,' Emma pleaded. But there was nothing she could say.

Everyone believed they had their man. Emma hadn't put the right man away according to them. Reggie had been contained, but merely for his own safety rather than the safety of the rest of the manor – that was how they saw it anyhow.

Reggie was a guilty man in the manor's eyes and something had to be done about it. Emma refused to budge, but Henry stepped forwards.

'Make way, *detective'* – he emphasised her profession again as if to mock her for what use she'd been.

He had turned rampant. He strutted his way to the door, expecting to pass through without a problem with Emma.

'I cannot let you pass, Mr Smallhorn. I cannot let you lust for blood and take matters into your own hands. This isn't the right thing to do.'

Emma deliberated the best she could. She tried to speak reasoning into Henry and the rest of the manor. But they'd already made up their minds. Every man or woman was innocent until proven guilty and Emma lived by those vows. The manor had already made their decision and by the look in Henry's grief-stricken eyes, there was no changing his decision.

'This is my home and this is my family. My wife's brother has been murdered and we are standing around doing nothing whilst the murderer is still running free.'

Henry yelled the loudest Emma had heard. He no longer cared that she was his daughter's friend. The emotions were high and the stubborn man had had enough.

'If you are not to do anything, then we will.'

Henry forced himself out of the door. He knocked Emma away with his elbow and created a free path through the door.

At once, the rest of the manor followed after him. They each carried their weapons and each wore the same grizzled, determined face, ready to brave the storm again. Even Madeline's grandparents were prepared to walk to the barn in the storm. Their determination enough would keep their feet rooted so not to be swept away by the might of the storm.

Emma looked on. The manor charged for the barn like an army of angry villagers to a monster that had killed the mayor's daughter. They were furious.

Emma had become saddened by the chaos which had warped the manor. She could only thank her lucky stars that Reggie had escaped to buy himself a little more time. She didn't know what to do. She couldn't stop them.

Emma could only pray that the power would come back on and she could call the nearest police station to send help. But it was a long shot.

Madeline stood behind. She waited to speak to Emma until after her family had cleared the room. They hadn't noticed she'd stayed behind with her friend.

Madeline huddled up to Emma. She listened to the detective sigh and she watched her place her hands upon her hips. Emma shook her head; she couldn't believe what the family had become. But fear had manifested and placed a guiding hand on each of their shoulders.

'They are going out there to kill Reggie, you know that, right?' Emma said.

Madeline didn't know. She hadn't the faintest clue what her family were capable of, but the Smallhorn name was reputable for violence from medieval times. The Smallhorns were a proud and forceful family, as well as the Lightfoots. It wouldn't surprise Madeline if her family marched upon the barn to root out the town monster.

'My family wouldn't kill him. I don't think they would. But tensions are high, Emma, and their time relying on you has run out,' Madeline admitted.

'I can't just find the murderer like that. It takes time and a procedure of detail to put the *right* person away,' Emma pleaded.

'When I go down there, will you help me? We need to speak reason to them.'

Madeline nestled her hands to her hips. She cocked her head a little and her mouth scrunched. She was unsure. She didn't want to go against her family, nor did she want to lurk around the eye of the law.

'I guess I can help. They are my family though, and I can't out myself against them like that.'

Emma understood.

'If they hurt Reggie, *or worse*… I will have no choice. You know that, right?' Emma confronted her friend with the information.

She knew her father had high passions and that her mother was terribly distraught. Revenge was the tiger-esque of the Smallhorn name. Blood for blood. An eye for an eye. Nothing could be better dealt with than revenge matching a crime. On Mr Smallhorn's inherited land, he became arrogant that it was his law to carry out. There was no telling what they would do, but Emma rest-assured that whatever harm they dealt which she couldn't stop, consequences would come.

Madeline agreed with a grunt. They could now see the scorches of flashlights outside of the office window. They were on their way already.

'Whatever you try to do or say to them, I'll stay by you.' Madeline finally had the courage to make up her mind. She was with her friend and on the side of the law. She could see now by the way her family marched on their way to the barn that it was the wrong thing to do.

'Thank you, Madeline.'

In a strange moment, Emma found she could smile. Before the two could turn on their heels and make their way to the barn, Emma mentioned the doctor.

'We should get Dr. Gottfried. A man like him could be just the right kind of voice of reason that we may need to back us up,' Emma advised.

Madeline agreed. He was only next door in the main office. Emma hoped that with some luck a distress call would have been made already. Thinking about the doctor had left

Emma with another thought. She hestitated at the door with the thought in mind.

She remembered seeing the doctor come up when she had investigated the darker end of the hall. Even still, she couldn't figure out which way he'd come up.

'Madeline?'

'Yes?'

'Dr Gottfried... Did he come up after I began investigating upstairs?'

Madeline paused for a moment. She didn't understand where Emma was trying to go with the conversation. Her eyes fluttered and she looked to her feet. She looked for an answer and with an unsure tone, she said 'Just after, I think."

'Just after?' Emma replied.

'What is it?'

Emma thought back to the very moment the doctor emerged from the darkness. He crawled out as if his body was created in the murkiness. She remembered his smile and the silent elegance in which he walked past her and down the hall, then finally towards the main office.

It was kind of spooky. The more she thought about it, the more she wondered if it had even happened to begin with.

'I saw the doctor. He came down the hall as if from nowhere. He looked at me and smiled a little. He never said a thing.'

Madeline raised her chin a little. When Emma described the situation, it was then that she had an inkling to what may have happened.

'He just drifted down the hall and I watched him go. That's when he entered the main office, like we discussed.'

Madeline pressed her hands upon her hips. She had enough to go off what happened. It was something that Madeline had been very used to growing up. She had seen something very similar for years.

'Remember what I said about this place, how it's haunted and whatnot?' Madeline said.

'Well, there is this ghost... No one knows who it is, but my father used to call him Peter. Peter likes to come down this hallway. When you see him, he impersonates people or things.'

Madeline was serious. Emma didn't quite know how to respond. She checked to see if there was any smirk in Madeline's expression, like it was a big joke or something, but Madeline didn't budge.

'This *"Peter"* is a ghost... That's what I saw?' Emma gawked. Her memory had become clearer, now she knew what it was. Now she knew why she was strangely unsettled. She didn't know it at the time and now that she did, a shiver ran up her spine.

'I used to see him all the time. He'd come down the hall, often with a smile but he'd never say a word. He'd emerge from the dark and look translucent in the moonlight. He was one with his milieu, the way the moonlight shimmered with a light glow along the centre carpet. It always frightened me.'

Madeline paused. She immediately returned to her childhood and the many nights she'd hear things coming from the kitchen and the dungeon. From her room she would hear thuds and clanking of chains outside the shield of her blanket covers. It was more than just *"Peter"*. But she always felt that Peter was kind. He had been a gentle soul.

'Peter often imitated my father or someone else. He'd walk into his study and I'd think it was him. Then I'd see Peter looking back at me, transformed from who I thought was my father. Over the years, it was something I'd just gotten used to.'

Emma was left flabbergasted. There was no way to interpret what she'd seen after what she had been told. She bordered along the thought that it simply hadn't happened. That way it'd be less complex and less frightening.

Madeline noticed the strained look of fear on Emma's face. It was her first and only ghost experience. Only one night in the Smallhorn manor had done it. She wanted to comfort her.

'Peter is nothing to be weary of. He is part of the home, really. It's quite safe.'

Madeline made light of the paranormal situation. It seemed to comfort Emma a little, but all she wanted was to get out still.

'Well, let's go and get the doctor. We don't have much time.'

With haste, the two ditched the second office and raced down the hall.

Chapter 12

There was a dead body in the office to welcome the detective. Slain over the desk, blood dripping from the table top, Dr. Gottfried had been struck.

When Emma and Madeline entered the main office, the doctor hadn't been dead for fifteen minutes before he was discovered.

The doctor's hands had turned cold. The telegram had been placed before him, the brass key pooled with blood and the outer plating littered with specks of red. His body lay over the desk, his head turned sideways as he drowned in his own blood.

Madeline was told to keep her distance. She stood in the doorway and let Emma come around to the desk. She tried to investigate, but the shock was immense.

Madeline stood with her hands upon her mouth. She couldn't contain herself and when she asked how could this have happened, Emma returned with an answer.

'There is a knife lodged deep in his back.'

The blade was still there. It was the exact type that had been used to murder Billy Javers, the exact type found in the riverbed. Much like the method which had killed Billy it had been done to Dr Gottfried in the same way.

It was so sad.

The way the doctor had been left there, his body taken of its life in a gruesome, horrible way. He was such a kind and loving man. He was a doctor for goodness sake, a man who'd dedicated his life to helping people and making them better. He didn't deserve to die in such a murderous way.

'How could someone murder him?' Madeline didn't know where to begin. Only a monster could murder someone who'd served their life saving people. It was a terrible thing to do for anyone, but with Emma and Madeline, it struck a nerve.

'Isn't it clear why he has been murdered?' Emma said, turning to her friend.

Madeline returned with a blank glance to which Emma began to explain.

'The doctor had a chance to contact his office. He had a chance to get help, perhaps he did even. But the murderer knew that. It's possible that the doctor was never part of their plan, but by signalling for help, he instantly painted a target on his back to be the next victim.'

'You mean the killer murdered the doctor to try and stop him from contacting his office?' Madeline reiterated, beginning to understand.

Emma shuffled her way to the body, stepping widely over the blood which had begun to soak into the carpet. The floor had done its best to absorb it, and no matter how far she stepped, a squelching noise sounded when she laid her foot down.

Emma came to the corner of the desk. She morbidly stood beside the doctor and picked up the papers beside his stiff arm.

She brought the papers up to a candle and read them under the flames. Her hand smudged the blood staining to the corners of the papers. She didn't care. All she cared for was the notes that the doctor had written before his death.

'What does it say?' Madeline asked. She continued to hover by the door. Emma wouldn't let her come any closer.

'It's an account of what has occurred tonight. Dr. Gottfried has written most things down.'

The notes had begun with mentioning the storm. *"It was the worst we'd ever seen. In my lifetime, it was probable that bad omens would soon follow. Up here in Northern England, away from any main city, it proved to be worse."*

The notes had also mentioned the guests. Dr. Gottfried had the time to write a profile on each person he'd listed. It wasn't anything spectacular. It was only brief, but she applauded the doctor for his detailing. She hadn't been sure if he had found the time to get everything on the telegram machine. Perhaps it was just in his notes, and he hadn't sent out anything at all in time before his murder. Emma wasn't sure.

She read the notes further. Dr. Gottfried had explained what happened. He noted the time that Reggie had been found in the barn and how it hadn't looked good for him. He also mentioned the time Howard Banks crawled to the manor and when Billy Javers was murdered. He dotted down Frank Lightfoot's strange disappearance, but he hadn't known so much about it. It, in every aspect of the matter, had very much been a mystery.

'The doctor has written everything from the evidence. He even mentioned a slight report on Howard's injuries. He has given a little report on everything so it seems,' Emma declared.

'Do you think that he got the signal off in time? You know... Before he was' – Madeline stammered with an awkward swallow. 'You know... *Murdered?'*

Emma wasn't sure. She looked at the telegram machine. She didn't know how it worked. She didn't know where to begin, she had never used one or much less seen one before.

'I'm not sure. It's possible that he got something off. If he did, someone in his office could have seen it by now,' Emma granted.

Madeline relished the idea. She hoped that Emma's words were true. With another murder at hand, they'd need all the help they could get.

'Who could have done this? We have all been together for the most part after uncle Billy's murder,' Madeline wondered.

'You didn't see anyone slip away whilst I was gone? You didn't see anything?' Emma asked.

Much to her expectation, Madeline shook her head. She hadn't seen anything suspicious, but Emma did remember looking down from the staircase to see the fluttering shadow across the hall. She wondered if that movement had anything to do with the murder.

'Emma,' Madeline stubbornly called her name.

She turned and looked at her friend with a due sense that something serious was on her mind. She'd been right. Madeline's face was flat. She looked like a woman who'd given up and had been worn down to join the majority. She just wanted everything to be over.

'Perhaps it really was Reggie. I mean, he was the only one up here when you were. Unless of course…' The words trickled out from her mouth uncontrollably. Madeline had alluded to Emma being the only one upstairs too.

Emma knew what Madeline was going to say, even before she stopped herself from saying it.

'Don't even go there,' Emma warned. 'I had nothing to do with murdering the doctor, or anyone else for that matter. What do you think I'm here for, Madeline?'

Madeline nodded. She felt embarrassed for bringing the idea to light and she couldn't believe that she had. It wasn't like her at all to turn on her friend like that, but once Emma understood the thought in her words, she had already forgiven her.

'I'm sorry. But not just for that... I suppose I am the one who invited you here in the first place. It was my idea.' Madeline grew sombre. She beat herself up for it, but Emma didnt let it weigh on her friend's mind.

'It's alright. There has been much trouble this night, but I feel as if it's coming to an end.'

Emma hinted to the fact that perhaps the rest of the manor was right. She'd now found herself believing that it could have been Reggie even more so than what she did. The manor had come under such distress. Perhaps no more would continue if a culprit had been selected. Emma wondered if she should arrest Reggie. Emma couldn't help but think it was possible. She took a moment to think before the pair left the study.

With Reggie gone – he'd escaped out of the window – it was possible that it was him. Why else would Reggie run away and how could he travel so quickly if he had only just left when the rest of the manor stormed upon his door?

Emma and Madeline rushed down the staircase to get to the barn. They hadn't heard or seen anything from the office window but the rest of the family continued to march upon it. They just hoped that nothing had been done or said yet.

By now the storm had cleared. It was still damp and windy outside, but it was much less unbearable. Emma could hear the wind converge upon the walls of the manor. It hit from time to time, shaking the foundation as it had for much of the night. A winding coo sounded through the gaps and alleyways of the manor, sounding much like a wailing ghost. It was barely raining, so Emma didn't need to find her coat to brave the outdoors again.

As the two reached the bottom of the staircase to face the entrance, Emma and Madeline could see the sunlight peeping through the side windows. It was morning.

Emma didn't know the time, but like the weather, darkness had left.

Emma opened the front door. Fresh air flowed into her nostrils and flew down her throat. The air had a forestry scent to it and it had mixed in with the smell of fresh rain. She could smell the grass and the bark of each tree and the nestles in between. She could smell the rain which had soaked the pebbles on the drive. It smelled like winter. A scent she loved. By now, the unbreathable, oily scent of Fillius's motor car had long evaporated.

It was silent, much like it was when she had first arrived. An eerie silence came with the country air, making it perhaps its biggest difference from any city Emma had been used to.

Emma peered down the valley towards the woods. The grass was smeared with rolling fog where white smears lifted from the patchy heaths. The lands were spooky. It was chilling, like vampire country.

Emma stopped in the front entrance doorframe. She turned to Madeline who had put her coat on. She struggled to get it comfortable over her shoulders, but when she did, she was ready to head outside to the barn.

The wind carried the shouting of the guests that had already made it to the barn doors. It was tough to comprehend what they were saying. Emma poked her head out to see the mass of them with Robin standing at the back. He seemed laconic. She hadn't heard him speak much and when she met him in the hall with his fishing poles, he didn't speak so much to the point where it was almost rude. She wondered as she stared at Robin if that's just how he was, or if it was that he didn't like the idea of marching upon Reggie. Like anyone, he kept quiet for fear of being turned out of the group.

Nevertheless they were all there already. A short chance had been given to Reggie to come out of the barn, if not given, they'd be in to find him already.

Quickly, Emma turned back to Madeline when she heard her footsteps coming towards her.

Like magic, the power unexpectedly restored itself. The manor was brightly lit once again.

Emma gazed up to the ceiling where the lights blared. A big, bright yellowness infiltrated the shrouding darkness of the entrance hall and with it, the entire manor opened in brightness. It was warm and soothing. Emma listened to the electricity surge through the walls, bringing the manor back to life.

'The power is back on. My goodness.' Madeline was happy. A laugh escaped her mouth.

'That must mean that the phone is working. We can call for help at last.' Madeline sounded excited.

Finally, this terrible night had been put to an end. One simple phone call to Sherrington and the manor and everyone inside will be saved. The bodies will be taken away and a proper, more experienced and thorough investigation would be put in place.

Emma was relieved. She let a gasp escape her mouth.

'Thank goodness.' Emma joined her friend in a little chuckle.

Their plans had now changed. Emma asked Madeline where the phone was. If the late doctor hadn't placed his urgent message in time, they would have the phones now in operation again.

Now they wouldn't head straight for the barn, but for the phone instead. Madeline set her torch aside on a nearby side table; she hadn't the use for it any longer.

'I'll show you to it.' Madeline waved Emma over. As she picked up the pace to join her friend, Emma listened to the advice that Madeline had to say.

'You know I did think it strange about what the doctor had to write about Howard Banks.'

'Yes?' Emma pried.

'Well, in his notes, he mentioned the injuries of Howard Banks,' Madeline stammered and stumbled over her words. She now sounded like she didn't know what she was talking about, but Emma urged her to keep going.

'Well, from what he wrote down, it just wouldn't seem to me that he'd be acting like that, you know all cold and shivering. I always thought that it was just the weather that did that, not the attack. The doctor mentioned how non-harming the attack was, yet Howard acted as if he was on his last legs for most of the night.'

Madeline gulped. She stood still by the staircase as she carefully explained. It had played on her mind since Howard arrived and was placed in the sitting room. It didn't settle well with her.

'What do you mean? The blade cut him up pretty good. Damage which was inflicted could make anyone feel a little woozy without being cold,' Emma encouraged. But something else was wrong. It wasn't just about Howard any longer, but now about Madeline.

She spoke as if she meant to say something, like she had meant to clue Emma into something she knew about.

Emma stared at her friend. Her eyes glazed over her plain expression as her mind took over.

When did I ever tell her about what Dr. Gottfried's report said about Howard?

Emma hung onto that thought, letting it roll around her head. That's when it clicked. She never did let Madeline see the blood-soaked report on the desk. There was no way she could have known, unless she had seen it before.

That of course would mean…

'Madeline?' Emma gulped. Her blood fizzed with nerves to the revelation she'd figured out. Madeline had inadvertently revealed to Emma that she'd known all along. Instead of squirming, she stood there, looking as if she was testing Emma into seeing what she would think. There was only one possible reason for knowing what the doctor had written.

'How did you know what the reports said? I never showed you what the doctor wrote, nor did I tell you.' Emma watched for the flicker in Madeline's eyes. There, she could see that she knew that her friend had found her out. Madeline had said the wrong thing and Emma had leaped upon it.

'How do you mean? You are scaring me,' Madeline stumbled. She stepped back a little from her place. Her hand gently fell from its rest against the side of the staircase. When she bridged a distance between them, Emma only matched her escape by inching closer.

'Madeline... Why did you *really* want me to visit tonight?'

Emma's words struck a fear in Madeline. She knew now that Madeline had discovered that Emma now knew what she had done.

Madeline quickly dropped her awkward smile. She shook her head and dropped her chin to her sternum. Her glossy hair dangled over her eyes and when she gazed back up, it cast a dangerous shadow over both her eyes.

The shape of her eyes turned fierce and the corners of her mouth turned up, making her look sharp and angered.

'So now you know, do you?' Madeline gave in. She let her veil drop and instantly, her whole look, mood and voice changed.

She knew that she could since it was only her and Emma alone in the manor. It was the right place at the right time and now Madeline had her friend right where she wanted her.

'Madeline… You killed your uncle, and the doctor. Why did you do it?' Emma was astonished. She lifted her tone to be as shocked and disappointed as she possibly could. She saw her friend of more than fifteen years standing before her, but now it was a different person. Some evil force had churned Madeline into a villainous, murderous monster.

'How could you?' Emma asked forcefully.

'I didn't kill them, Emma. God, I still can't believe that you haven't worked it out,' Madeline chuckled hysterically.

'You had the entire night to work it out. Trapped in by a storm with a room full of people you have never met seems a difficult task, I'll grant you. But this is your profession, is it not?'

Madeline toyed with her friend. She played with her food like a pod of orcas with a ray. Emma noticed that for as long as Madeline spoke, she never showed a slice of remorse for her uncle nor the doctor. There was still Frank Lightfoot which she had not yet uncovered.

'No, I believe I have worked it out.' Emma proudly stepped closer towards Madeline. Her shoes clicked upon the floorboards as she pounced on her.

Emma had only let it be a thought for as long as she'd known about it, but she could never be sure. When Howard arrived and she helped him over the drive, she had her very first suspicion.

'When Howard first appeared, I noticed the grease on his arms away from his cuts. The grease was off the motorcar when he'd previously cut the fuel line, I know it. But no one else noticed before I did and when the doctor blindly cleaned them away, the hint was gone. I also noticed the glances between you and he when the land dispute between he and your family occurred. You played the part of being angry quite well, but I saw your plans. There was also the unbroken latch upon his gate where the cattle had escaped and the moment I learnt that he'd been moving around from where he'd otherwise said he remained in the siting room all night, I had my suspicion on Howard Banks.'

Emma hadn't been purely sure that it was Howard all along. All she needed was the last piece of information which Mary the maid had given her to know for sure. That indeed Howard Banks could swiftly move around the manor when everyone thought that he couldn't. She could only wait until she could march down to the barn to tell the other guests.

She kept this valuable information all to herself. Though Reggie also had his claims to trouble her.

When Emma had finished explaining what she had learned, she heard footsteps outside. They were running, crunching upon the pebbles to finally enter the frame of the open entrance doors.

Emma wasn't entirely shocked to see that the man who had come was none other than Howard Banks. He had a pained look upon his face – from when he'd ran all the way from the barn to sneak back up the rolling hills to the manor to meet with Madeline.

It would seem as if this very moment in time had been planned. With everyone gone and with Emma alone, Howard could talk to her.

'Howard,' Emma announced.

'Hello,' he greeted with an innocent voice.

Right before Howard was about to make up an excuse for something else, he looked to Madeline to get the signal that the time was now. He breathed heavily and slightly nodded when Madeline did.

'So, you know, do you?' Howard asked.

With his large body, he blocked the doorway before Emma could even think about escaping. Like magic, his pain had been swept away, like it had never troubled him.

'She knows, Howard. But not everything,' Madeline informed him.

Madeline turned back to Emma. Caught in a crossfire between the two, she stepped back a little to gain some space against the wall, but only for the villainous couple to invade her space even more .

'If you haven't worked it out by now, Howard and I are in love.'

'What?' The news turned Emma on her side. Her eyes pinched tighter than they ever had. And when Howard chimed in to say that they had been for a long time, her hands found her hips again.

'But you hate the Smallhorns,' Emma said to Howard.

'I still do, but I love Madeline,' he replied.

The two smiled as they gazed at each other, looking over Emma's shoulder. They shared a joyous moment, one that didn't belong in such a catastrophe. But it was love.

'The fact of the matter is that with most of my family dead, I will gain the inheritance of this manor. If I were to marry Howard, he would have his land back and we'd both be rich.'

Madeline's words packed a lot of venom. She only cared for the money and the inheritance she'd receive. She didn't care for her family at all.

'So, you began systematically murdering them. That was your answer, was it?' Emma said.

'My family would never understand our love if I were to tell them the truth. This was the only way which I could, you see. As much as I wanted to, I couldn't murder them. I left that part up to Howard.'

Emma came back to Howard. The truth had been told and now she wasn't looking at an innocent, hurt man that she had helped up the drive. Now she was looking at a murderer. It didn't sit well with Emma, and nor did she feel right about her best friend any longer.

Howard Banks had come a long way from his farm. He'd braved the storm and crossed the river upwards towards the manor to play his part at the very beginning. The man played injured – though he truly was to some extent, but not to the amount that everyone in the manor thought. He even had the doctor under his spell. It was quite clever of him.

What Emma and the rest of the manor had done, was in fact welcomed in a man who'd planned to murder his girlfriend's family.

'I had my suspicions about you, Howard.' Emma referred to the time that she and Emma had investigated his farm. The latch had not been broken like Howard claimed. Emma explained to Howard that the latch – although it was hanging by a thread, as was the rest of the fencing – was fine, and the gate had been *purposely* left open.

'Your cattle were left to escape, thus creating a perfect alibi for you to venture into the woodlands and cross into the Smallhorn's property. Once you did, all you had to say was that you were attacked by someone, thus making us think that one of us would later murder the victims and had injured you.'

Howard Banks nodded to Emma's claim. She had it perfectly correct.

'You got it in one, *detective.*' Howard sneered at her profession. By now it had been too late. People had been murdered, the secret couple's plan had worked and now

Reggie was to be framed for everyone else's eventual murder.

When the police would be called as soon as the murders were complete and the power restored, they'd arrive upon a bloody scene and Reggie would be responsible. That was their plan. That was to be their great cover up when the time came.

'I should have immediately put an end to your plan once the maid told me that you had moved about the manor, fetching things out of the doctor's bag,' Emma said with wishful thinking. Then the doctor might have survived the night.

'Yes... Thankfully nobody paid much attention to her. You only did when she decided to steal then return that necklace. I saw it happen myself, right when I zipped off to the dungeon to find my dagger.'

Howard explained that in the gaps between Dr. Gottfried's routine fifteen-minute check-ups, he had timed his run perfectly. When the doctor had left for the second time, Howard knew how long he had to move around.

When the doctor left, Howard leapt at the opportunity. A little hurt and cold still, he did have trouble moving, but the coast had been cleared. Half of the manor had retired to the outdoors in search of Frank Lightfoot and the detective was a long way away at his farm by then.

Howard stormed the halls. He kept close to the darkness, using the lack of light and the sound of the fiery weather to his best advantage.

Dodging the lingering guests, he entered the dungeon. There, he saw Mary, who had in fact robbed Mrs Smallhorn of her precious necklace.

The two had exchanged secrets as not one of them was meant to be doing what they were.

Mary ran away – at which point she should have taken her first scare as an indication that she'd been wrong. Howard had said that *"If you'd been a cat, that would have counted as one of your nine lives."*

Now Howard had the dungeon to himself. He rattled around for something... *anything.*

That was when he found something quite peculiar. In a glass cabinet were an arrangement of antique daggers. They looked Turkish or Arabian, he wasn't sure.

He smashed the glass and took one out. He liked the patina on the blade and the way it curved a little. It was sharp and menacing. The blade looked like it hurt more than most by the way it curved. Looking at them made murder feel sweeter. He had his next weapon. It was a fearsome little instrument and one that he thought he'd enjoy using.

Once he took it, he stuffed a few chairs in the cabinet's way so it would not easily be discovered, and he quickly made his way back through the manor halls and to the sitting room.

He barely made it back in time. The doctor would make his routine check on him soon.

Howard had set himself back on the fainting couch. He placed the dagger by his side and stuffed it down the cushioning to hide it. When he placed the covers back over his body and fell asleep – or at least pretended to, that's when Billy Javers had come in.

'Billy Javers saw everything, didn't he?' Emma recited.

'He saw you lurking through the manor, avoiding everyone. He saw you break the glass cabinet and take your weapon. He saw you scurry back to your room and hide it in the couch, didn't he?' Emma asked.

Howard nodded. He gritted his teeth a little as he thought about that moment. He rather wished he hadn't been seen and for the longest time, he thought he had gotten away with it. He heard Madeline's grandfather talking boisterously about the war from the dining room and he took that as a fact that everyone was busy listening to him to ever notice anything. He believed everyone had barricaded themselves there as they waited for the outside venturers to return.

But Howard didn't count on Billy seeing him.

'That's when he attacked me. He saw me the entire time. He wanted to get the knife out of my hands by trying to kill me or something. I don't know. When everyone came in, Billy was taken off me. To my luck, the poor man had trouble speaking when he got a little anxious. When he said he saw me, I thought that was it. When I realised you wanted to talk to him, I thought you'd get it out of him, so I had to make Billy my next target.'

Howard Banks had yet again fooled the entire manor – even as everyone had returned after the brawl. When half of the manor had retired to bed and when Billy had come down to the kitchen for some water, that's when Howard had struck.

'I snuck up on him. I placed my arm around his neck from behind and closed off his screaming. I pressed my blade into his back and pierced his heart. I killed him and that was it.'

Howard again found himself running throughout the manor halls. He returned to his room and pretended to sleep. Once the detective had discovered the body a minute later to the noise, the rest of the manor had been alerted to the murder. Howard had gotten away with it.

'When Madeline came to *"check on me"* she told me that no one had seen a thing.'

Howard sounded rather proud as to how he had gotten away with it. He had thought for sure that his luck would run out. He had gotten risky with his every move, yet he still played the injured patient to fool everyone.

'And what about the doctor?' Emma asked.

'Again, it was tricky and risky of me. I had to find the exact moment when nobody could see me leave and where I could return to my place like nothing had happened.'

Emma nodded. She proceeded to say that the doctor was someone that was never part of the plans. He hadn't been a family member and his life could have been spared. But he played a pivotal role.

'You murdered him because he announced that he could signal his office with the telegram machine, didn't you?'

Howard nodded. He looked over to Madeline. She was scared and nervous. But she also remained strong with her plan and what she had done.

'We needed to do something. We couldn't let the doctor give an account of what happened here tonight,' Madeline intervened.

'Again, when nobody was looking, you snuck upstairs. Perhaps at the time when I entered the Smallhorn's bedroom to catch Mary.'

Howard again nodded. Now he was impressed by Emma's intelligence. He had predicted her to be something far less than what she was.

'That's right. I followed you. In fact, I saw you looking down the staircase and I feared you saw me.'

Emma remembered the shadow dashing from hall to hall. It was Howard after all. She knew it wasn't her mind playing tricks on her. It wasn't just the dark manifesting things for her eyes to see. It was indeed Howard making his way down the hall, preparing himself to come up.

'Once I knew you had entered Madeline's parent's bedroom, I took the chance and entered the main study.'

Howard recounted the very moment he opened the door and saw the stunned doctor. When the two exchanged stares, Howard knew that the doctor had known why Howard had barged in. He could see it on his worried face.

"Don't do it Howard," the doctor pleaded. But it was too late.

Howard swooped around the back of the desk and stabbed him in the back – close to his neck. He blocked the doctor's mouth with a cushion to stop him from yelling. Howard waited for him to bleed out – which didn't take him long.

He had taken a knife from a stand in the main office – something rather similar to the antique dagger he had stolen in the dungeon.

He murdered Dr. Gottfried, but it had been too late. The doctor had already sent his communication out to his office. Described in great detail upon his notes upon the desk, was what happened. It noted how Howard's injuries hadn't appeared as serious as he was acting. It wasn't much, but Howard knew what it meant.

In that moment, Howard shivered that the truth had indeed been sent off. It was only a matter of time now, but it only made him want to kill the doctor even *harder.* Now he didn't have the stress or adamants to do it.

Howard had left the blood-soaked papers and the blood-drowned desk in a hurry. He knew that he had to return downstairs to join the rest of the manor before he was found out. Henry Smallhorn had long ago organised a meeting for the manor once Emma had left to investigate on her own.

They banded together and everyone believed that Reggie had been the culprit.

The only person who seemed to have a close eye on Howard had been Robin. From then on, Howard thought about Robin as his next victim when the time came.

Howard had returned, managing to slip back down the staircase and into the sitting room. Robin and Henry had in fact caught him standing up before he could reach the fainting couch. Howard played off the occurrence coolly as he reached for the packet of matches to affix a well-timed blown candle.

The meeting had then begun.

'It was all built upon luck so it seemed. My timing was tested, but every time I managed to escape. It left both I and Madeline nervous throughout,' Howard admitted.

'Was it you two that had fanned the flames for the rest of the manor against Reggie?'

'It was quite easy in fact,' Madeline said.

'With a mixture of fear and conviction to a cause, it was easy to say that Reggie had done it. Of course, he was there with Frank Lightfoot at the very beginning and he was away from everyone most of the time. It was easy for anyone to think that he was the one moving about, plotting murder.'

Madeline sounded evil and with the smirk which never abandoned her face, Emma could both hear and see it. Richness and a formal standing of her family's name and the inheritance of her land and the history of the manor had plagued her mind in thinking that the only thing in her way was her family.

Of course, Howard Banks didn't help. He had been in her ear from the very moment the two had met. He had convinced her that it was the right thing to do. He even promised that he'd be the one to murder them and she needn't worry. All she needed to do was formulate a plan to get him in and keep any suspicion off both him and herself. It had worked out perfectly.

'And what about Frank Lightfoot? What happened to him?' Emma asked. It was the only thing she didn't know about. Frank Lightfoot was still very much a mystery.

Howard Banks would tell Emma what had happened to Frank Lightfoot. He explained it as if it were happening before their very eyes to paint a picture of the encounter.

Chapter 13

An hour before Emma had arrived at the Smallhorn manor, Madeline had finalised the plans she was going to carry out. She hadn't seen Howard all day, but the night before they spoke at his farm as he had rushed out in the moonlight at the dead of midnight. Knowing that her parents had fallen asleep, she crossed the woods with nothing but a simple lantern and a stick she found fallen from a branch for protection if needed.

They spoke in his farmhouse. They went over the plan like they had many weeks before.

Cunningly, Madeline had placed a knife inside the barn for Reggie to find and toy around with. It looked like his old knife, but it was different. When Madeline had claimed his old one and replaced it with hers, it looked like nothing ever happened. Reggie had resumed using this knife, thinking it was his old one for half a year now.

Of course, the knife which Madeline had left in the barn for Reggie to pick up was strikingly like the one Howard had intended to use. All he'd need to do was throw his away at some point, and then when Reggie was found with a similar knife it would seem clear cut that he was responsible.

The plan was fool proof.

When Madeline and Howard were proud of their plan and when they believed that everything was set right down to the last detail, they'd returned home and waited until the next day.

The family had to be murdered and both Madeline and Howard had their eyes set upon Henry Smallhorn first.

Henry would go out for a smoke before dinner. He usually did it all by himself. He too had a little problem that he intended to give up. Stopping smoking from his pipe was like a child giving up sweet soda for him. It couldn't be done and he often smoked to relieve himself of a hard day of work. Sometimes it got his thinking juices going. He liked it as a hobby. He was just like Frank Lightfoot, and with Madeline knowing of her father's routine, it made the perfect opportunity for Howard to kill him.

Howard came out that night as the manor settled down for dinner.

He let his cattle free from their yard.

Howard followed his cattle up from his farmhouse. When the storm had gotten worse, he'd barely made it to the cover of the woods where he let his cattle spread out between the trees.

The heath of the woods smouldered with thick fog from the cold. The ground had turned mushy where he stood and his cattle had some trouble moving about. But eventually, the cattle had spread enough to the point where their groans and mooing had almost sounded eerie as he looked out to them and listened from the river's edge.

Looking into the darkness of the woods, only seeing flickers of shimmering eyes and hearing their patchy moans behind the trees would make for a horrific night. Much like the horror that had not yet been committed.

The last of the sun had died down on the horizon and Howard crawled out from the woodland path. He followed the path – the trail his girlfriend's family had only just walked back to the manor from their fishing at the river.

Howard waited. He waited in the thickets of nature in the outskirts of the woods. He ducked down and stared at the rolling valleys of grass lapping outward from the Smallhorn manor.

Madeline had said that her father would come out for his smoke, but it had been a half hour more than he expected.

Howard had grown restless. There were other things that he needed to attend, but he continued to wait for another five minutes longer. He had in fact trickled up the hills silently to cut the fuel line of Fillius's vehicle as planned. It was only too easy.

At last, his patience had paid off. Up the grass knolls, away from the manor and even closer to the barn was Madeline's father. Henry Smallhorn had come out for his smoke.

It was dark and difficult for Howard to see, but he was sure the man smoking was Madeline's father.

Howard was sure that he had his man. He watched the fire flame from the pipe in his mouth. He saw that pipe lit and he came for him.

Howard ducked to the grass. He emerged from his hiding and slowly traipsed his way towards the unsuspecting victim. Howard Banks, with murderous intent and Henry Smallhorn with nary an inkling as to what was coming his way. Howard had gotten close enough to begin to run to snatch him like a cheetah on an unsuspecting antelope. But Henry turned.

He had his body half-cocked and half-facing the manor in the woods. He had seen a figure moving towards him from the corner of his eye. He turned and faced Howard.

He wasn't aware of who he was or what he was intending. Henry billowed hot ashes from out of his pipe. It lit his face, but not enough for Howard to see him.

Now Howard was spooked.

'What are you doing? Is that you, Banks?' he grizzled.

He didn't like Howard Banks. But yet not as much as Howard didn't like him by the looks of things.

He spoke to him like the scum he'd always thought he was. *Get off my land!* Were the words Howard really heard him say. It spooked him.

The course of smoke pumping through his body, swirling through his lungs and tampering with his voice had made him sound rugged and rough. It stirred Howard.

He stepped back before he could do anything. *By God… I'd forgotten to even draw my knife.*

The thrill was too much that Howard couldn't think straight. He couldn't believe what he was attempting to do and once he knew he'd lost the high ground, he turned on his heel and fled back to the woods. It was his first attempt at murder. He hadn't committed enough. Howard was scared.

He slackened. His boot had turned in the slush of the wet grass, rendering him sluggish enough for Henry to catch up to him.

Howard felt stiff and hard hands pound him in the back and when they hit, he tumbled down the path of the woods and landed close to the jagged rocks and pebbles of the river edge.

He got up. His body was bruised and he felt blood rolling down his arms. The moonlight was strong. He looked down at them and noticed that he was right. He was bleeding.

Howard heard the footsteps of Henry come down the path before him. He gazed up and stared at the tunnel-like path and at last, a figure came out.

But it wasn't Henry as Howard had suspected all this time.

It was a man he'd never met.

Howard looked at him. His eyes twitched and his brows crossed.

'Who are you?' Howard asked, thinking that it was even stranger that the mystery man had seemed to know him by how he had addressed him.

'My name is Frank Lightfoot,' he said.

'How do you know who I am? You mentioned my name,' Howard asked. As he made small talk and cunningly set his timbre to a weaker one, Howard recoiled his knife from his back pocket while pretending to feel his back for pain.

'The Smallhorn's have spoken about you many times before. I could only assume a mossy, woodland sprout quite like yourself would resemble that of one Howard Bank's.'

Howard didn't react. He'd let his knife do the talking for him. It wasn't the man he was originally after, but it was a member of the family that Howard would have pleasure in taking out just as much.

With Frank's arrogance, he even chuckled a little as he stood tall and manly before the hurt Howard. Rain beaded down on both their heads, turning their hair and clothes soppy and wet. They didn't care, nor did they mind the storm.

Thunder rocketed in the night sky, stirring Howard's attention to drawing him closer to act upon his intentions.

Howard remembered that chuckle and the grin set upon Frank's face. He wondered if Frank would still be smiling when Howard's blade would slice him up. For now, Frank saw

Howard as nothing. He thought him to be weak and feeble, a man that couldn't fight and that Frank would have great pleasure in beating if it came to it.

'Get up you low-life. Trickle off to your deteriorating barnyard. And by God, mend the walls so that it doesn't blow away with the storm.'

When Frank Lightfoot spoke, he couldn't help but wonder if he'd heard cows mooing in the distance. He looked over Howards bent body. His eyes crossed the river. He was sure of it. Frank also had come to Emma's later conclusion. The cows sounded frightened and sad. It was ghoulish and strangely terrifying to hear it in the woodland darkness.

When he was busy thinking was when Howard took his chance. Before Frank had even known it, the steel of Howard's knife slitted into his stomach.

Howard held the knife in. His teeth gritted and he looked up to Frank who stood astonished. But Frank fought back.

He punched Howard as hard as he could and ripped the knife from his belly. Blood poured from his wound, wetting his hand and causing him to drop it.

Sore of cheek, Howard stood right back up and picked up the fumbled knife. He attacked again, this time slashing Frank's body over and over again.

Howard didn't know what he was doing. He had his eyes closed whenever he seemed to strike and with the pelting rain and the chaos of the storm, everything was like a car crash in his head.

He kept slashing and slashing. With each swing, Howard noticed that Frank had grown weaker and weaker.

At last, Frank toppled over onto his back. He lay there, his arms cut and his stomach and chest leaking with blood. He could hardly breathe, nor could he talk. He lay there, twitching and scared of Howard now.

Howard stopped. He stood over what he'd done. He panted heavily, but not because of the violent thrashing, but of what he'd done. The thrill of murder and what he'd committed had now made it normal. It only took a second, but he didn't feel scared or cagey anymore. He could do it.

Frank lifted his hands forward and mimed a plea, but Howard didn't entertain it, not one bit.

He scooped up his legs and dragged him along the pebbles and jagged rocks – a pain which hurt almost as badly as the knife.

Howard jumped into the river. The water was strong, almost enough to carry him downstream, but his footing had him rooted to the bed beneath.

He dragged Frank's body across the river where he'd take him to the other side in the deeper part of the woods.

When they crossed, Howard set Frank by the river's edge where a pool of rocks created a sort of circle for him to rest him. It was there where Emma would later discover the rockpool of blood.

Howard left Frank there as he wandered into the woods to find a place to bury him. He took his knife and started cutting at the loose ground. It would take some time, but the adrenaline had seen his time cut in half.

The earth was muddy and the soil beneath was loose by the rain and the cold. By the time the manor had even noticed Frank's disappearance, Howard had got the grave dug.

Howard returned to Frank – who was barely alive still.

He took his knife to his throat and slit it. Frank's lifeline had been cut.

Drenching the ground with blood, Howard dragged the dead body all the way to his shallow grave and buried him.

When the ground was covered and Frank was hidden, Howard made sure to clean the rocks trailing from the river edge to the grave. He carried handfuls of water to splash them away as quickly as he could. The rain would do its bit, but it wasn't enough, so he had to help.

When he came to disperse the rockpool of blood, he then noticed the flashlights before him on the other side of the woods, peaking through the trees. People were now looking for Frank and the grounds of the manor had become mayhem.

In a panic, Howard abandoned cleaning the rest of the blood. In haste, he threw his knife in the river, but not before he committed to his plan.

He hated the thought of it, but he had to make himself look injured.

He looked at the knife like it was his worst friend. He cleaned the blood and dirt off with the river water and without thinking about it for a second longer, he slashed at his own arms and legs.

He dug the blade in deep enough to look like an inflicted attack, but not enough to bleed out. He swiped at his stomach, lifting his jacket up to do the worst. He winced and clenched his teeth. The pain was unbearable, but it was what he had to do.

When Howard was done, he tossed the knife into the river, like he was getting rid of his evidence overboard.

He hoped that no one would find it, thus getting everyone to believe that the knife used to kill Frank was indeed in Reggie's hands all this time. But of course, Emma did find it.

Howard leaped back into the water, somewhat cleaning his wounds for them to only bleed even brighter when he got out. He wanted to look drenched for the story he was about to give.

Howard burst out of the woods. He ducked away from the searching flashlights and took the swerving long way up the manor hills to reach his checkpoint.

He was bleeding, cold, sopping wet and startled. The mushy grass had splat water into his boots and now his feet were cold and they began to turn wrinkled. The dirt off the knife and the blood stained from Franks and now into his had turned him sick. But he still played the part as planned and the rest was history.

Emma had let the killer into the warmth of the manor as Madeline and Howard planned and from then on, Howard played the part of an injured patient, all the meanwhile learning the patterns of each and every guest and planning each of their murderous ends with Madeline always in his ear.

Chapter 14

It would come to this.

Everything in the plan had been executed and now it was coming to an end. Madeline and Howard didn't have much time to kill the others. Day had come, the storm had eased and the power was returned. Everything had come as a sign that time had run out for Madeline and Howard. Once more, nobody truly knew if Dr. Gottfried's message had been received, but Howard could only assume it had.

An ambush of police officers could be on their way right now. Time was of the essence and the last of Madeline and Howard's plans would need to come into effect soon.

Madeline would speak to Emma with less aggravation this time. It wouldn't seem possible, now that Emma saw the monster she'd become. Her skin was etched tight over her face and a croaky, evilness peaked through what she thought of Madeline all along.

For this, Emma felt stupid. She couldn't believe that her friend had organised murder. Her hand hadn't been at the blade's handle, but it may have well been.

For all this time she'd been confiding with Emma, learning valuable information and being there at every turn of her investigation. She had her on her shoulder, in her ear throughout most of the investigation. Little had she known until this very moment that in actual fact, she could have been helping her all along.

Madeline was granted an insight into every step of Emma's investigation. She knew where she was going, what she wanted to ask and what her mind had become fixated on. It had all been a façade, yet Madeline still considered Emma her best friend.

She sounded to her as she always did. Madeline confessed and turned to Emma like they did when they were kids.

'You are my best friend, Emma. What we have done here is against the law, I know it. But you can help us and in return, we can reward *you.'*

Madeline's words sickened her as she tried to justify what she'd done. Even worse, she tried to sweeten it with a deal. Emma hadn't been sure of it, but she could tell that somewhat of a deal was coming her way. Even before Madeline could say it, she could read it coming from her lips.

'We *needed* you, Emma. Now we have an opportunity to take all the riches and heritage of my family's name. And with you on our side, we would surely get away with it and live happily ever after.'

Madeline smiled widely. She was giddy with each and every word like it was the best idea she'd ever thought of. She even thought it best to bounce on her toes when she spoke. What she and her hidden lover had planned was brilliant in their eyes.

'We want you to clear our names. Once my family is dead, we ask you to prosecute Reggie. No one will ever have to know,' Madeline encouraged.

'I don't understand…' Emma staggered. In fact, she understood everything that her friend was saying. She just needed more time on her side to think of something to delay them.

'We had set up everything to go against Reggie Jackson. Now that my family had followed my lead into accusing him, it will be easy to gather up your evidence to put Reggie away for murdering my family, whilst we walk free and collect everything. All we need you to do is to prosecute Reggie as a detective and abandon any true evidence to stray us away from this mess. Reggie is accused of killing my family, we collect the inheritance and you will get a sum for putting the heat on Reggie and away from us. Simple.'

All whilst Madeline spoke, Emma needled her eyes at a space between Howard Banks and the front door. There was a small opportunity where she could squeeze through and escape from their madness.

Emma coolly hung onto her intentions. She didn't let it be known that she wanted to flee. She turned to Howard who'd huddled up closer towards the wall where the staircase turned. His right arm was stuck behind his back, as if hiding something.

'We never intended to hurt you, Emma. We just wanted to find the right moment to tell you our plan. Together, we can do this, and for your help, we'll reward you greatly.' Madeline promised. Her words were candy to anyone desperate and up against the ropes. For anyone seeking a fortune in exchange for sidelining the law, it was an opportunity some may take. But Emma didn't want it. Her loyalty was to the law and the good of people. Murder for the prosper of riches did not bode well with her, no matter how hard her friend tried to push.

'We need a detective; someone within the law to verify everything for us. It is the perfect plan. No one will suspect a thing. I *need* you, Emma'

Madeline kept a hold of her joyful tone in hopes of luring Emma in on her side. She rather thought that Emma would take the bait. Emma was young and naïve. It wasn't as if she'd pledged her full allegiance to solving crime in Madeline's eyes.

As she waited with bated breath to hear her answer, Howard grudgingly reminded Emma to speak up.

'Well… What say you?'

Emma's eyes flickered. She took in a deep breath and hurried down an awkward swallow.

'No, I will not do it for you.'

Madeline's smile had erased and Howard's grip had tightened behind his back.

'No? What do you mean *"No?"'* Madeline's voice changed. Her sickly-sweet voice disappeared for a more brutish one once again. Emma could see that her friend's blood fizzed in her body. With it, her entire mood and look changed. A volcano of anger began to erupt inside at her friend's lack of help.

'I will not help you get away with this.' Emma stood firm and strong. She was backed by an education and dedication to law. She hadn't truly begun, but she wasn't about to become a crook. Madeline and Howard had committed their crimes and with Emma or not, they'd continue the massacre.

'You have murdered three people tonight. You have become monsters. I will not stand here and let you walk away after this, nor will I join you and help you hide amongst the good of mankind.'

Emma's words did not amuse Madeline. She didn't like one bit of them. When she knew that Emma wasn't going to change, she exchanged a look to Howard without Emma's knowledge. The signal was given and once Emma decided not to side with them, then she too must be eliminated.

From the staircase, Howard then pulled a dagger from a chip in the wood big enough to hide it. It had remained there for this very moment when he needed it. It slithered out like a gun to his holster. He gripped it and dragged it around to his hip. He awaited Emma's final response.

'Do not make this foolish decision. You can get us out of this, and we, with you.' Madeline pleaded with her. She did not want to see her friend murdered. But if Emma did not wish to help, then they'd have no choice but to silence the truth.

'You claim to know what a foolish decision is, but yet, here we are,' Emma cunningly said. But that was the signal. Her last worst would be her final decision. Madeline had given her but one last chance to change; one more chance than what she'd give anyone else. But that was the final straw.

'Bad choice,' Madeline hushed. When she did, Emma realised that Howard had rushed towards her. She turned on her heel and saw him lunging towards her.

A stark, murderous look was painted upon his face and his eyes widened with horror. Now she was seeing what their victims had seen before their death. Now Emma was next.

He brought his knife out to reveal it to Emma. He held it high over his shoulders and intended to slash Emma with it as he did with Frank.

Emma screamed. She closed her eyes and waited for the hot death of the steely blade. But nothing came. All that did was a gunshot.

It sounded from the front door.

Bang!

Emma heard the blast and she opened her eyes. She looked up to see that Howard's chest was open. His innards were turned to mush and blood piled heavily to the floorboards before his feet.

Emma witnessed his stone-cold face. He was still alive for a second and there he stood, but the moment he hit the ground, he was dead.

He hit the ground hard with a thud. Blood burst from the fall like a blood-soaked pumpkin, coating both Emma and the walls with specks of red.

Emma quivered. To come so close to death, she thanked her lucky stars that by some miracle she'd been spared. She gazed up over the body to find the trail of smoke which coursed out of a gun barrel. Holding the shotgun was a young man she recognised.

'Reggie?'

Within an hour the police department from Sherrington had arrived at the manor, courtesy of a phone call made by Emma herself.

In quick concession, the grounds flooded with officers from every rank and the horror of the Smallhorn manor had been uncovered.

Moments after the gunshot, the family converged upon the scene, halting Madeline in her place. Her partner had been killed and Reggie was the man with the shotgun. But when Emma had explained the truth, Reggie was soon a hero.

Reggie had in fact used his smarts to elude the rest of the manor. He didn't escape through the window but remained hidden in the room. Once everyone believed he took refuge in the barn, he crawled out and found a gun.

He said to Emma what he'd done to save her life.

'There was something off from the moment I noticed that Madeline decided to stay with you. She was the one who instigated the whole façade that I was the murderer. She only made her father look like he was the one who started thinking it. I knew it.'

The two spoke on the steps of the manor outside an hour after the sound of Reggie's shotgun.

Emma had been cleaned of blood and Reggie sat rather comfortably. She admired how calm and well-balanced the young teenager had been all this time. He had killed a murderer. Even killing the bad people for the *right* reasons was tough enough for anyone. But luckily for Emma, Reggie understood the urgency.

'Thank goodness you were there, Reggie. If not for you, I'd be dead and likely everyone else would be too now.' Emma smiled. She respected Reggie for remaining strong throughout all his troubles.

'I heard what you said by the way.'

'What was that?'

'I heard what you said about being loyal to the law and caring for the good of mankind. You could have taken the easy way out to save yourself. But even when you thought no one was there listening, you still stood strong to your ethics. It was more of you than me, I think.'

Such words warmed Emma. If she hadn't known already, now she knew that justice had been served and that Emma's dedication to doing the right thing trumped all.

Reggie smiled and left with a wink. When the chief of the Sherrington police department came beside Emma, it was Reggie's cue to leave.

Emma got up for the man. She hadn't been hurt, just a little *"rattled",* she confirmed when she was asked.

Chief Hoover had served for the town of Sherrington for some forty years. His hair had grown grey and his moustache a little curlier and nothing within his time had equated to what Emma had dealt with in just the one night.

'In the wind of last night's storm, it could drag up all kinds of evil people and malevolent intent.' The chief spoke with a northern accent. It was a grizzled *Toony voice*, but somewhere more Northern in Newcastle, if Emma's dialect was worth its salt.

'It did not come from any wind nor storm. The evil came from within, sir. For all this time.'

'It was their mistake, bringing a detective to the table. I found that Reggie' fellow's quick thinking was quite courageous also,' the chief said.

He'd seen the damage upon the manor's entrance. Before the forensics could cover Howard's body up and take away the others, Chief Hoover had seen everything.

He couldn't begin to conjure up what kind of night the innocent had suffered, let alone the culprit and her intentions which were then exposed.

When he did take the weeping Madeline away, he felt the heart drop of every person in the room who'd seen it happen. From that moment, her family had become completely detached from her. Madeline was seen as a cruel, plotting woman who would care more for the wealth and inheritance of her family than her family itself.

Madeline didn't even look at them as she was taken outside and into the patrol vehicle to be sent away back to Sherrington where indeed her fate for conspiring to murder will be later dealt with in London.

The rest of the family had been taken back to Sherrington for questioning. Millicent Gottfried was sad to see. She hadn't known about her husband's murder until Emma had declared it. Emma hadn't seen a broken heart tear so much in the flesh in her life before. Her broken heart would scar her for the rest of her life and would surely add an indent as being the saddest victim Emma would ever encounter.

Grief came with the trade, Chief Hoover mentioned. By now, their conversation had strayed away from the manor and into the woods where they walked.

The two stood by the edge of the river, away from the blanket of trees. When Madeline had confessed where the body of Frank was located, there had only been one thing left to do.

Emma and Hoover stared over the water and into the outskirts of the woods on the other side. Where the ground was mushy and recently broken, an assembly of diggers had already got to work on digging up the last body.

'To say that you aren't a true detective yet is utterly gobsmacking.'

By now Emma had informed the chief of her true position. She had not yet become a detective, but she hadn't told him that she'd been studying for a number of years.

'Have you thought about looking into it? I think you'd make a bloody brilliant one, miss Squier,' the dotty, less formal now chief encouraged.

The chief had a little sway to his posture and a smile arose from under his bushy moustache. He focused back upon the diggers who'd hit a stubborn object in the shallow grave.

'Actually, what I meant sir is that I've studied criminology for a number of years. This year I graduated and I'm looking for work. I have much to study still, but work experience will help me along my way.' Emma hinted at the chief. It was obvious that if he hadn't said it already that he was impressed with her work, but instead of offering her a place in the Sherrington police force, he believed she could do better.

'With what you did last night, London will be calling you as fast as the papers reach their hands. If they don't, I'll at least make sure of it.'

At the time of their speaking, Frank Lightfoot's body had been discovered and excavated in his grave. The broken roots beneath the soil coiled around his greying skin. He'd been dead for some hours and an assortment of underground critters had already begun to nibble at his hardened body.

Even with such a morbid sight before them, Emma couldn't help but match the chief's smile to his encouraging words.

A great travesty had been set upon the manor. People were never set to be how they'd always been and Emma had to learn it the hard way. Her friend had been lost to the temptation of evil's many lures.

To lose a friend and to be a witness to seeing such innocent people die in the company of grief was a terrible thing. But to put away the *right* people was the only thing Emma could settle for.

At that moment, as Emma gazed back over Frank's exhumed body, she realised it was all over. The irony of it being calm before the storm spoke volumes to her and a night at the *manor of murder* would only start to describe what the rest of her career would entail.

Emma's next case is near…